MUSIC OF THE WANDERING STARS

Music of the Wandering Stars
By Elena Clark

Cover Design by Michelle Vymenetz

2nd Edition
Copyright © 2014, 2018 by Elena Clark

ISBN: 0-9937975-7-1
ISBN-13: 978-0-9937975-7-6
L&V Publishing Company
Published in Vaughan, Canada

MUSIC OF THE WANDERING STARS

Elena Clark

L&V Publishing Company
Vaughan, Ontario

ELENA CLARK

Table of Contents

BOOK I

Love at First Sight

They met on June 29th, 1982, during Nina's annual recital. Actually, Anton had noticed Nina, immediately fallen in love with her, and decided that this girl must become his wife, even before she knew about his existence. After all, what Anton wanted Anton was sure he could get. It had always been that way: with his music, with the women – why would it be any different now?

Scarcely hours before, Anton's heart belonged only to his career. In the morning, Anton had passed his last exam of the year. One more year in the Moscow Music Conservatory and he would be ready to conquer the world. He would be the most famous, or at least one of the better known, brilliant concert pianists, on the world stage.

Anton had every right to be proud of his achievements and to be confident about his future. He had been touted as a major talent and a brilliant piano player from his early school days. His professors, even the strictest and the most demanding ones, always had words of praise and encouragement for him.

Moreover, the stage loved him. Anton had a *presence* about him when he was performing. He was told again and again by his teachers and his fans that his performing technique was emotional, strong and captivating. He was a big man, tall and athletically built, and he liked *big* music. Quiet, lyrical pieces were not for Anton; he loved playing Beethoven and Rachmaninoff. His handsome features did not hurt him either. Anton let his blonde wavy hair grow long, almost to his shoulders, and that head of hair nicely framed a sculpted face: large blue eyes, strong, well-shaped nose, and a chiselled chin.

Yes, one more year of studies and the world would be at Anton's feet – women and all! There was no doubt in his mind about his future. He would be performing as a piano soloist in the best concert halls of the world. He could already envision himself on the stages of New York, London, and Vienna, Berlin...

However, one chance meeting changed everything. A new passion began to burn in his heart: Nina!

On that fateful day, in the late summer afternoon, Anton went to look for his best friend and roommate, Boris. Anton was in an excellent mood. During the exam, he performed his piece with the confidence and the skill that a future concert pianist must possess. Anton received the highest grade on that exam (no surprise there), so now he was officially a graduate student of the Moscow Conservatory. He was ready to celebrate the successful end of the school year and the beginning of the summer holidays.

Anton found Boris outside the Conservatory at the flower stand. Boris was carefully selecting a bouquet of flowers.

"What are you doing, man?" Anton inquired. "Today is a day of celebration. Let's do something extraordinary. We deserve it!"

"I can't, Anton," Boris shook his mane of bright red hair in negation. "Larissa has her annual recital today. I promised to be there. Do you like this bouquet?" Boris pointed at a large bouquet of mixed flowers.

"Yeah, sure, but what do I know about flowers?" Anton responded in a disappointed voice. "Aren't you getting a bit too serious about Larissa?"

"I am very serious, Anton. I proposed to her yesterday," Boris replied, his large dark eyes shining with excitement and anxiety.

"No way! Are you out of your mind? Why would you think about marriage at the age of twenty-two? We're too young to get married. It's our time to enjoy life, to be free, to 'sow those wild oats', as people like to say."

"You go ahead and sow," Boris replied with a laugh. "Women are attracted to you as bees are to honey. I'm a simple Jewish boy. I want to marry Larissa and live happily ever after in a small *shtetl* called Toronto, Canada."

Boris paid for the flowers and the two friends headed back to the Conservatory.

"Has Larissa already agreed to marry you, you loser?" asked Anton, with a bit of a chuckle.

"She told me that she will give me her answer after the recital," Boris replied worriedly and then added, "Anton, please go with me to the recital. If she says *yes,* we'll go out together to celebrate my engagement. If she says *no*, I'll need a shoulder to cry on and you have a big one."

"Well, you *will* need to get drunk in any case and I'll gladly help you in this endeavour. Honestly, Borya, I hate the soprano screeching you have to endure at these recitals, but I'm ready to suffer for a friend." Anton then asked, "What are you planning to do in Canada? Do you think it'll be easy to get a good job?"

"I know that it will be difficult, very difficult indeed, to get any job. But my family emigrated three years ago, and I feel I have no choice but to join them. They left me behind only to finish my studies."

"Does Larissa want to emigrate?"

"To be honest, I'm not sure about that. But I've decided to take it one step at a time."

"But, Borya, if you don't get a job, what will you do?"

"I don't know, Anton. But I have a dream. Do you want to hear it?" Without waiting for an answer, Boris continued, "I want to organize a band. I will play piano and maybe even compose some songs. Larissa will be my soloist. She's very good at singing blues and soul music. I want you to hear her today."

"So, what will you call this band of yours?" Anton

asked good-naturedly. He was in an exceptionally good mood, so why not to indulge his friend, that incurable dreamer? After all, Boris was a good musician. Well, not in the same league as Anton, and the career of a concert pianist was out of Boris's reach - so let him dream about that band of his.

"I didn't even think about it," Boris replied. "I'm not in Canada yet, and Larissa hasn't yet agreed to marry me, never mind to emigrate with me."

"I have a great name for you. Do you remember the book you gave me a year ago, *Wandering Stars*? You'll be wanderers and you're planning to be stars, right?"

"*Wandering Stars*... I like it," Boris mused approvingly.

Ω

An hour later the two friends were sitting in the Conservatory, waiting for the recital to begin. For them, it was a very familiar environment: an audience consisting of nervous but proud parents, bored friends who promised to attend, and several die-hard lovers of classical music.

When the recital began Anton felt fidgety. He was a bit sorry that he had agreed to attend. It was a shame to waste such a nice evening listening to familiar, boring arias sung by students. Anton idly began to scan the audience, hoping to discover a pretty face. Anton liked women and had had his share of conquests, but had never had a serious, long-term relationship. No need for that yet. First, he had to develop his career, establish himself as a major piano player, and then... he could have any woman he wanted.

Just now however, Anton was feeling a little bit sad. Boris had always been a willing and eager partner in all their adventures. Now it seemed that Anton would be on his own.

He was checking out a pretty girl sitting in the fifth row when he heard the most beautiful and enchanting voice imaginable. Never before had Anton heard anything so captivating and as magical as this voice. Slowly, he turned his face toward the stage. He was not disappointed; the singer was as lovely as her voice. She was tall and slim, with beautiful straight, long, and very light hair, reaching almost down to her waist.

Anton wasn't sure what he liked best: her voice, her large bright green eyes, her lovely heart-shaped face or that aura of style, elegance and poise that was emanating from her presence. He was totally enthralled.

"Who *is* that girl?" he asked.

"That's Nina. She's in Larissa's class. But I think she has a boyfriend. At least I always see some guy waiting for her after classes."

Without giving a second thought to the actual purpose of the flowers in his friend's hands, Anton snatched Boris's bouquet and made his way toward the stage. When the girl stopped singing, Anton bravely ascended the stage, approached her, presented her with the flowers, and whispered, "I love you, Nina, with all my heart. One day you will be my wife. Please take my words seriously." Without waiting for a reply, Anton turned around and left the stage, leaving the astounded Nina holding her bouquet.

When Anton returned to his seat he found an angry Boris waiting for him.

"You are a selfish pig," Boris hissed. "You have destroyed my life!"

"Don't worry. I'm on my way to get flowers for your beloved Larissa."

"She's singing after the next three performers."

"Plenty of time," Anton said and ran outside.

Larissa was already singing when the by-now very worried Boris, anxiously looking around and sitting on the edge of his seat, spotted Anton who had returned with a beautiful bouquet of white lilacs. Mollified, Boris took the flowers and grumbled, "You're crazy, but for this bouquet I will ask Larissa to introduce you to Nina."

It was Boris's turn to march to the stage and present the flowers. He quietly whispered something to Larissa, and observing his friend's wide and happy smile, Anton guessed the answer.

Larissa is not a bad looking girl and she has a decent voice, but no comparison to my Nina, Anton reflected. In his mind, Nina was already his.

Meanwhile, backstage, Nina was trying to find out something about that arrogant (but very handsome) young man who had made such a preposterous proposal.

"Does anybody know the name of the guy who gave me these flowers?" Nina asked.

"Who doesn't? It's Anton, the future Franz Liszt. Unfortunately for all of us, he's in love only with himself and his piano," one of the female students responded.

"Nina," another added, "all of Anton's relationships are short-lived; *very* short-lived."

"But they're fun while they last," a red-headed girl, who was a popular beauty of the faculty, commented dreamily.

"Oh, stop it, all of you," snapped a stately girl with wavy dark hair, equally dark eyes and very luscious red lips. "Nina, Anton is my Boris's roommate. Anton's parents live in Leningrad, so he lives in the dormitory. He's OK."

"Thanks, Larissa. And I understand that you are to be congratulated."

"Twice – first for catching such a great guy as Boris and secondly, for guaranteeing my future in a civilized country. Boris's parents and sister live in Toronto, Canada, so we will join them after graduation. Mind you, Boris never asked me if I want to emigrate, but I know his plans and I really do want to live in Canada!"

Ω

After the conclusion of the performance, Boris and Anton hurried to the stage door from which all the performers appeared upon leaving the concert hall. Boris quietly pointed out to Anton a young man who was standing with flowers, close to the door. The chap had a nice, kind face but he frowned when he noticed Anton.

"That's Anatoly Kuznetsov, Nina's steady," Boris whispered. "They're always together. Anatoly is in the conductor's class."

Anton glanced at Anatoly and quietly responded, "No problem. This guy isn't even serious competition."

The door came open and the first group of performers emerged. Anton felt his heart beating furiously and took a step closer to the door. Anatoly took a step forward as well. Nothing was said, although both men understood that a battle for a woman's heart was on.

Finally, Larissa and Nina, smiling and both holding their flowers, emerged through the doorway. Anton's and Nina's eyes met for a second, but then Nina looked at Anatoly, stepped towards him and asked in an anxious voice, "Tolya, was the middle of the aria a little flat?"

"Not at all, Nina," Tolya reassured her, "but if you want, we can work on it tomorrow."

"Thanks! Tolya, we have great news. Larissa is engaged!"

"Congratulations! Who's the lucky man?" Tolya asked, somewhat perplexed why this news should make Nina so happy. As far as he knew, Nina and Larissa were classmates but they hadn't been very close.

Larissa made the introduction, "Tolya, please meet Boris, a very fine piano player, a casual composer, and my fiancé."

"Why *casual*? That's bordering on an insult,

Larissa! But I do like the sound of the word *fiancé*. A pleasure to make your acquaintance, Anatoly," Boris said, extending his hand.

Anatoly shook Boris's hand and repeated, "Congratulations."

"Boris, I agree with you," Anton joined the conversation, "I like the word *fiancé* too. It's the word *husband* that frightens me."

"And this buffoon is my roommate and best friend," Boris introduced Anton jovially.

"Anton," he said and nodded curtly to Tolya and respectfully to Nina.

Anton noticed at that moment that quite a few of the students had not left, but rather were standing around and listening to the conversation.

"Hey guys," Larissa suggested to Anatoly and Nina, "I would like to invite you to celebrate our engagement with us. Boris promised to take me to some amazing new restaurant."

"Thank you, Larissa. Maybe some other time. I have invited some friends to my cottage for an end-of-the-year party. We should be going to the 'dacha' now." Tolya replied.

"Oh, that's too bad," Larissa answered. "Have a good time."

"Where is your dacha?" Boris inquired. "It's getting late. How will you get there?"

"On a commuter train. It's only a forty-minute ride." Tolya explained politely.

"But how will people get back?" Boris persisted. "Commuter trains don't run all night."

"We're going to party all night and then everyone can go back on the first morning train," Nina said lightly, and as an afterthought, she added, "Tolya, dear, why don't you invite the happy couple to join us? It's quite romantic near the lake."

"Yes, of course, if they would like to," Tolya

reluctantly agreed.

"Thank you, Tolya, we would love to come," Boris enthused. "Would you mind if my friend joined us?"

"Oh, not at all. You're all invited," Anatoly said, carefully watching Nina. In fact, he did mind. He minded very much.

Ω

Half-an-hour later, the merry company was sitting on the train and heading out of Moscow. Anton looked around and concluded that at least half of the passengers in the coach were Anatoly's friends. It was a happy and noisy crowd. Students were celebrating the end of a gruelling school year, and quite simply, their mood reflected the fact that they were young and full of energy and had all their lives ahead of them.

Anton was sitting across from Boris and Larissa, thinking about nothing else but Nina. He tried not to stare at her and not to appear too obvious or even rude, but he just couldn't take his eyes off her.

There were quite a few students sitting in Nina and Anatoly's compartment. One of them had a guitar and started to play a popular folksong; one by one the other students joined in, and soon the entire train-car was filled with the sound of student chorus.

Even in this crowd, among many voices, Anton could distinguish Nina's melodic and powerful voice.

"Larissa," he implored, "please tell me everything about Nina."

"Poor Anton, you're smitten!" Larissa wanted to keep the conversation light.

Anton's eyes were sombre. "No, Larissa, it's worse than that. I am in love."

Larissa looked intently at Anton and said, "Please understand, Anton. I have never been Nina's close friend. But I've been her classmate for four years and I can tell you that Nina is a very special person. She's caring and considerate, very honest and very straightforward. I think she's too trusting and maybe even a little naïve. Nina thinks that the world is made up of only good people. She treats everybody nicely and in turn, expects the same treatment from other people. I think that if she loves Tolya, you are out of luck. Nina is not a person to play games or to flirt lightly. Whatever she's doing in the Conservatory is done wholeheartedly. She always dedicates herself fully to every project she's involved in. I believe, in her relationships Nina would behave the same way - all or nothing. Anton, it's very easy to betray Nina, but you should never betray somebody like her. Do you understand what I mean?"

"I wonder," Boris ventured, "if her back is itching?"

"Why would her back itch?" Larissa asked irritably.

"Well, you've described her as an innocent angel. Angels have wings, so I wonder if Nina's wings are sprouting?" Boris chuckled at his own joke and added, "I'm sure you're exaggerating. In this day and age, you'd have to be a complete idiot to think that we're living in a perfect world and surrounded by virtuous people. Nina doesn't look stupid to me."

"I never said that she was stupid! I simply said that she was a nice person. Apparently, this concept is foreign to you," Larissa snapped, and the newly engaged couple found themselves getting into a lover's spat.

Anton didn't pay much attention to their bantering but he thought to himself, I wouldn't be able to stand such constant needling. Being with someone as sharp-tongued as Larissa would drive me crazy. I need my sweet Nina.

Soon the train reached their destination and everyone began making their way to Anatoly's dacha. The dacha itself was not impressive – a small, two-story summer cottage, but the location was truly amazing. The dacha was standing on the shores of a forest lake, amid huge oak trees. The cottage was covered with flowering vines and surrounded by flowerbeds. Anatoly's parents emerged from the cottage and greeted the students and the other guests.

"It's so beautiful here!" Larissa exclaimed when she was introduced, "and the cottage looks like it came straight out of a fairy-tale."

"Thank you," Anatoly's mother replied, "the flowers are mine but the cottage was built by Tolya and his father. Would you like to see the inside?"

"Yes, of course, thank you," Boris responded, as he was led with Larissa into the cottage by the proud parents.

Anton had no desire to see the cottage. Instead, he waited for the moment when Tolya went to tend to the grill and left Nina unaccompanied. He took this opportunity to strike up a conversation with her. "Nina," he said in a downcast voice, "I want to apologize for my offensive behaviour. It was rude of me to speak to you so presumptuously."

"Don't worry, Anton. I didn't really think that you meant what you said and didn't take your words seriously," Nina said, trying to sound casual. "But next time you want to meet a girl, I suggest you find a less dramatic approach."

"But I meant every word I said," Anton replied, as he looked intently into Nina's eyes.

Neither of them spoke another word for a long, awkward moment.

Then Anton solemnly said, "I have learned today the true meaning of the expression 'love at first sight'. But I didn't know then that your heart was already taken. I envy Anatoly. He's a very lucky man."

"My heart is not taken," Nina said in a very soft voice. "Tolya is a good friend of mine. I've known him for ages, ever since I began music school. But we are only dear friends."

"Nina, don't deceive yourself. For Anatoly, you are much more than a friend. He loves you. It's so obvious!"

"I know that. But I don't love him. However, it does not mean that..." Nina observed Anton's silly and happy grin and started to laugh.

Then they joined the others in the group who were sitting around the bonfire together. Everyone ate the traditional shish-kebabs, drank dry white wine, sang songs, and told stories. Most of the stories were horror stories involving alleged monster professors and innocent, hardworking students in distress.

During one of those stories, Anton discreetly motioned Nina aside and invited her to go for a stroll with him around the lake. Nina nodded her head slightly and followed Anton.

Those two would-be young lovers could not have enjoyed a more romantic evening. The full moon was shining on the smooth, dark waters of the lake and the sky was sparkling with bright stars. The sweet voice of a nightingale drifted through the otherwise quiet forest. Anton and Nina randomly talked about everything and about nothing in particular. They quickly discovered that they read the same books, loved the same composers, preferred the same actors, and cheered for the same soccer team. It did not seem to matter what subject they touched on, they agreed about everything.

They spoke about their families too. Anton had parents and a married sister in Leningrad, while Nina and her family were from Moscow. She was living in a two-room apartment with her mother. Nina's brother was married and lived with his family not too far from them. Nina's father left them when she was only three years old. He moved to another city, got married again and had a new family. Nina had seen him only a couple of times and even that was long ago. Her mother had never remarried and instead dedicated her life to raising her two children.

Nina and Anton continued strolling slowly around the lake, listening to the sounds of the forest and the distant sounds of the party. Suddenly, Nina inquired, "Anton, you must have a goal. What is it? What do you want to accomplish with your life?"

At this moment, Anton wanted only her; nothing else in the world mattered but Nina. Even so, he forced himself to focus and gave her a considered, less spur-of-the-moment answer.

"I want to be a concert pianist. I suppose most of the students in my class have the same goal. But will any of us achieve it? My professors tell me that I have a very good chance. Nina, I want you to hear my playing. Your opinion is very, very important to me."

"Of course, Anton, I would like to very much."

"Tomorrow, then!"

Nina smiled and responded agreeably, "That's great. Tomorrow it is."

Then in a more serious tone of voice she asked, "Anton, have you heard about the International Competition that will take place in Moscow next April?"

"Oh yes, it's basically *a must* for me. Every successful performing concert pianist has been a winner of one or more of those competitions." Anton replied.

For the next half-hour Anton and Nina talked at length about the competition. They knew that at the end of October, the administration of the Conservatory would decide who would be its representatives for the next April competition. After all, it was one of the most prestigious international competitions and the Moscow Conservatory was very scrupulous in the selection of its favoured candidates.

"I hope to be selected," Anton confided. "I plan to practice hard all summer. My entire career may depend on that competition, and I intend to win it."

"Me too," Nina asserted. "There's a vocal competition as well. I want to sing in the Bolshoi

Theatre, but as you said, so does most of my class. A victory in this competition would greatly increase my chances of being invited to work for the Bolshoi."

"Nina, it will guarantee their offer! I heard you today and I can tell you - you are fantastic. You will be selected and you will win. I'm certain of it!"

They sat down on a large rock and Anton took Nina's hand in his. He turned toward her and said, "Ours is not just a whirlwind romance, Nina. It's destiny." Then he gently pulled her towards him and kissed her softly. Nina's body tensed for a moment but she didn't resist. That first sweet kiss was like magic. Nina softly whispered, "I didn't know that I could be so happy. But how long will it last?"

"A lifetime, Nina. I promise you a lifetime of happiness."

On the early morning train back home Nina was sitting beside Anton. Boris and Larissa looked in astonishment at the happy couple and Larissa pointed out, "It took you more than half-a-year to propose to me, Boris. Your friend was much more decisive!"

From that moment on, Nina and Anton were together every possible moment. The very next day, as they had planned, Anton performed for Nina and she enthusiastically declared that he was the most talented pianist of their generation. Anton asked Nina to sing for him and tried to accompany her, but found that he did not have the aptitude for it. He couldn't just play for somebody else, making his music a secondary aspect and allowing the vocal sound to take precedence. It just wasn't his cup of tea.

Throughout the summer, Nina continued to work with her usual vocal coach and sometimes with her old friend Tolya.

At one point Nina tried to have a heart-to-heart conversation with Tolya but he assured her that it wasn't necessary. She was a free woman and entitled to give her love to anyone she chose. However, he assured her that he would remain her friend and that she could rely on him, as always.

Some of Tolya's friends called this position *noble*, but the majority agreed that he was quite stupid to let Nina go without a fight. Only Tolya's parents and his closest friends knew how devastated and how heartbroken he really was.

Young love is selfish. Nina and Anton weren't worrying or even thinking about Tolya. They were too happy to let even the slightest unpleasant thought diminish their bliss.

Larissa was right: Nina didn't play 'hard-to-get' games. Her love was unfettered and irrevocable and she did not disguise her feelings. Because of the friendship of Anton and Boris, Larissa and Nina started to spend more time together and by the end of the summer they became close friends. Nina's open display of her feelings and her surrender to all of Anton's desires and whims seemed to Larissa to be naïve and even dangerous. She tried to give her friend some sound advice. "Nina, you shouldn't always be so agreeable. A man should never take a woman for granted. When that happens, it's the beginning of the end of the relationship. Win Anton's respect first and foremost, and then his love will last."

Nina just laughed dismissively at this advice. "Larissa, every man is different. What works for Boris will not work for Anton. Anton loves me and I don't have to play with him. Our relationship is built on love, trust and mutual understanding."

Larissa was left shaking her head.

That summer was truly magical for Nina and Anton. It was filled with romance and passion, although that did not preclude both of them from working hard in their chosen and beloved musical fields. The only slight 'fly in the ointment' was the reaction of Nina's mother. She was civil and polite with Anton when she met him for the first time, but it was evident that she was upset.

"Nina," she asked her daughter when they were alone in the kitchen, "what about Tolya? Why did you dump him?'

"I didn't dump him, Mama," Nina asserted. "Tolya was always my very good friend and he still is. But I don't love Tolya. I love Anton."

"Well then, the topic is closed."

"Mama, why don't you like Anton? You just met him."

"He's too good-looking."

"And since when are good looks considered to be a crime?"

"It's just that good-looking men rarely make good husbands."

Nina understood very well where this remark had come from. She moved close to her mother and hugged her. "Mama, Anton is different. He's a good person, a very fine person. He will do everything to make me happy."

"If you're happy, then I'm happy too. Let's go back. Your *Prince Charming* is waiting."

Galina Georgievna's (Nina's mother) attitude towards Anton changed somewhat for the better after she met Anton's parents. They came to Moscow in the middle of August to visit their son and a meeting between the parents had been arranged. Galina really liked Anton's parents. In her opinion, they were 'salt of the earth' folks - dependable and unpretentious. Their love for each other, even after so many years of marriage was apparent, and Galina hoped that Anton would be as good a husband to her daughter as his father had been to his mother.

Meanwhile, Anton's parents were enchanted with Nina. "That's my boy!" his father exclaimed jubilantly. "Anton, you have as good a taste in women as I do!"

The meeting between the parents went smoothly

and all the involved parties decided that Nina and Anton would get married right after graduation, in June of the following year.

September and October passed by in a blur. Between the pressures of graduate year studies and preparation for competition tryouts, Anton and Nina hardly had enough time for food or sleep, but they still managed to find time for each other. At the end of October, the tryouts took place and they were both selected to participate in the competition in their respective categories. There were two other student pianists from Anton's class selected as well to represent the Moscow Conservatory, although everyone was betting on Anton to be the eventual winner. Nina was the only student selected from her classical vocal class.

In the middle of November, Boris and Larissa got married. Larissa's parents rented a large banquet hall for the occasion, and over two hundred guests were invited. Larissa was resplendent in her magnificent, custom-made dress.

"Our wedding will be much more modest," Anton whispered to Nina.

"Who cares? I'd even agree to elope, as long as it's with you," was the joyful, enthusiastic reply.

Ω

Boris's wedding impacted Anton's life, and not for the better. Boris moved to Larissa's apartment, and Anton found himself with a new roommate in the dormitory. The fellow, who had transferred to Moscow from the Perm Conservatory, was two years younger, and Anton considered him to be a backwater provincial. The new roommate was extremely irritating with his persistent questions about the Conservatory, the teachers, and about life in the capital. Everything about him annoyed Anton. Nina jokingly commented, "I think you detest him simply because his name is not Boris."

Anton conceded the point. He and Boris always got along well, always supported each other, and shared many happy memories. But there was another factor, and as Nina suspected, this aspect was the real reason behind Anton's frustration.

It was not possible for Anton and Nina to be alone together in Nina's apartment. Her mother was retired and stayed at home most of the time. In addition, many years ago, her mother had asked Nina never to spend time with a man in their apartment until she was properly married. Nina promised, and therefore being together with Anton in the apartment was never up for discussion. Furthermore, renting a hotel room for an unmarried couple was impossible in the old Soviet Union.

When Boris was Anton's roommate, all Anton had to say was, "*Borya, you need some fresh air. Go for a walk and don't come back for at least two hours. Nina's coming.*" Boris always obliged. There were quite a few times when Anton returned the favour, leaving Boris and Larissa alone in their room. It was a normal, accepted practice between friends. Now, when Anton hinted to his new roommate what was being asked of him, the young man frowned.

"A woman? In our room? Isn't that against dormitory regulations? I'm sorry, but I'm not going to risk my place in this dormitory. I would have no other choice but to inform the authorities if you bring your girlfriend here."

Anton was furious. He needed to concentrate on his studies; the competition was approaching, and yet all he could think about was his longing for Nina and his loathing of his new roommate. A month after Boris's wedding, Anton asked Nina, "Why are we waiting for the end of the graduation year? Why can't we get married right now?"

"But our parents wanted to make a wedding for us next June. It takes time to properly organize a wedding."

"Nina, do you want a wedding, or me? Or do you have some reservations about marrying me?"

"Of course not, Anton, but I don't even have a dress."

"How long does it take to get a dress?"

"I can ask my mother to help me and I suppose we could make my dress in a couple of weeks," Nina replied hesitantly. "However..."

Anton didn't give her a chance to finish her thought. "Thank you, darling. I knew you would understand."

Two weeks later, Nina and Anton were married. They had a very informal reception in Nina's apartment. Anton's parents and sister came from Leningrad. All through the evening the students from the Conservatory were stopping by to congratulate the newlyweds. There was always somebody playing piano or guitar and somebody singing. Anatoly arrived with a large bouquet of flowers and wished Nina and Anton a lot of love and happiness.

Anton was more than satisfied: granted, Boris's wedding was more formal and grandiose, but his own was much more fun.

Anton moved into Nina's apartment and they settled into a happy married life. But there was no question of a honeymoon; with the winter's semester exams approaching and the looming competition, there was just no time for holidays, not even for a short getaway.

The International Music Competition

The winter exams had been passed successfully, and before they knew it April had arrived and it was time for the competition.

In the category of female vocalists there were over seventy contestants. In Anton's category there were over sixty hopeful pianists. The competition was comprised of three *rounds,* and traditionally the small number of contestants who survived the two elimination rounds before the final round were already considered to be winners in their own right. It could be expected that if they were Soviet citizens, the best and the most desirable companies of the Soviet Union would woo them.

Nina's competition round started a day before Anton's and so he decided to forgo his practice for a couple of hours and attend her performance. One after another, the young female candidates ascended the stage and sang well-known opera arias. Some of the contestants were very good. Boris, Larissa and Anton carefully discussed each candidate and alertly observed the reactions of the judges. However, when it was Nina's turn to perform, it was immediately apparent that she was in a league of her own. Her voice, her technique, and her presentation on the stage were vastly superior to all the other competitors who had preceded her. The affirmative nods of the judges and the thunderous applause of the audience confirmed the judgement of Anton and his friends - Nina was simply the best.

After her performance, Nina quickly changed, washed off her stage make-up, and joined her husband and her friends. "I want to hear Miller and Kowalski. I've been told that they are my most serious competition," Nina whispered.

The rumours were true: both of those young women were very talented vocal performers and stood out from the other candidates, just as Nina had done. Anton was quite surprised to see the reaction of his wife: her eyes were sparkling and alight with excitement and her cheeks were flushed. Anton frowned, "Nina, aren't you worried? Those two are good, very good."

"Sure, I'm worried, but that's what the competition's all about. I felt that I might be the best in the Conservatory, but I always wondered how I would rank on the international level. Now I know - I'm on a par with the best. Let the battle begin and may the best competitor win!"

However, when a very attractive brunette appeared on stage and began to sing, Nina grimaced with anger and hissed to Larissa, "What is she doing here? She wasn't even selected to participate!"

Larissa and Nina exchanged furtive glances and Larissa murmured, "Well, that's the end of the competition. The first place is taken. Now the three of you will have to fight it out for second and third place."

"Why do you say that?" Anton inquired. "Her voice isn't that great."

"It doesn't have to be! Her connections are superior to her voice. I am sure her papa has promised her the gold medal," Larissa grumbled bitterly.

"Who cares?" Nina responded hotly. "For me the gold medal is a step on the road to success, an important achievement. For her it's just one more toy that papa will procure for her. I'll just do my part and the rest is up to the judges. In any case, the world needs more than one good singer."

The following day, it was Anton's turn to show the judges what he was capable of. Nina, Boris and Larissa were sitting in the audience, nervously holding hands.

They were not disappointed. Anton performed with the poise of a master and a world-class recitalist. When he re-joined his friends, Boris whispered, "Consider the medal in your pocket, mate," and then he asked, "are we going or staying?"

"Staying," was Anton's response. "I want to hear the rest of them."

Nina fondly kissed her husband and apologized. "I must go; my professor is waiting for me."

"I'm going with you," Larissa whispered, and the girls left the concert hall. Anton listened to the succession of contestants with growing confidence - so far, he was the best. His classmate, Konstantin Sorokin, performed very nicely and Boris commented, "You know what they say in Canada: 'close, but no cigar'."

Another new contestant was now trotting to the grand piano that was standing in the middle of the stage and Anton commented derisively, "Look at that bunny-rabbit. I wonder if they'll have to put a book on the bench to help him reach the keyboard."

The figure on the stage looked almost comical: a small young man with outsized ears and an ill-fitting suit, too large for his small frame. He didn't approach the instrument with a confident stride either, but rather with small steps and indeed, it practically looked that he was hopping.

Anton's musing was right - the bench had to be adjusted. Finally, the *Bunny-Rabbit* got comfortable on his seat and began to play. From the first note, Anton and the entire audience immediately forgot about the diminutive stature and the oversize ears of the contestant. He was unbelievably talented. Every note was defined and perfected, and together, all the notes and chords blended into effortless and beautiful harmony. Anton was hearing a familiar musical score, yet it seemed as if he was listening to it for the first time. He felt shivers travelling up and down his spine.

The judges were not just nodding this time. It was much more emphatic than that: they were spellbound. When the music stopped, the audience sat in rapt silence for a moment and then broke into wild applause. Anton tensed.

"OK," Boris said as casually as he could, "so there are two serious competitors. As Nina would say, the world needs more than one good pianist."

The appearance and stage manner of the next contestant was the antithesis of the *Bunny-Rabbit*. He was very tall and lanky and looked like an lamp-post. He reached the piano center-stage in three large steps, shook his mane of curly black hair and started to play.

Each chord that rippled from the piano struck Anton's consciousness like a sharp knife. All his senses became alert, and with growing apprehension he observed every nuance of the judges' reactions, every smile and nod from the audience. Someone behind him whispered, "These last two competitors are virtuosos." Those words were akin to the pronouncement of a death sentence for Anton. Never had the label *virtuoso* been applied to him.

After the final contestant finished playing, a subdued and pale Anton quickly excused himself and went home. He felt angry. He felt betrayed by his teachers and by the music itself. Why had nobody forewarned him about those two? Why had nobody even suggested to him that such a high level of performance was physically possible?

When Nina arrived home, she found her husband lying in bed, fully clothed.

"Anton, darling, Boris told me that there were two other strong contestants. That's great! The challenge is on. Now it's between the three of you."

Anton looked incredulously at his wife. How could she be so insensitive and stupid? "Nina, the competition is over. I am not on a par with either of those two."

It didn't matter what words of encouragement Nina tried. Anton was inconsolable.

Early the next morning, Nina gingerly suggested, "Anton, you need to practice."

"What for?" was the bitter response, but finally he pulled himself together and went to the Conservatory. His beaming professor was waiting for him. "Very well done, my boy! Two more performances like that and you are a winner!"

Nice try, Anton thought, but he didn't reply. For the first time, he didn't believe his teacher.

Eighteen vocalists and twenty pianists had advanced to the second round. Nina and Anton were among the group of surviving contestants. They had their next performances scheduled on the same day so they could not sit in the audience and cheer for one-another.

Again, Anton was playing ahead of his two main opponents. This time his interpretation of the music sounded a bit strained. It was still a good, powerful performance, but Anton inwardly knew that the tone was shallower and more mechanical. He was playing on inertia; the spark was not there. When he was walking back from the stage, he noticed that his professor was looking at him with dismay and concern.

The *Bunny-Rabbit* and the *Lamp-Post*, as Anton has christened that pair, both performed brilliantly again, and there were even some added tonal nuances and a new magic in interpretation of their music.

As Anton listened to his rivals, he experienced a genuine fear of failure for the first time in his life. He broke out in a sweat and his hands became cold and clammy. Boris glanced at his friend and said, "You need a drink." Anton did not protest.

However, if Boris had in mind one drink to calm Anton's nerves, Anton was ready to drink himself into oblivion. He wanted to drown his sorrows and to forget all about his failure, his humiliation.

He didn't remember how he eventually got home or how he got to bed that night. The next morning, he even forgot to ask Nina how she had fared with her performance. Again, Nina suggested that it was time to go to practice, but this time Anton refused. "The competition is over for me. I played lousy yesterday. I'm out of the running for any medal."

Nina left the apartment without him and Anton remained in bed for a long while. He actually hoped now that he would not be advanced to the third tour. He just could not go through this routine one more time; it was too embarrassing for him to perform, knowing that he would not be counted among the best.

Five vocalists and six pianists were ultimately selected to advance to the third tour. To Nina's delight and Anton's chagrin, they both made it. Everybody was congratulating them. Just to have advanced to the third and final round was considered to be a great achievement.

Anton remained dispirited, but he reluctantly resumed his practice routine.

By the luck of the draw, this time Anton was the last contestant to perform. He listened to the performance of his classmate Sorokin, then the performances of the two virtuosos. Finally, it was his turn. On heavy wooden legs, Anton approached the piano like a man walking to his own execution. When he sat down on the bench, he felt that his hands were sweaty and shaking slightly. He did his best to gain control over this nervous tremor and began to play. Anton played more poorly than he had in years and even made several technical errors. That had never happened to him before during any major recital.

The competition was over. In the piano category, the gold medal was awarded to the *Lamp-Post*, the silver to the *Bunny-Rabbit* (Anton had finally learned their real names but still thought about them in those derogatory terms), and the recipient of the bronze medal, to everyone's surprise, was Konstantin Sorokin, Anton's competent but less talented classmate.

Anton stood aside and watched how the representatives of different companies went to talk to the other five pianists who were in the third tour. Not one person approached him. People avoided his eyes and quickly brushed past him.

Anton went to see his professor. "I made it to the third tour, Professor. Why hasn't anybody offered anything to me?"

"There are a lot of challenges and demands in show business, Anton. Companies cannot afford to hire a musician who could so easily crumble under pressure," the professor explained with a pained expression on his face. There was undisguised disappointment, frustration and bitterness in his voice.

"It would be better if I had never attended this competition!" Anton exclaimed.

"Yes," the professor sadly agreed, "much better for everyone," and he walked away.

Larissa and Boris came to Anton to give him the news: Nina had performed *Casta Diva* from Bellini's *Norma*, one of the most challenging arias in the soprano's repertoire, to a standing ovation. She and the contestant with high-level connections shared first place, so they both received gold medals. Kowalski was awarded the silver medal and Miller got the bronze. Nina was currently talking with the representative from the Bolshoi Theatre and had asked Anton to wait.

"Good for her," Anton mumbled. "Give her my congratulations. I'll see her at home."

For several days, the relationship between the young couple was severely strained. Anton simply could not understand how Nina could be cheerful when all his own hopes and dreams had been shattered and his entire future was cast into doubt.

For her part, Nina was bitter that Anton could not be happy for her. Eventually, it was she who approached Anton, hugging him and kissing him, and telling him how much she loved him and believed in him.

The furor over the competition finally settled down and normal studies resumed. By the time the graduation exams were held, Anton had recovered from the unfortunate competition experience and performed well.

Mundane Reality

Shortly after his graduation, Anton was summoned to the office of his professor. He found the professor engaged in a discussion with a distinguished looking man. Anton's heart skipped a beat - he recognized the Director of the *Moscow Philharmonic,* Alexei Nikolayevich Parchomov.

Parchomov was blunt. "You performed poorly during the competition. Anton. This is a fact and everyone knows it. I'm only talking to you out of respect for my old friend," and he nodded toward Anton's professor.

"He believes in you and assures me that it was a one-time weakness and it will never happen again. I hope he's right, because I am offering you a job. We are organizing a troupe of classical performers to tour around the Soviet Union. You will not be touring in New York and London, but in Poltava, Ryazan and Tula. You will be sleeping in awful local hotels and eating lousy food. You will perform before audiences who may be hearing a classical concert for the first time in their lives. Accordingly, you will not be playing your favourite complicated and challenging pieces, but what we call 'light classics'. But you will be playing, Anton, and playing solo."

Parchomov looked intently and critically at Anton and added, "If you excel, and only *if* you do, then you may get an opportunity to play in Moscow. There is still a good possibility that you could eventually be playing solo on the best stages of the world, but you will have to earn it, Anton, with years of gruelling work ahead of you. Now, I am only going to ask you once: do you want this job?"

"Yes!" Anton replied emphatically and without

hesitation. The elder musicians looked at each other and nodded their heads in satisfaction. Anton had understood that the slightest evidence of indecision on his part would have lost him this vital opportunity.

At home, Anton explained to Nina, "The most important thing is that I will be part of the *Moscow Philharmonic*. All the concerts and all the tours originate from there. The idea to educate the masses in the provinces and to introduce them to the beauty of classical music is not a new one. If they want me to play in the small cities, I don't mind. I am sure that it's only temporary. Before long they will recognize that it's silly to waste such talent as mine and will engage me for concerts in Moscow and abroad. They want me to pay my dues for my failure in that stupid competition. Fine, I'll pay my dues. Nina, in a year I'll be playing in Vienna, not in some isolated Vologda... you will see."

"I have no doubt that you're right, sweetheart. You will have to work very hard to prove to the administration of the *Philharmonic* how dedicated you are. But your position is not any different from mine. In the Bolshoi, I am starting in the chorus. It will take time before I become a soloist. The most important thing is that we're both working and doing what we've been trained to do. It's only a beginning, but it's a good beginning," Nina said cheerfully.

"Nina," Anton said ruefully, "we should wait to have children until you are promoted to soloist. If you leave the theatre before your promotion, you will have to start all over again when you're ready to return, or you may not even have a job to go back to. If you take a maternity leave as a soloist, you return as a soloist."

"I completely agree with you, Anton. We are very young. Let's wait."

In early July, Boris and Larissa emigrated to Canada, Nina started her job at the Bolshoi Theatre, and Anton departed on his first tour. The carefree student days were over and they began their adult working lives.

Ω

Within several months, Anton found himself having to cope with a growing dissatisfaction. He was trying to reassure himself that these tours in the small cities of Russia were only temporary, that he must not pay attention to small irritations, but think instead about 'the big picture'. In truth, he hated leaving Nina and Moscow. He hated travelling in the smoke-filled trains and sleeping in the cheap hotels, and he detested spending his days and nights with the constantly quarrelling members of the troupe. Most of all, he hated to play the same 'light' pieces again and again.

He was not permitted to select the pieces for his performances, or even to suggest them. He played only what he was told to play. He despised the small cities' audiences, that bunch of provincial ignoramus who did not understand anything about classical music. Quite a few of the musicians in the troupe were drinking more than they should, and Anton found it harder and harder to resist the temptation. What's more, the pay was a mere pittance.

Big-ticket expenditures were out of reach for Anton and Nina. Anton looked with envy at the shiny cars gliding along the streets of Moscow and fretted that he would never own one of them. He wanted to take Nina for vacation to Crimea but it was not within his budget. He was also tired of living in the same apartment with his mother-in-law, but there was no other choice.

Yet among his former classmates, Anton was considered the lucky one: he had an apartment in Moscow and worked for the *Philharmonic*!

Another thing that annoyed Anton to no end was Nina's kind-hearted willingness to help everyone else. She had a knack for cutting and styling hair, and so her friends and neighbours were exploiting her shamelessly.

"Why are you doing this, Nina?" Anton asked her once. "You're a singer, not a hair-stylist. None of those people respect your time and never pay you a single penny."

"Anton, I'm styling their hair for fun, not for the money. I like to make people look beautiful," Nina explained. Nonetheless, she started to make sure that her 'clients' came to the apartment when Anton was absent.

The next summer, the graduate class of students gathered together for their one-year reunion and Anton listened to the stories about the experiences of other graduates. It had been a hard year for everyone. Nobody had really prospered or achieved much professionally within that year. In fact, quite a few of them envied Anton and Nina. After all, Anton was performing solo in concerts and Nina had started to get her first small solo parts at the Bolshoi Theatre. Konstantin Sorokin didn't attend the reunion: he was on tour in the United States.

Ω

Letters started to arrive from Boris and Larissa. Apparently life in Canada for classical musicians was not any easier than in the Soviet Union. They did not get any contracts with established Canadian companies, so Boris put together his own small band. They were working in a Russian restaurant and night club in Toronto and performing for weddings and other celebrations. In addition, Boris and Larissa performed for some charity concerts. They were not upset or disappointed; it was only a beginning. The most important priority for them, Boris wrote, was attaining everyday knowledge of English and they were studying very hard.

Nina and Anton sometimes discussed the contents

of those letters and tried to envision what it would really be like to live in Canada. However, by winter, when nothing had changed in their lives, Anton started to pay even greater attention to each letter.

Before the New Year, Anton was summoned to the administration office. He hurried there, hoping to hear some good news: that he would play in Moscow, or maybe he would be sent somewhere abroad. In any case, he would get to play real music, no more 'light classics'.

The news was quite disappointing, and frankly, humiliating. Anton was being asked to play in Moscow in several industrial plants and factories during their New Years' parties.

When he arrived home that day, he found the latest letter from Canada. Boris wrote that they had secured some engagements at an Ontario resort and had bought a used van. They were planning to use the van for travelling with their instruments, but in Toronto they were driving a car that they had bought from Boris's brother. Boris was lamenting that the car was quite old and had a high mileage, but that was all they could afford for now. In addition, he wrote, Larissa was dreaming of buying some townhouse or semi-detached house, so they had started to save and put some money aside for their first home. If they were very careful, in a couple of years they would have enough money for a down payment.

Anton couldn't believe his eyes - two cars! A house in two years! And he, Anton, was supposed to feel sorry for poor Boris that his life was difficult? With his pittance of a salary he wouldn't have a car in twenty years. As far as a house was concerned, Anton was convinced that he was destined to live his entire life and then die in the same dreary apartment.

1985 did not bring too many changes in Anton's life. He was still travelling within the Soviet Union. Several times he had more interesting performances: he was sent to Kiev, then to Riga and Vilnius. In the larger cities, he performed more challenging and hence more satisfying pieces. But these occasions were few and far between. Nina was by now receiving more serious solo performance parts at the Bolshoi, although officially she was still a member of the chorus.

The country had a new leader, Mikhail Gorbachev, and new words came into play in their vocabulary: *perestroika* and *glasnost*. The iron curtain had been raised, if only by just a little bit.

At the beginning of 1986, Anton decided it was time to have a serious conversation with Nina about their circumstances.

"Nina, when I was growing up," he was saying, "I imagined my life in terms of colours - bright colours. It's hard to explain, but in my mind I saw clear blue sky, green trees and a bright yellow sun. When I thought about performing, I envisioned a brightly lit stage with a shiny black grand piano in the center.

"Now, I'm still seeing my life in colours, but there are only two colours: white, which is you, my love, my only bright spot; and gray - gray trains, gray hotel rooms, gray stages, gray streets of gray cities, and gray people who surround me oppressively. Nina, I am suffocating. OK, I admit it's my own fault. I will never forgive myself for my collapse during that competition, but I'm not prepared to suffer my entire life for the sake of one past mistake.

"And what about you, Nina? You're a winner, the recipient of a gold medal, but how do they treat you at the Bolshoi? You should be singing lead roles by now. You should be the prima donna of the company, but instead they're feeding you with little solos here and there. Nina, we are wasting our best years."

"Anton, darling, what else are we supposed to do? We knew all along that the life of musicians and singers was not easy. We knew that we would have to work very hard and eventually…"

Anton interrupted. "I can't stand that word *eventually*. When? In ten years? In twenty? Just before our retirement? Just look at Boris and Larissa. They already have two cars, they're planning to buy their own house, they have their own band, and they're moving forward with their lives! Nina, let's face it: we are much more talented than our friends. I don't want to diminish their talent and ability, but there's no comparison with our level, right?"

"Maybe that's so, Anton, but they are in Canada and we are here in the Soviet Union."

"Precisely!"

"So, what do you suggest? Moving to Canada?" The idea was so outlandish that Nina started to giggle, but then she noticed the sombre face of her husband and promptly stopped laughing.

"Nina, direct emigration to Canada and the United States is allowed now. Granted, it's not easy. We wouldn't be able to go via Italy as refugees and then arrive into the welcoming arms of family sponsors and the Jewish community, as Boris did. We would have to fend for ourselves from day one, but we would be living in the free world. We could go for auditions in New York, Boston, Philadelphia, Toronto and Montreal. We would be able to travel to Europe! I'm sure that there are any number of companies that need musicians and vocalists with our superior qualifications."

"Anton, please, let's not talk about it. It's impossible. I can't leave my mother and you can't leave your parents. We are simple Russian people and our place is here in Russia. The country is going through big changes and I am sure that these changes are going to be for the better."

"This country is going through turmoil," Anton countered. "It's going to be much worse before it gets any better. I'm not planning to sit around here and wait for better times. I want to live now. Nina, there's no need to worry about our parents. It's not like before, when people were leaving forever and weren't ever allowed to return. We would be visiting them and they would be visiting us from time to time. Maybe, once we're established, they would move to Canada too and live with us."

"No, Anton, I can't do it," Nina asserted and abruptly left the room. It was the first time since they met that Nina had said *no* to Anton.

Despite Nina's rejection of his proposal, Anton did not give up his quest. In fact, he became increasingly obsessed with the idea of emigration. Often, after making love with her, he would whisper sweet words in Nina's ear and talk about Carnegie Hall, the Lincoln Center, Roy Thompson Hall, and the Canadian Opera Company. He was painting illusionary pictures of recognition and applause and flowers from adoring fans. He also bought glossy lifestyle magazines and showed Nina enticing photos of American cars, and large houses, and Caribbean resort beaches.

Nina remained unmovable. She just could not imagine herself leaving her mother and Moscow and the theatre. She did not want to emigrate and that was that!

Anton altered his strategy. He became moody and sullen. He left on his tours without kissing Nina goodbye and didn't call her while he was away. Whenever Nina called him, he always sounded depressed. Anton started to drink too much as well.

All of this was more than Nina could bear. She hated to see her beloved husband so unhappy and she finally brought up the subject of emigration with her mother. The older woman looked sadly at her daughter and said, "The place of a wife is beside her husband. If Anton is so adamant about emigrating, what can you do? Do you want him to leave without you?"

"Oh no! Mama, I can't live without Anton."

"Then start packing, Nina. Don't worry about me. Your brother will take care of me."

"Will you come to stay with us, Mama?"

"Let's take it one day at a time, dear," was the melancholy response from her mother.

No sooner had Nina conceded than Anton miraculously became an entirely different person: energetic, purposeful, and what was most important, cheerful. He decided to apply for immigration simultaneously into both the United States and Canada. In the United States, Anton surmised, there were more opportunities for musicians and singers, but in Canada they could be near their close friends, Boris and Larissa.

The necessary documents were assembled and the applications completed. Secretly, Nina hoped that they would be rejected, and so she went on with her life without thinking too much about the prospect of emigration.

The summer brought some good news for Nina: the next upcoming season, she would start as an official soloist for the opera company of the Bolshoi Theatre. Even more exciting was her assigned role as an understudy for *Mimi* in Puccini's *La Bohème*. All through those summer months she was busy rehearsing her first significant part, fully dedicating herself to this challenge.

At the end of August, Anton and Nina were called to the Consular Section of the American Embassy. The interview was short and conclusive. The Consul General asked them a few questions and then announced his decision.

"There are a lot of competent musicians in the United States of America, and every year a new group of young and talented students graduate from our fine schools and colleges. They all need jobs. They have everything that you have to offer, but in addition they have competency in English. You don't have those language skills, unfortunately. In the States, you would just become another statistic, relying on the unemployment and welfare programs. Go home and develop your professional talents and skills here. It's an exciting time for your country and you should stay and be a part of it."

Nina couldn't have agreed with the Consul more. She hoped that the result of this interview would diminish, if not extinguish Anton's enthusiasm for emigration. But she was wrong.

Ω

Two more months passed and then they were called to the Canadian Embassy. The beginning of their interview followed much the same pattern. The Consul General began by asking them questions to verify their credentials and more importantly, their knowledge of English. But this time Anton behaved differently; evidently, he came better prepared.

In quite adequate English he started to talk about the history of the Canadian Opera Company and the Toronto Symphony Orchestra; he cited the names of the directors of those companies, the conductors and the leading musicians as if they were his personal friends. He admitted that he recognized the difficulties lying ahead of them and cited Boris and Larissa as an example of ambitious immigrants who became self-sufficient without being dependent on the government. He assured the Consul that he was ready to do whatever it took and that he was not afraid of any work opportunity in the world of music.

The Consul and the interpreter were visibly impressed. Nina was shocked. She knew that Anton had been studying English and that he took along all kinds of English books and magazines on his tours, but still, his interview performance came as a total surprise.

The Consul then directed his attention to Nina and asked, "And what is the young lady planning to do in Canada?"

At that moment, Nina knew that their future was in her hands. If she failed now, Anton would never forgive her. One part of her wanted to mutter something so inappropriate in her terrible, broken English that the Consul would immediately deny them further consideration. Then they could continue living in Moscow and she could perform that solo role that she was working so hard for. But she was nonetheless a loving wife and felt that it was her ultimate responsibility to support her husband.

Nina rose from her seat, assumed the stance of a singer on stage, and in her enthralling, beautiful voice sang the first stanza of *Si, mi chiamano Mimi* from *La Bohème*, her newly rehearsed aria.

The Consul was overwhelmed. He rose from his chair, stepped around the desk, came forward to Nina and kissed her hand graciously. Then, still grasping her hand and looking straight into her eyes, he proclaimed, "It would be a crime not to admit such a talented woman as you to Canada. Well, Russia's loss is going to be Canada's gain."

He returned to his seat, looked intently at the young couple and proclaimed with a broad smile, "Welcome to Canada."

Ω

Nina and Anton didn't need much time for preparation. They had no furniture to sell, no apartment to dispose of, and by the middle of November they were ready to depart.

When Nina resigned from the Bolshoi, the reactions of her colleagues were quite varied. Some were jealous - Nina was escaping the turmoil of a country in a period of drastic change. Others were shaking their heads in amazement and disbelief. Nina had just been promoted and she was on the path to a great future with one of the best opera companies in the world. One of her vocal coaches, an older gentleman, came to Nina and bluntly informed her, "Nina, you are making a huge mistake. Some species of plants are very sensitive and can't be replanted. They wilt away and die. Your roots are in Russia, Nina, and I'm afraid that you are one of those kinds of plants."

Anton's departure from the *Moscow Philharmonic* was less dramatic. His colleagues wished him good luck, but nobody seemed to be surprised and none of them encouraged Anton to stay.

The day before their departure, Nina's old school friend, Anatoly, stopped by to say goodbye. "Nina," he asked, "are you sure you know what you're doing? Do you really want to leave Moscow and the Bolshoi?"

"Tolya, let me be totally honest with you," Nina replied. "No, I don't want to go. But a wife must be beside her husband and support him. I love Anton. I love him more than I love my own life. He makes me a very happy woman. All that I wish for you, Tolya, is to find a love as big and beautiful as mine. Good luck, my dear friend."

"Good luck to you, Nina. I wish you the best of everything and I want you to know that I will always be your friend," Tolya said while looking into Nina's eyes. And in his eyes, Nina could see such a deep sadness and all-consuming love that she felt a momentary pang of regret. She was relieved when Tolya took his leave. Anton, busily chatting to other well-wishers, had paid no heed to Tolya or his parting conversation with Nina.

Anton's parents came from Leningrad to say farewell to their son and daughter-in-law. Anton's mother was weeping, virtually non-stop. His father sought one last serious talk with Anton and Nina. He tried to discourage them from leaving, drawing upon everything in his arsenal, ranging from painting a horrific picture of life in a capitalist country, to reminding them of the poor state of health of both of their mothers.

But the impassioned urgings and arguments of Anton's father were to no avail. The following day, Nina and Anton bade a final farewell to her mother and his parents, and then they boarded a flight to Toronto to begin the new life that awaited them in Canada.

Hopes and Travails of New Immigrants

Boris and Larissa were waiting for the new arrivals at the airport with welcoming flowers and happy smiles. Boris was looking smart in his stylish Canadian clothes and Larissa looked very big in her maternity outfit.

"Larissa, you didn't write anything about your pregnancy!" Nina exclaimed, hugging her friend.

"One more month and I'm a mama!" a joyful Larissa declared. "Let's go to our car," she said. "There is so much we have to tell you."

They piled into Boris's car and he confidently drove away from the airport parking lot. Once they were on the highway, Boris enthusiastically started to tell Anton and Nina about the arrangements he and Larissa had made on their behalf. "We may have an apartment for you... We finally bought that semi-detached house that we were writing you about," Boris was saying.

"It's very close to the apartment building we used to live in," Larissa added.

"That's right, so we decided to keep our apartment for now and sublet it to you. It's a one-bedroom unit with a living room, bedroom and a small kitchen," Boris explained.

"Now," Larissa cautioned her friends, "please understand, it's nothing fancy, but quite satisfactory for a start. When we moved to Canada we bought some furniture, but most of it we received from our relatives and it's staying in the apartment for you. For our new place, we decided to buy all new furniture," she proclaimed proudly.

Boris continued, "So, we're driving you to the apartment that we were living in for almost three years.

Now it's yours, and if you don't like it you can find something else. But at least for now you have a place to stay. Today is the eighteenth of November and the rent is paid until December. You have two weeks to find some work."

"This is great!" Anton exclaimed. "I'm sure that it's more than satisfactory. You Canadians are spoiled rotten, but for us a one-bedroom apartment is a dream come true."

"Oh, thank you so much, my dear friends! I can't wait to see this apartment," Nina piped in joyfully.

"You can apply to the government for social assistance, but we suggest you become self-sufficient as soon as you can," Boris advised.

Larissa interrupted her husband and said. "We have an idea, Nina. Boris decided I shouldn't be singing anymore in the restaurant."

"You should have stopped singing a long time ago." Boris interjected and looked fondly at his wife. Then he addressed Nina.

"It's too difficult for Larissa in her condition. We were postponing looking for a new singer because we were hoping that you wouldn't mind substituting for Larissa. What do you think, Nina?"

"Do you actually want me to sing in a restaurant?" Nina cried out in total shock. "What would I sing? *The Marriage of Figaro*? *Rigoletto*? *Tosca*?"

"Nina, welcome to the world of immigration and to the world of capitalism," Larissa teased. "You need to pay rent and buy food like everybody else. Work is work."

Boris then added, "Nina, the pay is not bad and Larissa will show you the songs. Believe me, there is nothing to it.

"And as far as you are concerned, Anton, there is another restaurant being opened and one of my friends is forming a band. His name is Alex and he's a graduate of the Kiev Conservatory in the violin programme. He needs a keyboard player and I've asked him to wait for you. The money that you both would make is not that great, but at least it would be enough for necessities.

"Now, let's talk about real jobs for the future. Anton, you should meet with talent agents and start looking for some gigs. I have a list for you and I made some preliminary phone calls. I wanted to organize an audition with the Toronto Symphony Orchestra for you, but they have no openings just now. They suggested that I should inquire again before the next season.

"Nina, Larissa organized an audition for you at the Canadian Opera Company. It will be at the beginning of February, so you have enough time to prepare."

"Guys, I don't know what to say. You have done so much more that we could possibly have hoped for. We will never forget your kindness. Boris, Larissa, we owe you, big-time!" a grateful Anton exclaimed.

"You owe us nothing," Boris laughed. "We're very happy that you're here. You will soon learn that in early stages of immigration it's very easy to acquire an acquaintance, but..."

"Very difficult to find a real friend," Larissa finished the sentence for him.

"But we *do* have real friends, so we're one step ahead. I'm sorry for my initial reaction. I will do whatever it takes to make our life in Canada successful," Nina added.

Soon they arrived at their new home on Fishersville Street in Willowdale, a northern suburb of Toronto and near the center of the Russian immigrant community neighborhood. They took an elevator to the fifth floor and entered the apartment.

"Nina, it's bigger than your mother's place in Moscow and it's all ours!" Anton exclaimed. "No more sharing with the mother-in-law."

"Yes, it's great," Nina replied, thinking for a fleeting

moment about her mother and how much she already missed her.

They looked around the apartment and at the furniture; then they opened the fridge and the pantry, only to discover to their delight that both were fully stocked. Boris and Larissa had bought them enough food to last for several weeks.

A new life had begun on a truly positive note for Anton and Nina.

Ω

The next day, Anton and Boris went to meet Alex, the founder of the new band. Meanwhile, Larissa started to coach Nina on the restaurant's entertainment repertoire.

It seemed that lady luck was smiling on the new immigrants. Their start in Canada was easier than for most other newcomers. Anton landed the position of keyboard player in the new band based on Boris's recommendation. In addition, their visit to a local agent proved to be successful too. With the approaching Christmas season, piano players were needed to perform carols in office towers and in the malls. These were not the places where Anton longed to play, but he would be making money practically from his first week in Canada and still have time for practice on the piano. Anton knew that he must spend several hours playing each day in order to maintain his skills for better job opportunities and he fully intended to do so.

Nina easily became acquainted with the songs within one day, under Larissa's supervision bought some new outfits appropriate for the restaurant, and was ready to start her new job.

On the very next Saturday, Nina sang with the restaurant's band for the first time and it was a resounding success. Patrons loved the new, beautiful singer and her easy-going manner. The members of the band befriended Nina and praised how comfortable it was for them to work with her.

Likewise, Anton's carol performances were very enjoyable for both the audience and even for himself. He liked playing the easy and merry tunes while observing the professionally dressed Canadian business people walking by and pausing to listen. During the lunch hour, quite a large crowd gathered around Anton and he tried to play his best for his first Canadian audience.

The rehearsals with the band, however, were not going as well. After the first rehearsal, Alex mildly pointed out that Anton was playing his part too loudly. "Anton," he said, "take it easy, man. You aren't playing on the big stage." Then after the second rehearsal, Anton was reprimanded. "It's hard for our vocalist to sing. You're trying to outplay everybody else."

After the third rehearsal, Alex dismissively announced to Anton, "It isn't working out as I expected, Anton. You're out."

Anton was not overly upset. Playing in a restaurant band was hardly his idea of a dream job in any event and he was otherwise busy enough.

However, after the New Year, engagements with the agency had almost dried up, although Anton was still called upon to play occasionally. He was introduced to the priest of a Russian Orthodox Church and was sometimes invited to play for wedding ceremonies. Unfortunately, this was not enough to support a family and it certainly wasn't bringing him any closer to the fulfillment of his dreams: headliner engagements in classical concerts on the serious stages of the world and the comfortable life of a wealthy man.

In February, Nina went for her scheduled audition at the Canadian Opera Company. Her loyal friend Larissa left her small baby, Michael, with Boris and accompanied Nina. For her audition, Nina decided to sing an aria that she had performed during the third tour of the Moscow competition: *Casta Diva*. She sang majestically and the adjudicators could be seen enthusiastically nodding their heads and smiling their approval.

After the audition, everyone shook Nina's hand and she was told that she would be informed of a decision shortly. It was not a question of her qualifications, she was assured, just a matter of budget and verification of the available positions. Nina was ecstatic. She was certain that she had made it! She went looking for Larissa and found her in the lobby of the theatre. Surprisingly, Larissa was looking gloomy.

"What's wrong, Larissa? Aren't you happy for me?" Nina asked worriedly.

"There's nothing to be happy about yet," Larissa replied.

"Why not? They said…" Nina started.

"That they will inform you. They didn't offer you an actual contract, right? Nina, while you were schmoozing with two of the committee judges, the other two men on the panel were leaving and I overheard their conversation."

"What did they say?"

Larissa explained. "One of the members of the audition committee was saying to another with unrestrained enthusiasm, "Wow, what a talent! A real diva. How many sopranos do you know today who can sing *Casta Diva* like that?"

"Yes," the second man acknowledged but then added, "it's too bad we can't hire her."

"What are you saying? We can't afford *not* to hire her. She is so superior to our leading women…"

"Precisely. We've painstakingly built this company and if we hire this Russian woman we would have a real revolt on our hands. She's different; she will not fit. If she was a prima in some other company and came here as a guest performer, that would be a different story."

"But..."

"Then the two men disappeared. I hope that the enthusiasm of the other two judges that you were speaking with will prevail, but your position with the Company is far from certain," Larissa concluded.

Nina suddenly felt utterly deflated. Perhaps, if she had picked an easier aria and didn't try so hard... It had never occurred to her that she might be 'overqualified'.

"Larissa, let's not tell Anton about that conversation. We'll just tell him that everything went smoothly. I don't want to worry him, maybe for nothing."

"As you wish, Nina," Larissa agreed, but she couldn't help but think how different her marriage was from Nina's. If it were her, Larissa would go directly to Boris and tell him every little detail about the audition and about that worrisome conversation she had overheard. They would discuss it for hours and Boris would comfort and reassure her. *Isn't it hard to keep everything inside and not to share such important matters with your husband?* Larissa pondered. Then again, maybe it would simply be selfish to burden her husband with her problems. Generous and kind Nina was much nobler. In fact, too noble for Larissa's taste.

Three weeks later, Nina received an official letter from the opera company: "*We appreciate your interest in our company. Unfortunately, currently...*"

Nina was stunned; Anton was furious and severely disappointed. However, two weeks later, Nina received a surprise call from one of the men on the panel of judges who had listened to her audition. He assured her that her talent was noticed and appreciated and that the rejection was a simple matter of the current year's budget.

Nina couldn't understand more than half of what the man was saying. Nonetheless, even her limited

English was sufficient for her to comprehend the reason for his call. The man gave Nina his name and credentials, as well as the names of the people in New York that he suggested she should see. He instructed Nina to use his name as a reference and wished her the best of luck in the United States.

Meanwhile, Anton went to another agency, and then another. Agents praised his talent and his qualifications and promised to find a serious engagement in no time at all, but nothing concrete materialized. Anton tried on his own to arrange for an audition with the Toronto Symphony, but he received the same answer as Boris: there were no openings. He had several auditions with smaller companies and even played with them several times, but still nobody had offered him a permanent placement or even a short-term contract. He met a number of Toronto musicians and befriended several of them. Only after being in Canada for some while did he realize how difficult it was in this country to achieve meaningful success in the field of music and how slow and tortuous the road to fame was going to be.

Anton contemplated Boris's life from a new point of view and he did not like what he observed. Boris was working six, sometimes seven days a week. His working hours were erratic and so was his income. Boris was playing weddings and bar-mitzvahs; he was working in the restaurant; and he was picking up any other engagements that the agencies could provide for him. Despite all of this, soon after the baby was born, Larissa had to take on several vocal students to make some extra income for the family.

This was hardly the life that Anton yearned for himself. He calculated that even with Nina's income from the restaurant, it would take years before they could even hope to buy a new car or to afford a good vacation. As far as their future house was concerned, it was simply not in the cards.

Anton was still hoping for some major contract or some other opportunity that would provide a steady income with interesting and exciting work. He was considering a trip to the United States and Nina needed to follow up on the New York references she had been given, so they applied for a visitor's visa. Meanwhile, they needed to pay rent every month, buy food and pay for transport. Money was very tight.

One day, Anton approached Nina with an idea. "Nina, you always liked to style women's hair and everybody loved your work. Why don't you take on several clients?"

"Anton, I already work several evenings a week with my vocal students and I must practice every day. I want my voice to be in the best possible shape when we go to New York."

"I agree with you, Nina. But just a few clients would not take much of your time. It would be a real help. You know how hard I'm trying. One of these days I will get a solid contract and our money problems will be behind us."

Nina acquiesced and made a small advertisement flyer, posting it in the elevator of her apartment. In addition, she invited several women acquaintances to come to her apartment for a free trial haircut. Slowly but surely, Nina started to build her clientele.

In the late spring, Nina and Anton bought their first car. It was a small, seven-year-old Honda Civic with more than a hundred thousand kilometers on it, but at least it was wheels! They had to take out a small loan and Nina's extra money from her hairdressing activities went to cover the insurance on the car and the monthly payments.

On Sundays, Anton liked to take Nina for a leisurely drive. They passed through the most upscale areas of Toronto - Forest Hill, the Bridal Path, and Post Road, wondering who was living in those mansions and what kind of life they must have. They also drove through the suburbs of Metropolitan Toronto and the new subdivisions. Anton liked to drive between Bathurst and Dufferin streets, just north of Steeles. That was the area preferred by those immigrants from the Soviet Union who had lived in Canada for several years and could afford to buy a house.

"Nina," Anton would say, gesturing at the rows of two-story houses, "immigrants like us are living here. Are we less capable or less talented than they are? Why can't we live in such a house?"

"Anton, please don't get frustrated over this. We are new arrivals to Canada. Give us several years and we will have a house too."

"With the money that we make now, Nina, we will be stuck living in our one-bedroom apartment forever."

"Anton, just a few months ago you were ecstatic to have this apartment."

"Is there something wrong with wanting a better life for both of us?"

"Of course not," Nina hastily agreed, seeking to bring that subject of conversation to a close.

In May, Boris was celebrating his birthday and an unexpected guest came to the party. Konstantin Sorokin was on tour in Toronto and took that opportunity to visit his old classmate. After the other guests had left, the five graduates of the Moscow Conservatory sat down to talk about the good old student days and their current lives.

Boris poured everyone a glass of wine and the conversation began in earnest. To Anton's surprise, Kostya was complaining more than he was boasting. He related to his friends how difficult it was to get invited on a good tour; about the fierce competition between the leading pianists; and, how tired he was of constantly travelling and sleeping in hotels and eating in restaurants.

Kostya said that his first record had been a commercial failure and passed on the news that the winner of that ill-fated Moscow competition, the tall man that Anton had mockingly nicknamed 'the Post', had given up classical music altogether. He had formed a jazz band and his first recording release had been quite successful. Apparently, jazz was vastly more popular than classical music. The second-place winner, 'the Bunny-Rabbit', was still touring and it was not easy to compete for bookings with such an accomplished performer, Kostya was saying.

Sorokin lamented that more and more theatres were using pre-recorded music instead of a live orchestra. Even for some ballet and opera galas, recorded music was being used to substantially reduce the operating expense, he explained. This meant that the opportunities for professional musicians were becoming few and far between.

Anton listened carefully to Kostya's story and again felt betrayed by his life-long devotion to classical music. He was thinking that even now, Kostya's life was not that much different than his own mundane touring days back in the Soviet Union. Even though the hotels and the restaurants were better and the musical pieces were more exciting, it sounded all very much the same.

"What are your plans, Kostya?" Boris asked. "Do you intend to continue touring?"

"Yes, of course, as long as somebody invites me, I will continue. However, I've been admitted to the grad school of our conservatory. In three to five years I hope to graduate and eventually land a professor position there."

"Good for you!" Nina exclaimed, and then she started to quiz Kostya about the dramatic changes taking place throughout the Soviet Union and especially in Moscow.

Anton listened to their conversation attentively and

later, when they were walking home, he irritably commented, "Nina, you should stop thinking about Russia as your country. We are Canadians now. You would be better off learning English and adapting to the Canadian lifestyle, rather than constantly yearning about Moscow."

Anton was right in one respect: Nina's English was not improving. She was spending her days with Russian-speaking clients and her evenings singing in a Russian restaurant and at Russian parties. In her limited free time, Nina practiced her vocal work on her own.

When little Michael was half-a-year old, Larissa resumed her regular position in the band, so there was no longer a place for Nina. There were no current openings in other bands either, and so, in order to compensate for that lost income source, Nina was obliged to take on quite a few more hairdressing clients.

Betrayed by the Music - or Betraying the Music?

The visas for the intended trip to the United States finally came through, but Anton kept postponing the trip. One day in July, he sat down with Nina and boldly informed her that he had decided to quit music altogether as a career objective and seek a new profession. While Nina stared incredulously at her husband in total disbelief and shock, Anton explained his rationale.

"Nina, Canada is a great country and there are a lot of opportunities, but not in the sphere of classical music. I have applied for and have already been admitted to the Herzing Institute. There's some special government program for new immigrants that I qualify for, so the government will pay for my education. I will study for one year and at the end of the year I will graduate as a computer programmer-analyst. I've met some people who are working in the information technology field and they tell me that there's always demand for qualified staff. Programmers can make up to thirty thousand dollars a year as a starting salary. It would be steady income and it's a nine-to-five job."

"But Anton, you are a talented musician, so how can you give up on the piano so easily?" a visibly upset Nina persisted.

"I will still play piano; I can't *not* to play. Music is in my blood, but it will be as a hobby, not a source of income. We would be able to start living like other people and to start saving money for a house. Nina, I know that you want to go to New York and you will, but can you help me for a year? Only one year, Nina. As soon as I'm working regularly, you will be free to concentrate on your career, to travel to auditions, and do whatever you need to do in order to sing. If you find a vocalist job somewhere else, I'll move with you. Programmers are needed everywhere. Nina, we're a family. Please support me now for a year and then by the next year I'll support you."

"Anton, if I work full-time for a whole year with all these hairdressing chemicals, I might lose my voice. If I don't practice enough, I will be out of shape and nobody will hire me. I'm a singer, not a hairstylist. I want to sing, not cut hair. It was fun to do it for my friends as a hobby but I never envisioned anything like that as my main occupation."

"Then go, Nina. Go to New York or wherever you want. I am staying in Toronto. I will rent some basement apartment, maybe with a roommate, study in the daytime and find some job in the evenings. Of course it will be very difficult for me. If I want to become a programmer in one year, I must study very hard. And if I have to work simultaneously, it will be next to impossible, but somehow I will manage. You'll see, Nina! I'm going to succeed this time."

"Anton, please don't talk like that," Nina pleaded. "I would not go anywhere without you."

That was the end of the planned audition trip to New York.

In September, Anton began his studies and Nina doubled her clientele. She was working every day, even Saturdays and Sundays. She had clients arriving from early morning to late into the evenings. It was a difficult challenge to live on one modest income, but it was only supposed to be for a year.

"It's the responsibility of a good wife to support her husband," Nina would say to Boris and Larissa, but she knew that they strongly disapproved of Anton's studies and her decision to postpone auditions for a year.

Anton usually came home late. He preferred to

study with friends or at school. It was too difficult for him to concentrate on his studies at home with the noise from the hairdryer and the constant chatter of Nina's clients. They had dinners late and Nina, tired from standing the whole day on her feet, liked to sit down and just listen to Anton's school tales. Sometimes she would tell Anton the stories and gossips that she heard from her clients too. They discussed the lives of other Russian immigrants, their successes and failures. However, whenever Nina wanted to talk about music or her vocal practice, Anton would just clam up.

During that trying year, Nina became very close to Boris and Larissa. In the daytime, whenever she didn't have clients, Nina liked to go to their place for a visit. She played with little Michael, practiced with Larissa, or listened to Boris's new compositions. He was still dreaming of making his band, *The Wandering Stars*, into something more than just a local restaurant band. He was writing soul music and blues, and Larissa and Nina were his critics and admirers.

Before the end of the year, Boris became involved in a new project: he was organizing a New Year's concert for senior citizens. He insisted that Nina must sing at the concert and she readily agreed. She welcomed any opportunity to perform. Anton was asked to play too but he declined, claiming there was too much studying for him to do before the winter exams.

The concert was a great success. People liked Boris's songs and Larissa's performance, but Nina was predictably the biggest hit of the show. However, in some ways the many compliments that she received were quite frustrating. One lady dragged her husband along to meet Nina with the words of introduction, "This is my hairstylist. Isn't she divine?"

And in turn, the woman's husband congratulated Nina by saying "You sing very nicely for a hairstylist."

Another of her clients asked Nina, "Where did you

learn to sing so beautifully, Nina? Did they have a choir in the hairdressing school?"

When she related these comments to Anton, he was amused and a bit concerned at the same time. "Nina, you're just confusing your clients. If they think that you're not a professional hairstylist, they'll go to someone else. You can't afford to lose any clients. Please, Nina, just forget about singing in public any more for another half-a-year."

The second semester was proving to be difficult for Anton; mastery of computer programming was not coming easily to him. Anton had befriended a couple that had graduated from the Moscow University. They were working as professional programmers and he arranged with them for some additional private lessons. Nina had to increase her clientele even more to pay for these lessons.

What worried Nina most of all was that she felt estranged from Anton. It was nothing that she could put her finger on, but the former closeness was just not there.

"It's only temporary," Nina would say to Larissa, mostly trying to reassure herself. "Anton is under tremendous pressure. He needs to have really high grades in order to be recommended for a job by the College."

"Nina, that's enough dwelling on about Anton. He's a big boy and he can take care of himself. Consider your own future," Larissa insisted. "You have to start singing again as soon as possible or otherwise you will never be able to do it."

"I know, Larissa, and as soon as Anton receives his first job..."

"Nothing will change. He will not leave his job to go to New York, and you will not go anywhere without him. You should get a job in Toronto. I have a plan..."

Nina listened attentively to Larissa's plan as she

outlined it and thought that it would be worth pursuing. However, her immediate problem was Anton's diminished interest in her. They spent less time together and almost never talked. Anton started to avoid talking about his studies, reasoning that it was too hard for Nina to understand anyway. Whenever Nina was telling him about her day, he would complain that he was tired of listening to immigration gossip and didn't care who slept with whom, and who was divorcing or getting married to whom.

Something drastic had to be done, so one day a desperate Nina stared at her reflection in the mirror, took a pair of scissors in hand and cut her long hair. Then, she streaked her hair in several colours ranging from platinum blonde to almost bright orange. When she was finished, a new woman was reflecting at her from the mirror: younger looking, more modern and attractive in a new and different sort of way.

When Anton arrived home, he took one look at Nina and began to laugh. A moment later he said, "Now you look the part, like a real hairstylist - cheap and sexy."

"What do you have against hairstylists? Why do you think that hairstylists are cheap?" a frustrated Nina shot back in self-defence.

"Hey, Nina, you talk like one too! All right, all right, I take back the comment about *cheap*; but you definitely look sexy," and Anton pulled Nina closer to him.

Ω

Anton graduated with high grades but not at the top of his class. Anxiously he began to look for a job. He knew that the Herzing Institute was no competition against the University of Toronto, or the University of Waterloo, or even Seneca College. To secure a position in the world of information technology, Anton, with the 'guidance' of his Russian tutors, had created for himself an impressive resume. According to the resume, he was a graduate of the Computer Science Department of the Moscow University with two years of work experience in Moscow.

"Two years," his friends were rationalizing, "are not enough for employers to expect great results right away, but more than sufficient to get you in the door. Nobody ever asks for a diploma. Don't worry about it. Act confidently and always respond with a *yes* to any question."

Anton sent his creatively conceived resume to several organizations and was waiting for invitations for interviews. Meanwhile, Nina was growing impatient. She needed to talk to Anton about quite another subject and she couldn't postpone telling him her news much longer, so she hoped that he would get a steady job very soon.

Anton failed the first two interviews because he could not adequately describe his duties associated with his alleged work experience. He related to his friends the nature of the questions that he was asked and they coached Anton with appropriate responses.

The third interview was conducted by a young project manager named Carol Walker. From the first moment they met, Anton was impressed with Carol - her impeccable grooming, business-style clothes and professional manner. He was even more attracted by the strong and distinguished features of her face, her slim figure, and her long legs which were further enhanced by high-heeled pumps.

Anton, in the presence of such a woman, immediately became his most charming self.

Carol's questions were short, crisp and to the point. Anton thought in admiration that Carol was a commendable woman. She would not whine and complain. She looked like she knew what she wanted and how to get it. *A woman like Carol would be an asset to any man*, Anton mused.

For a moment, he envisioned Nina in her habitual black flat shoes, leggings and oversized sweatshirt. *It is so much more pleasant to look at the professionally dressed woman*, Anton mused, while observing Carol with growing admiration.

He thought carefully and deliberately about each of his answers, trying to match the style of his responses to her questions.

Carol was equally impressed with Anton. After several questions she began to have some doubts about those two years of alleged work experience on his resume, but he looked eager and enthusiastic and coachable; and, not the least consideration in Carol's decision process, he was certainly not too hard on the eyes.

"OK, Anton, I will give you a chance. The first three months will be a trial period. Employee benefits will start after the trial period is over. Our project is very demanding and dynamic. If you are looking for a nine-to-five job, this is not it. But if you are ready to work long hours, learn the business and contribute to the project, then welcome to the team!"

"Thank you very much, Carol. I can assure you that I won't let you down," was Anton's enthusiastic response.

Anton was driving home in a state of euphoria. He made it! No more poverty for him, and no more dependency on ineffectual agents or working for a pittance. Now he belonged to the Canadian middle-class mainstream and all the opportunities and comforts that Canada offered were within his reach. Anton was not at all worried about the trial period or about his contrived resume. He would work as hard as necessary and he would make certain not to lose this prized position.

Along the way, he drove to his favourite area in the northern suburbs where many new houses were being built. He parked the car near one of the construction sites and got out to take a closer look. He walked around one of the unfinished houses, surveying it with admiration and thinking that in a year or two he would live here and would own a house just like that one.

Anton went back to the car but didn't drive off immediately. Instead, he took a paper and a pen and started to make calculations. If Nina continued working and made the same money for one more year, during which they would live only on her income, then at the end of that year he would have enough savings for a down payment.

We would still have to continue to live very frugally, Anton reflected, *to pay down the mortgage, but in three to five years we would be in good shape financially.*

Days of Drama and Trauma

There was only one problem with Anton's home ownership plan - Nina's unrelenting desire to return to singing. He wished that she would stop dreaming; there was no future for a Russian-trained classical singer in Canada, and most likely not in America either. Anton had no inclination whatsoever to move anywhere from Canada and Nina's constant chatter about her singing career and a trip to New York for auditions irritated him to no end. It was time to put a stop to it, he firmly decided.

At the same time, Anton was not unduly worried about convincing Nina to continue her hairstyling business. After all, he had always managed to persuade her to do what he wanted. After reflecting on how he would bring Nina around to his way of thinking again, Anton started the car and finally headed for home.

At the last moment, he stopped near a florist shop and bought a large bouquet of flowers. Flowers always put Nina in a good mood and he needed her to be in a good mood today.

But when he arrived home there were three ladies sitting in his living room and Nina was busily styling one of them. *One more year*, Anton thought, *and you will all be in the basement of my house when you're getting your hair done, so I won't have to see you ever again after that.*

He smiled nicely to everyone, presented Nina with the flowers and went to the bedroom.

"What a nice husband you have," one of the ladies commented.

"And so handsome," another added. "What does he do for a living?"

"He's a programmer," Nina said with a bit of

uncertainty. She still couldn't get used to the idea that Anton was no longer a musician. "Please wait for a second," Nina excused herself and went to the bedroom.

She hugged Anton and asked, "How was the interview?"

"Excellent! Nina, I got the job!"

"Oh, Anton, I'm so happy for you! Thank you for the flowers; they are lovely and so appropriate! I have some exciting news to tell you."

"What news?" Anton asked, suddenly worried by her words.

"Good news! Actually, two things happened and both are good news. Please wait. Give me an hour to finish work."

An hour later, husband and wife were left on their own. "Please tell me about your new job," Nina started.

"I'll be working on a big project for *Advance Electronics*. They're developing a new Order System. I'll be on the reporting team. They're doing the project in stages and the first implementation is in just two months from now. I'll have to work very hard, Nina, long hours and maybe even weekends. I will have to prove myself there. I'm sure you understand. Now, please tell me your news."

"Anton, I've decided not to go to New York or anywhere else for an audition. I'm quite sure that now as you begin your first job, the last thing you'll want to do is to leave Toronto."

"Nina, thank you so much! That's my smart girl. I knew that you would finally realize that singing is not a career."

"On the contrary, Anton," Nina enthused, "in September I will start singing with the Canadian Opera Company, right here in Toronto!"

"So, they've hired you after all. To be honest, I *am* surprised. Did you audition for them again?"

"Well, they did not exactly hire me..."

"I'm confused, Nina."

"It was all Larissa's idea! She went with me to see the Artistic Director of the company and I asked him to allow me to join the chorus. I told him that I understood the company's previous hesitation to hire me - different background and education, lack of fluent English, and so on. But I told him that I want him to give me a chance, to allow me to prove that I can fit in. He told me that there's no money in the budget, but I said that I was willing to work as a volunteer without pay during this trial period and he has agreed. I will work with them for four to five months and then, hopefully, they will offer me a contract. The Artistic Director was very positive and enthusiastic about this arrangement."

"Why not?" Anton shot back sarcastically. "It doesn't cost him anything and he's not obliged to hire you next year anyway. How many hours a day are you planning to waste on this hair-brained idea of Larissa's? When would you have time for your clients? Will you be home on time for your evening appointments? Or do you think all your clients will wait until January for their next haircut?"

"Anton, I am not planning to work in January. In fact, I am planning to quit very soon. I just wanted to tell you first."

"Nina, are you out of your mind? Why would you quit?"

"Because I'm pregnant!" the triumphant Nina joyfully exclaimed. "Anton, you're going to be a father soon!"

For just the second time in his life Anton felt trepidation bordering on genuine fear. He broke into a sweat and then he felt a chill. This could not be happening to him... All his dreams were destroyed by this announcement. His reaction was so extreme that he started to hyperventilate.

Nina tried in vain to read the reaction of her

husband and asked, "Aren't you happy for us, Anton?"

Anton finally mastered his emotions and as calmly as he could said, "Nina, I'm afraid this is not a good time for a baby. I am just starting a new job. The first three months is a trial period. What if they fire me?"

Nina stroked his hand. "Mama always said that God sends a child and God provides for a child."

"Let's be real, Nina. It's not God whom you expect to provide for you and your child, but me. I am afraid that it's out of the question this year. Please go to the doctor tomorrow and schedule an abortion."

"I can't, Anton. I will not do it," a despondent Nina replied.

"Why can't you?" Anton was feeling growing irritation with her stubbornness.

"It's a child, Anton - our child. I love him very much already. I will not kill him."

"Oh, don't be stupid! It's not *him* or *her*; it's *it* - an unfeeling sliver of meat. I don't want this *it* to destroy our future, our opportunity to build a good life in Canada. Don't you want to have a house, Nina? A brand new car? Go to the Caribbean Islands for a vacation?"

"No, I don't! I want this child and I don't want to work as a hairstylist any longer. And furthermore, I want to sing," a sobbing Nina stammered.

That resolute response was the last straw. Anton lost his patience and began to shout heartlessly at his wife. "You are naïve and stupid! You're not a singer, you're a hairstylist and you'd better accept that reality, Nina.

"Forget about singing once and for all; I don't want to hear about it ever again. You have a pleasant but small voice. You will never be able to sing an entire opera and you will never be a lead singer in any company. Don't you realize that in the chorus, even if they ever hire you, you will not make even half the money you're making now? How would we be able to save the money for a house? We must have a house! How long do you expect me to come home and see all those clients of yours occupying our living room, or to sit on a sofa covered with somebody's hair, eh? We need a house to build you a nice studio in the basement. That's it. I'm tired. Tomorrow I will take you to see the doctor myself." Anton got up, marched off to the bedroom and slammed the door behind him.

Anton collapsed on his bed, shaking with anger. He tried to calm himself so he could think more clearly.

This is the price I'm paying for my brainless mistakes, Anton pondered. *I was naïve: world stages, the adoring public at my feet... What a pile of rubbish! People don't care about serious music, not in Russia and certainly not in Canada. Just the same bunch of old farts attending all the recitals. Even for the musicians who make it to the big stage, it's such a cut-throat business. Everybody is waiting for you to fail and just to take your place. I was smart to realize it fast and get a real profession.*

Poor Boris! Him and his pathetic band - The Wandering Stars! He will entertain drunken Russian immigrants in the nightclubs and restaurants forever. That is where his beloved Larissa with her pitiful voice belongs - in the nightclubs, where everyone is too drunk to care what they are even listening to. Thank goodness, I'm out of that rat race!

Anton envisioned himself sitting in a fancy Russian nightclub, dressed in a designer suit and with a beautiful companion by his side, offering Larissa and Boris a modest tip and requesting that they perform a particular song, just for him. Just for Anton. What an enthralling picture!

But who is my companion? That was my worst, the stupidest mistake: to marry young - to marry Nina. Anton clearly realized it now.

How could I be so easily seduced by a pretty face

and a pleasant voice? We have been living in Canada for almost two years and what has she achieved? Nothing, absolutely nothing! She doesn't even have rudimentary English. So now she wants to saddle me with a baby to entrap me forever. I'm not going to let that happen!

His anger of the moment was somewhat spent and Anton concluded that perhaps he was overreacting. After all, eventually Nina always abided by what he asked her to do. Why should it be any different this time? Feeling somewhat more self-assured that his wishes would ultimately prevail, Anton drifted off into a deep sleep.

Nina remained sitting and crying for a long time in the living room. *What has happened to us?* Nina asked herself. *Why is Anton so angry with me? What did I do wrong? He asked me to support him for a year and I did. Or is Larissa right when she says a woman can't give a man her entire affection, her heart and her whole life without asking anything in return? Should I be thinking more about myself and less about Anton? But who am I?*

I am an opera singer with a passion, a love of music, and I have real talent. What am I doing working as a hairstylist? I'm Russian and I love Russia, so what am I doing in Canada? I'm my mother's beloved girl but I haven't seen my mother for almost two years. I'm Anton's wife...everything else hung on that. Nina's troubled thoughts had come full circle and she was back to her dilemma with Anton.

The next day, Anton and Nina went to the doctor. They sat together in a waiting room crowded with patients. Nina looked at the radiant faces of other pregnant women with a pang of envy, while Anton observed their protruding bellies with disdain. Finally, Nina was admitted and Anton sat for a long time, impatiently glancing at his watch while Nina was with the doctor. Eventually she emerged, quietly said something to the receptionist, and then motioned to Anton that they could leave. In the car, they were both silent until Anton asked, "So, when is the procedure going to take place?"

"I'm not sure yet. I have to do all kinds of tests. They will call me," Nina replied meekly.

"Have you told the doctor that you want to terminate the pregnancy?" a suspicious Anton asked.

Nina remained silent and Anton became enraged. The fight started as soon as they got home - if it could be called a 'fight'. Anton was screaming and Nina was crying.

Nina was relieved when Anton started his job - at least she had some peace during the day. She avoided telling her clients anything about the pregnancy or about her intentions to quit her business. She was afraid to aggravate Anton even more. Nina furtively hoped that after his initial violent reaction, Anton would become reconciled to the idea of fatherhood.

Anton, meanwhile, was busily strategizing. He had to convince Nina to give up her silly idea about singing for nothing without any concrete assurance that she would be hired for the next season. Equally, he had to persuade her to terminate this unfortunate pregnancy. It was not that he didn't want to have children, oh no! But just not now. The time was all wrong. Maybe in three or four years when they were better established in Canada, but certainly not now.

The next two months proved to be exceptionally difficult for both spouses.

Ω

On his first day of work, Carol introduced Anton to the team. "Hi everyone. We have a new programmer joining us today. Please welcome Anton Gorchichniy."

Then Carol looked at Anton, smiled and posed a question. "Anton sounds foreign and rather formal. Would you mind if we call you Tony?"

In fact, Anton did mind. He was very proud of his name; it had a certain 'masculine' sound about it. *Tony* sounded like a wimp. *Well, when in Rome, do as the Romans do*, Anton thought and responded cheerfully, "Not at all, Carol. Tony it is."

Anton soon realized that there were a lot of additional skills and knowledge he must possess if he wanted to survive his first trial period in the world of information technology. He was surprised and even astonished when he came to understand how little he really knew and how much more he would have to learn in a big hurry to survive on the project. His team was in the midst of preparations for an August implementation, and he had to write and then test several important report programs.

Carol was running a very tight ship and the words 'delay' and 'missed deadlines' were not in her vocabulary. The trial period was not just a bunch of empty words to incent a new hire work harder - it was a fact. Either Anton would deliver or he would be out. During these two months before implementation, Anton was working long hours and weekends, just to avoid falling behind. What made him especially angry was the fact that his stubborn and selfish wife did not want to understand that he was under tremendous pressure and did nothing to support and help him.

Surprisingly, the only person who encouraged Anton and gave him moral support was his Project Manager, Carol. She was always strict and demanding with her team, but several times she stayed behind into the evening and discussed Anton's tasks with him and gave him some good advice about how to develop his reports. They went for lunch a couple of times too, but only talked about the project. That was until one evening

Carol invited him for dinner, and during the meal she revealed a little bit about herself. She was from a well-established family that had settled in Canada generations before Confederation. Her parents and brother were still living in Calgary where she grew up. She moved to Toronto after she got married and stayed, even after her marriage collapsed.

"Why did you get divorced?" Anton asked impulsively, before he had time to realize that the question was too personal. He hastily apologized. "I'm sorry, Carol, that's none of my concern."

"It's OK, Tony. Actually, it's very simple. He cheated on me. I found out about it and the same day I packed his stuff and filed for a divorce."

"Are you living alone, Carol? Why wouldn't you go back to Calgary?"

"I'm not alone. I have my four-year-old son and a live-in nanny. I want to gain more experience as a manager and then I might go back. Right now, I just want to implement this project and I want it to be successful. I would want to return to Calgary, if I decide to go back at all, as a winner, not as a weak and despondent divorcee. My career and my self-esteem are of utmost importance for me."

There was nothing inappropriate or untoward in their relationship. Some days Anton briefly harboured the feeling that Carol was attracted to him, but then he would chastise himself for thinking that way. He realized that he was the weakest link in her team and concluded that she wanted to make sure that he was not going to fail her and jeopardize the entire project. There was seemingly nothing personal in her attention.

He, Anton, felt a deep respect and admiration for his manager. He genuinely wanted to excel and to prove to Carol that she had made the right choice when she hired him.

When Carol innocuously asked him about his wife,

he simply said that he married young and that his wife was a hairstylist. As much as possible, Anton avoided talking about himself, his past, or his marriage. His resume was a lie and therefore his past, as Carol knew it, was a lie too. Anton was leery that he might inadvertently say something that would reveal that he had graduated from the Moscow Conservatory, not the Moscow University, and that his field of study was piano, not computers.

Without consciously realizing it, Anton was constantly comparing Nina with Carol and the comparison was not in Nina's favour. In the office, he observed an energetic, accomplished woman who cast an aura of confident authority; at home, a pale, lethargic woman was waiting for him every evening.

People say that a woman blooms during pregnancy and becomes radiant. It's a lie. Pregnancy makes a woman really unattractive, Anton concluded. He didn't even feel sorry for Nina. He was surprised by her unflinching stubbornness. The pregnancy was difficult for her. She had severe morning sickness. *One more misnomer,* Anton thought. *This morning sickness seems to be lasting the entire day and evening.* As far as he was concerned, her predicament could be easily resolved with a quick procedure before it was too late.

Anton continued to employ various strategies to convince Nina to undergo an abortion. Some days he was tender and loving, trying to cajole Nina to agree to do it in the name of their love and future; other days he was screaming in a fit of rage, insisting that Nina must go through with it. And then there were some other days when Anton simply ignored Nina, knowing how much it distressed her. Throughout this time he remained uncompromisingly angry with her. Didn't she understand how important these three months were for him?

Nina understood very well. She didn't want to anger

Anton and she wanted to support him. In fact, she was ready to do just about anything for him, but despite all that she could not bring herself to even contemplate having an abortion.

When it was time for Nina to visit the doctor again, she spent the entire morning before the appointment repeating her prepared response, like a school child studying for a test: "*Doctor, I want to terminate this pregnancy. Doctor, I want to terminate this pregnancy. Doctor...*"

The doctor examined Nina and before she had a chance to utter that fateful sentence, he said, "Your baby is developing just fine. What I don't like, dear lady, is how you look. You've lost weight and you look far too pale. You must start taking vitamins."

Nina lost her nerve as soon as the doctor said '*your baby.*' If he had said *fetus*, Nina thought that maybe she would have been able to bring herself to utter those fateful words. But the doctor had said '*baby*', and so Nina took the prescription for vitamins and the referral for an ultrasound and then made her way home.

A few days later, Nina underwent the ultrasound and brought home a first picture of the baby. She left it on the table and in the evening, Anton picked up the black-and-white image and asked Nina what it was. When she explained, Anton looked at her with open disgust and asked, "Is this supposed to excite me? You're a fool."

Anton gained only one small victory: he had insisted that Nina must stop seeing Larissa. As far as he was concerned, it was the fault of that bitch for meddling in other peoples' affairs and encouraging Nina to continue to pursue that unrealistic dream of becoming a singer in Canada. He even convinced himself that it was Larissa who was responsible for suggesting that Nina stop taking birth-control pills and try to become pregnant. Nina's assurance that it was an accident did nothing to lessen Anton's anger and loathing towards his former friends. Boris was deemed 'guilty by association'. In order not to enrage Anton even further, Nina avoided seeing Larissa and Boris any longer. In this time of her great need, Nina was left without support from anyone.

Then August came and Anton ceased his attempts to persuade Nina to have an abortion; it was already too late. Nonetheless, he could not reconcile himself to the idea of becoming a father. He left the apartment earlier than ever each morning and only returned late in the evening. Anton and Nina stopped communicating altogether. He never touched her or spoke to her. Several times Nina tried to strike up a conversation, but Anton remained unresponsive. She called him at the office one time, just to ask him what to prepare for dinner, and he instructed her never to call him at the office again, no matter what.

Nina was still working and hadn't even cut back on the number of clients she was servicing, so she was always exhausted and in the evening she would collapse into bed as soon as the last client had left.

Ω

The third weekend in August was the time for the project implementation. When Anton arrived at the office early on the Saturday morning, the entire team was already there. Carol gathered her troops and outlined the process they would follow. Everyone was given a copy of the implementation plan that consisted of literally hundreds of tasks. Each task had an assigned responsible person and was linked to a preceding, dependent task that had to be completed before the next new task could commence. Every aspect was documented precisely and scheduled minute-by-minute.

Anton's first report was intended to run after the

primary conversion program was completed. The estimated time for execution of his report was ten-thirty in the morning. He looked around the project room and observed some people were busily working, while others were quietly talking or looking over the shoulders of their teammates. Two men were playing a card game; their time to perform would come later.

At ten-thirty, several people, including Carol, were standing behind the team member responsible for the main conversion, trying to help him resolve some unexpected problem. It wasn't until noon that Carol indicated that Anton could run his report. The program ran without a glitch, but when Anton looked at the results he became panicky: the results looked wrong. It took him several minutes to calm himself down and then he called over his team leader and Carol.

Now it was Anton's turn to be on the 'hot seat'. Was the problem with the data or was his report faulty? Carol sat near Anton and intently observed how he was debugging the program. Ten minutes later the cause of the problem became apparent: the conversion program did not take into consideration some variations within the data. Again, it was time for Anton to relax and for other team members to get working again. Finally, at three o'clock, Anton's report produced the expected results and the remaining implementation steps could then move forward.

Anton observed and admired Carol's conduct 'in action'. She operated as an experienced music conductor, keeping all her 'orchestra' working in unison and harmony. At one o'clock, boxes of pizza had arrived for a working lunch and by seven o'clock in the evening a fast-food dinner was provided. Carol took pains to make sure that her team was comfortable and could focus their attention on the tasks at hand.

Nobody had left for home as yet. Finally, at eleven o'clock in the evening, Carol gathered the team together to thank and congratulate everyone. She asked a couple of project staff to stay behind to continue monitoring and running the remaining tasks, while encouraging everyone else to go home to rest and to be back on time in the morning. She looked fondly (or was that his imagination?) at Anton and informed him that he would not be needed before ten o'clock.

Anton drove home in a euphoric mood; now he was really a full-fledged part of the team. He had withstood the pressure and he did not fail. He felt as though he had passed some very important exam successfully.

He was not surprised to find the apartment in darkness. He was expecting Nina to be in bed at that time of the evening. But when Anton turned on the light, he frowned. A chair was standing in the middle of the room before the large mirror, the cushions were thrown haphazardly on the sofa, and bits of hair covered the mat around the chair. The room had a very untidy look about it. It was very unlike Nina to leave the living room in such a mess. Anton walked over to the chair to move it and noticed a large rusty stain on the floor behind it. Now becoming anxious, he hustled into to the bedroom. It was unoccupied and the bed was made up and undisturbed.

"Nina," he called, but there was no response. Anton then quickly moved to the kitchen, turned on the light, and observed a note that had been left on the table. He frantically read it. "*Nina had a miscarriage. She's in Branson Hospital. Boris.*"

A multitude of emotions overwhelmed Anton at that moment. Unexpectedly he felt an enormous tenderness and compassion towards Nina, and then sadness and a feeling of the loss of something or someone very dear.

He drove the short distance to the hospital in record time, parked the car and made his way towards the entrance. He noticed Boris and Larissa walking towards their car and called out to them. They stopped and

Anton quickly approached. "How is Nina? Where can I find her?" he asked, in quite a frantic voice.

"Why would you want to know?" Larissa angrily shot back. "Visiting hours were over long ago." She turned towards Anton and looked him critically in the eye. He observed that her face was puffy and her eyes were red. "Are you happy now?" she asked caustically. "You got what you wanted: there will be no baby. But don't kid yourself, Anton. This miscarriage happened for one reason and one reason only - because of all the stress Nina was under, thanks to you. You killed this baby. It was a boy, Anton. As far as I'm concerned you murdered your son!"

"That's nonsense!" Anton shot back. "Don't you try to accuse me. Nina had a difficult pregnancy and something went wrong. It's not my fault."

Before Larissa could reply, Boris intervened. "Larissa, please go to the car. Here are the keys. I will be along in a couple of minutes." She wanted to say something more to Anton but Boris implored her, "Please, Larissa, go now."

When the men were alone, Anton asked his friend, "Is this true? Did Nina miscarry because of too much stress?"

"We asked the doctor this question. He said that there can be a dozen medical reasons for a miscarriage, but stress is definitely a significant factor. He said that it's never a good idea to be overly stressed out during a pregnancy. He tried to explain something about the chemical reactions triggered by stress. I didn't understand the details," Boris said.

"When did it happen?"

"Supposedly, Nina had a lot of clients today. Around five o'clock in the afternoon, one of the women noticed that Nina was hemorrhaging. She had to lie down and the women called the ambulance and then they called us. Nina said that she didn't know your work number. Is this true, Anton?"

"I wasn't at my desk today. We had an implementation and we were all in one large project room," Anton replied defensively.

"Anton, I didn't say that we couldn't reach you. I said that Nina did not give your phone number to anybody, not even to us. Anyway, we drove to the hospital right away and we've been here ever since. Nina was almost four months pregnant, so the procedure was not so straightforward. I didn't ask for any details but Nina doesn't feel very well right now. Here's the room number." Boris provided the information to Anton and started to walk towards his car again, but Anton stopped him.

"Borya, please don't judge me harshly. You know how much I love Nina. I definitely want us to have children some day, even though now just wasn't the right time."

"Anton, that's between you and Nina," Boris replied coldly and then he strode purposefully in the direction of his car.

Anton hurriedly went up to the designated floor in the hospital but was intercepted by the night-shift nurse. Anton explained about implementation, smiled, cajoled, begged, and finally was allowed to see his wife.

He quietly entered Nina's room and approached her bed. Tall Nina somehow looked diminutive lying there in her hospital gown. Her multi-coloured hair-do looked silly and even scary when contrasted against the gown, the white pillow and her almost equally pale-white face.

"Nina," Anton called out softly, practically in a whisper, and when she slowly turned her head in his direction, he stammered, "I'm sorry, Nina. I am so sorry."

"My baby is dead. It's over, Anton," Nina said disconsolately, and for a moment Anton was not even sure if Nina was talking about the pregnancy or their marriage.

He gently took Nina's hand into his and started to apologize for his behaviour and for his lack of attention. "I love you so much. Everything will be fine, you'll see. One day we'll have children and I'm sure it will happen very soon." Nina listened to him attentively, but when Anton said that he was already reconciled to the idea of becoming a father and that now he felt very sad he had lost his son, she turned away. Anton couldn't get her to say another word. Soon after that, the nurse asked him to leave for the night.

Anton was back in the hospital first thing in the morning. He sat down near Nina's bed and tried to cheer her up. A good night's sleep had restored his good spirits and he had started to look at everything in a different perspective. For sure he felt sorry for Nina, but life must go on. When the time was right they would have their child. However, after an hour of non-responsiveness from Nina, Anton began to feel irritated. Didn't she see how hard he was trying? Why couldn't she be at least a little bit cheerful?

By quarter-past-nine, Anton had become fidgety. He didn't want to be late for work and he was just about to leave when the doctor came into the room. He examined Nina's chart and said, "Usually we allow women to go home on the second day, but in your case, there was a considerable loss of blood, Nina. I would like to keep you in the hospital for a while longer for observation while you recuperate."

Then the doctor turned to Anton and continued, "I am glad that I can talk to both of you at the same time. I would like you to be very careful during the next three to four years. Your wife, Mr. Gorchichniy, may have a difficult time conceiving again. But even if she does conceive, the pregnancy would quite likely end with another miscarriage."

"Do you mean to say that we will never have

children?" an alarmed Anton asked.

"I didn't say *never*," the doctor corrected. "I'm just suggesting that you should wait three or four years. For the next while your wife needs to be under a doctor's supervision and she may have to undergo some further treatment. Only after that we might be able to come to some conclusion."

The doctor turned his attention back to Anton's wife. "Nina, please don't despair. You are a young woman and today's medical science can foster miracles. I will come to see you again tomorrow morning."

The doctor left to continue his morning rounds, leaving Nina and Anton looking at each other in dismay and confusion. Anton was relieved that Nina's pregnancy was terminated, but the prospect of never becoming a father was devastating. When the doctor's prognosis finally sank in, Nina started to cry and Anton could not find the words to console her. Finally, he looked at his watch and told Nina that he had to go to the office.

Anton arrived to work around ten-thirty and Carol eyed him disapprovingly. However, the rest of the day went smoothly and by six o'clock that evening, the implementation was completed and the results had been verified. Carol gathered the team together again and said, "I want to thank all of you for your hard work and I would like to invite you to the bar to celebrate your success. The food and the first round of drinks are on me."

"Hurray!" someone shouted, and one by one the members of the team began to head out for the nearby bar. Anton called to Nina at the hospital. He informed her that he was almost finished work for the day and that in an hour or two he would be able to come to the hospital. After making that call, Anton joined up with the team to celebrate.

In the bar, someone gave him a gin and tonic and a

plate loaded with different appetizers was placed before him. He didn't take any of the food; instead, he nursed his drink and morosely thought that he must be leaving soon. He had no desire to go to the hospital to see his depressed wife and again struggle with searching for the right words to say to her.

Carol sat down near him and asked in a concerned voice, "Tony, what's wrong? You came late this morning and then you were in a withdrawn mood the entire day. Is there something the matter at home? Did you have a fight with your wife? I am not trying to pry, but I care about every single member of my team and it really concerns me to see you so obviously unhappy or distracted by some personal problem."

"Thanks for asking, Carol. I appreciate it. Actually, my wife is in the hospital and I'll be going there any minute. One more drink and I'm on my way," Anton said.

"What happened to your wife? I hope it's nothing serious."

"Nothing serious. Tomorrow she will be home. Nothing serious," Anton repeated and then added bitterly, "just the end of all my hopes and dreams."

"Tony, you're not making any sense. What dreams?"

"The dream of becoming a father, Carol. Nina had a miscarriage and the doctor said that she will never have children."

"Did you want this child, Tony?" Carol asked compassionately.

"It was a boy, Carol. My son! Yes, I wanted that child very much. But it was not meant to be."

"Tony, I am *so* sorry. You should have told me about this in the morning. You did an excellent job today, even being under such stress. I want you to know that I am very happy that I hired you. You fit in with the team and other people like working with you. You can consider that your trial period is over as of now."

"Thanks so much, Carol. That means a lot to me. I like my work and I do like working for you. You're a great manager. It's just that I feel very guilty today."

"Why is that, Tony? Is it because you were working today instead of being with your wife in the hospital?"

"Yes, that's part of it but there's much more. We'd had some difficulties lately. On the one hand, I wanted a child very much, but on the other hand..." Anton paused and became silent mid-sentence, not wanting to continue with the explanation, but Carol ventured to finish the sentence for him.

"You're not sure that you want to have a child with *that* woman. Am I right, Tony?"

"I'm sorry, Carol. It's difficult for me to talk about it. It's not right for me to burden you with my personal problems."

They both fell silent and a short while later Anton excused himself and left the bar. He drove to the hospital and tried to visualize the forthcoming meeting with Nina. She would be sitting in the waiting area in her ugly hospital gown, impatiently watching the elevator. As soon as Nina noticed him, her face would light up like a Christmas tree. In his mind, Anton was comparing Nina to a loyal puppy waiting anxiously for its master. So pathetic!

Anton was partially right. Nina was waiting for him, but when she saw him there was no expression of joy on her face, more-so one of apparent bemusement that he had shown up at all. For some reason, the fact that Nina couldn't even muster the slightest smile when she saw him was annoying. *Lately, everything Nina does irritates me,* Anton contemplated.

He remained in the hospital for a half-hour, telling Nina a bit about his day in the office, and then abruptly left. She didn't make any effort to encourage him to stay longer.

The next day, Boris and Larissa drove Nina home,

and just three days later she was already servicing her clients again. She still felt fatigued and light-headed, but didn't want to aggravate Anton by taking any more time off. In addition, Nina was worried about the rent money. Since Anton had started to work, he had not given her any money for normal expenses, having indicated that his salary was reserved for their future house.

Ω

Friday evening, Anton announced that on Sunday they were invited to a barbeque party at his manager's house, so Nina should rearrange her appointments to finish before four o'clock on the Sunday afternoon.

"Anton, I still feel quite weak so I'd rather just relax. Why don't you just go ahead without me?" Nina proposed.

"Nina, you always complain that we don't go anywhere, and now when there is an opportunity for you to meet the people that I'm working with and to enjoy a fun afternoon, you object. Carol specifically asked me to bring you along, so you're going."

"Anton, I have nothing to wear. Since we came to Canada, I haven't bought myself any new outfits. I don't want to show up looking plain and old-fashioned."

"Nonsense! I'm sure you can find something to wear, so stop looking for excuses. We're going to the party together so please be ready on time."

On Sunday, already exhausted from a full day of work on her feet, not to mention her recent ordeal, Nina started to get ready, soon after three o'clock. By three-thirty, Anton was agitated that Nina was still not ready so she tried to calm him down.

"Anton, why do we have to be there exactly at four? It's an outdoor party. I'm sure that the majority of the guests will come a little later."

"I'm not the majority! I'm a recent hire and if my

manager told me to be there at four, I'd better be there at four! And Nina, please, no talk about music or about singing."

Confused by Anton's outburst and his evident nervousness, Nina quickly finished dressing and they drove to Carol's house.

Nina was right: they were the first to arrive. But when she saw Anton's project manager and the abrupt change in his manner when he saw Carol, and when she observed Carol's telling smile directed at Anton, quite a few things suddenly became clearer to Nina.

Carol greeted them warmly and said, "The first guests to arrive get to help with the preparations for the party! Nina, please help me to bring the glasses and plates out from the kitchen. I hope you don't mind, dear?"

"Of course she doesn't mind, Carol," Anton promptly responded on behalf of his wife.

"Great! Anton, you're responsible for the barbeque - that's a man's job. Here's all the tools that you'll need."

In her typically efficient way, Carol positioned Anton beside the barbeque and explained what he was to do. Then she directed Nina into the kitchen, showed her the paper plates, the plastic cutlery, and the napkins, and explained in detail how she wanted the forty place-settings to be arranged. Each fork and knife was to be wrapped in a napkin and placed on a plate. The ladies then carried everything outside, but no sooner had they started to work on the first place-setting than some new guests arrived. Carol left Nina to prepare the table settings on her own and hurried off to greet the new arrivals.

Anton was elated. He had been assigned a responsible post which would allow him to see all the guests and exchange pleasantries with them. In a way, he almost felt like the host of the party. He glanced at the spacious backyard with the large porch, the flowerbeds, the small vegetable patch in one corner, and a large apple tree in another corner. This was the life. This was how he wanted to live.

He studied the architecture of the stately house with admiration and glimpsed through an open door at the large, modern kitchen, all the while feeling a longing to possess one just like it for himself.

Nina felt light-headed and wanted to sit down but instead, like a maid, she had to prepare those silly table settings. More guests arrived. Everyone had a beer or a glass of wine in his or her hand. A lively conversation started up around her but Nina was not a part of it. Apparently, everybody assumed that she had been hired to help with the party and paid no attention to her.

Nina felt insulted and wondered if Carol had purposely intended to humiliate her. Finally, she finished with her table-setting task and moved to stand close to Anton. If she was expecting that he would introduce her to his co-workers she was sadly mistaken. Anton was keeping himself busy flipping hamburgers and hot dogs and joking with everyone else and paid no heed to his wife. Carol was imperiously instructing Anton what to prepare next and he was obediently complying with all her directions.

She behaves, Nina thought bitterly, *as though he already belongs to her.* Nina put a small portion of food on a plate for herself and retreated to a free chair that was positioned near the fence. Before long, Carol approached her and asked, "How do you like the party, Nina?"

"It's very nice, thank you," Nina replied politely.

Carol sat down near Nina and said in an intimate voice, "I heard about your recent misfortune. Anton was devastated. He really wanted that child."

"Did he?" Nina asked briskly.

"Oh, yes. He's a very caring man. You're very fortunate, Nina, to have a man like him."

The very thought that Anton had been discussing their private life and especially her miscarriage with Carol was very disturbing. Nina couldn't help but feel even more humiliated.

Carol continued speaking in her confident and - as it seemed to Nina - patronizing voice. "I've heard that you're a good hairstylist. I should make an appointment and see what you can do with my unruly hair." Carol pointed to her perfectly groomed hair and added, "If I like it, I can recommend you to some of my friends. I could help you to build up a really good clientele."

"Thanks, Carol," Nina responded, again in a patient and polite voice.

In fact, the last thing Nina wanted or needed was to have Carol as a client or to have any new clients at all! And so she said, "I have quite poor English. I work only with Russian-speaking clients. If you'll excuse me, please..." Already tired and feeling even more stressed from this conversation with Carol, by now Nina felt dizzy and nauseated.

She rose gingerly from her chair and without saying a word to Anton, quietly left the party. Nobody other than Carol noticed Nina's departure.

Carol waited for about ten minutes, and then she discretely approached Anton and said in an offended tone of voice, "Tony dear, you are such an educated, intelligent man and a real gentleman. Sorry to say this, but I am puzzled what you could possibly have in common with that ignorant and ill-mannered woman?"

"What happened, Carol? What did she do?"

"I just tried to be congenial with her by starting a conversation but she spoke to me rudely and then stormed off down the street. I really don't know what I could have done wrong to offend her!"

"You did nothing wrong, Carol. I'm very sorry. It's just, you know, the recent events... Nina's not acting very rationally these days."

"Oh, I realize that," Carol said in a deliberately mollified and innocent tone. "I shouldn't even be telling you about this. After all, she's your wife."

"Hey, chef," one of the guests called out, "are there any more hamburgers left?"

"But of course, my friend! Here you are," and with that, Anton resumed his duties at the barbeque.

Nina walked slowly home alone, trying to suppress her sobs. She had no purse and no money. Carol's house was somewhere in the middle of suburbia and Nina wasn't even sure how to get to a main street. Eventually, a woman in a car stopped, opened the window and asked, "Lady, do you need some help?"

"Yes I do," Nina said haltingly, "if you can take me to some main intersection, I would be very grateful."

"Where do you live?" the woman inquired.

"Not far; near Bathurst and Steeles," Nina explained.

"It's on my way and I'd be happy to take you there."

"Thank you so much."

Nina didn't even have a key. She sat down on a bench near the entrance to her apartment building, resigned to patiently wait for the eventual return of her husband.

A couple of hours later, Anton arrived and immediately began to berate her. "How could you? What is wrong with you? I am working hard to build a good relationship with my co-workers and you are doing everything to destroy it! What gave you the right to insult my project manager? How do you think you made me look by leaving the party alone? Carol is right: you are an ignorant and rude woman! And let me tell you this too, Nina, you are stupid!"

It was all so unjust that Nina chose not to respond. She meekly followed Anton into the building and as soon as they had entered their apartment she went directly to the bedroom and collapsed on the bed, sobbing uncontrollably.

Ω

The next morning, a completely transformed, composed and enthusiastic Nina made her way to the opera house. Finally, she would be among people who could understand her and who could become her friends... she would be doing something that she loved to do and was good at it too. She would sing again.

The pattern of life in an opera company is repetitively the same everywhere in the world: lessons, rehearsals and recitals. But when Nina was riding back home on the subway after that first day and even through the first full week, she felt nothing but a sense of deep disappointment and emptiness. She wasn't made to feel in any way that she belonged. Seemingly, nobody cared if she was there or not. Not a single person addressed her by name or made any effort to speak to her. She was introduced on the first day to the troupe and that was it.

Nina listened to the conversation of other ladies in the chorus and surprisingly, she understood almost everything. Her well-trained musical ear had picked up more English than she realized. She wanted to be part of the conversation too, but by the time she constructed a sentence in her mind, the conversation would have already drifted along to another subject. Nobody tried to speak more slowly for her sake or to interrupt the conversation just to accommodate her. People were reservedly polite to her but it was apparent that they didn't really care about her one way or the other. As far as the teachers and singing coaches were concerned, Nina was just an apprentice so she wasn't really part of the company.

Anton was right, Nina thought, *this will not work.* But she couldn't bring herself to say anything to him about her thoughts and her problems; he would only insist that she must stop her folly and take on more clients instead.

Nina longed for support, not ridicule, and she was thankful that at least she had Boris and Larissa to turn to. After her miscarriage, Nina defied Anton's will and began communicating with her old friends again.

Working on their different engagements, caring for their small son, and what with recording Boris's vocal compositions, they were always very busy. But even so, every day Larissa found time to call and talk with Nina and to reassure her that it was just a slow beginning with the opera company.

Ω

The very next Friday afternoon, Carol approached Anton and asked him if he was busy on the weekend. "I need to work on next year's budget and I need somebody's help. Everyone else on the team already has some plans with their families. Tony, you told me that your wife is usually working on the weekends, so I was wondering if you could help me out?"

"By all means, Carol. I'll come into the office tomorrow morning," Anton co-operatively replied.

"Oh, I hate to work in the office on the weekends. Why don't you come to my house instead?"

On Saturday morning while he was driving to Carol's house, Anton couldn't help but wonder what this invitation really meant. He would know how to behave back in Russia if a woman invited him to her house – that was for sure. But he was thinking that perhaps Canadian women had a different mentality and this invitation actually meant nothing out of the ordinary. So, he wasn't quite sure what to expect.

The floor in the living room of Carol's house was littered with papers. She was sitting in jeans and a t-shirt in the middle of that mess and busily trying to sort through all the papers. She was demonstratively pleased to see Anton and immediately put him to work. That's what they were doing on that sunny September day - working on the budget.

They stopped for lunch and Anton again had an opportunity to admire Carol's house, the modern furnishings, and the expensive art-works on the walls. There was a piano standing in the corner and Anton asked, "Do you play, Carol?"

"No, it was my husband's. That piano and this house," Carol said rather cynically, "are the spoils of war."

"May I?" Anton inquired, and then quickly crossed the room, sat down on the piano stool and started to play. He deliberately selected an easy piece, and so, when Carol admiringly inquired about the origin of his skills, Anton had a ready answer. "I finished music school. Russian parents think that their offspring must play some kind of instrument. Mine were no different. They were actually disappointed when I decided not to make a career out of music."

"That was a smart decision, Tony. It's much harder to make a living and have a normal life in the world of arts than in the world of information technology. The piano is nice for entertaining guests but not for providing for a family."

"Carol, I couldn't agree more," Anton enthusiastically concurred.

They resumed working again until finally, when the sun was starting to go down, Carol decided to call a halt to the budget activity. "You've helped me so much, Tony. Please stay for dinner."

Anton readily agreed. He felt comfortable and content in this house and with this woman. The idea of going home to his apartment and his depressed wife didn't excite him whatsoever...but Carol did.

They had an enjoyable pasta dinner in Carol's dining room and shared a bottle of chilled white wine. Then they adjourned to the living room and Carol served coffee and brandy. They sat on the sofa and began listening to quiet, beautiful music on the stereo. Anton was about to comment on the performance and tell Carol everything about the history of this classical piece and its composer but prudently decided against it.

They spoke very little but kept looking at one-another with considerable intensity. Finally, Anton broke the ice by getting up and coming close to Carol. He took her hand and said, "I'm really attracted to you, Carol. I know that it's wrong but I'm thinking about you all the time."

"Then the decision is yours, Tony. I'm very much attracted to you too, but you're a married man."

Anton kissed her hand, said his good-byes and promptly left the house. He felt himself becoming aroused. He wanted Carol but he knew that she couldn't be his...at least not yet. The alcohol had heightened Anton's feelings and when he arrived home and found Nina in bed, he laid his hands on her body and pulled her towards him. She was half-asleep and surprised by his advances. But when Anton kissed her passionately, she gently pushed him away. "Anton, it's too soon after the operation. I can't."

"Well, I'm sure there's something you can do for your husband," he said hoarsely, but Nina replied, "I can't, Anton. Not today. Not like this."

Perhaps Anton had had more to drink that he realized because in retrospect, he was surprised by his own actions and his words. "What *can* you do, Nina? First, I discovered that you can't even deliver a child, and now you've just demonstrated that you can't be a proper wife either. You are such a loser, Nina!" the now-enraged Anton exclaimed and stomped away to sleep alone on the living room sofa.

Nina had never felt so low and so utterly humiliated in her entire life. She quietly started to cry. Soon she could hear Anton's snoring but sleep would not come to Nina. She had lost him, she thought. Why? She always tried to be a good, caring wife, supportive of her husband, and loyal to him. Tonight, Anton wanted a woman, but he did not really want her, Nina. How did it come to this? What had she done wrong? The answers would not come.

When Anton awoke the following morning, he knew exactly what he would do. The day spent in Carol's house and her words *"it's your decision, Tony"* were enough to prompt Anton into action. He went to one of the Russian deli's and picked up one of the free, weekly Russian newspapers. Then he walked to a nearby coffee shop and started to scrutinize the ads.

Soon he found what he was looking for: a single Russian man advertising that he was looking for a roommate for his furnished basement apartment. Anton called the number provided, made an appointment and was soon inspecting his future residence. The two-bedroom apartment smelled of alcohol and cigarettes. It was a dump, but Anton was not planning to live there for long. He agreed on month-to-month rent, paid a deposit and received a key. Now Anton was ready to start his new life. All that remained for him to do was to have a final, decisive talk with Nina.

He spent the day on Sunday buying groceries and other necessities for his new place. He hated to part with his money for something that in all likelihood would be thrown away shortly, but he wanted his rented basement quarters to appear not as the lair of a loser, but rather as the temporary dwelling of a desperate gentleman.

In the evening when he could be certain that Nina was at home alone, Anton returned to their apartment. He was startled by his own resolute frame of mind. Just the day before he had still been thinking about Nina as his wife and this apartment as 'his'. Today, she represented nothing more than a chain about his neck that he must break in order to start a new and exciting life. Entering the apartment for the last time, he was already thinking of it in his mind as just 'Nina's apartment'.

The confrontational talk that Anton had dreaded was much easier than he had anticipated.

"Nina," he started, "we must talk."

"Are you leaving me, Anton?" she asked impassively.

"Yes, but let me explain..."

"It's not necessary. Do you need my help packing or can you manage yourself?"

"I'll pack myself. Nina, but what about my financial obligations? You know I am still on my trial period and..."

This time Nina interrupted him. "Anton, I missed several days of working and still work only part-time because of my apprenticeship. I'll need a check to cover the rent for the next month."

"But Nina..."

"Anton, please just write the check and it will conclude your financial obligations and our marriage."

Anton quickly packed his clothes, wrote out a check to cover one month's rent and hastily left the apartment. No further words were exchanged.

On his way out of the door, Anton had glanced at Nina for the last time and thought, *actually she's still a rather good-looking woman. It's too bad that she's such a loser.* He was amazed how quickly his deep love and former passion for Nina could evaporate. Anton felt nothing emotionally towards that woman, not even pity.

Nina had sat quietly while Anton was packing and she didn't move when he left. It took her a long while to comprehend what had happened and only then she picked up the phone and called her friends. She could hear the phone ringing six times and then Boris's recorded voice came on the line and asked the caller to leave a message. "He left," Nina said, and hung up the phone. Then she started to weep. All the feelings she had been trying to suppress for the past several months - anger, disappointment and grief, she allowed herself to release now with this bitter bout of crying.

Finally, she stopped; Nina had no more tears. When her friends rushed to her apartment after hearing the phone message, to their amazement they found a self-possessed and calm Nina waiting to greet them.

Boris and Larissa urged Nina to concentrate on her future, to forget about Anton and the last two years of disappointment and frustration in Canada, but Nina was not ready for it. Her mind refused to absorb their advice or to consider any future plans. For all of the next week, Nina went about her daily routine like a robot, by inertia. In the mornings, she was going to the opera company for rehearsals and in the afternoons she was cutting, dyeing and perming the hair of the neighbourhood ladies, as usual.

Thursday evening, she received a large envelope, looking very official. It was delivered by a young courier and she was asked to sign a receipt for the package. Quite surprised, Nina asked the boy if he knew what was contained in the package. "I have no idea," was the indifferent response.

She opened the envelope to examine the set of enclosed documents. She only had to see one English phrase, '*Separation Agreement*', to fully appreciate the purpose and contents of the package delivery. She placed the documents in her purse and left the apartment to go and see Boris.

Boris read through the documents and commented, "According to these papers you are not entitled to any alimony or any part of Anton's future earnings or future assets. He's giving you nothing. Nina, I urge you to get a lawyer and fight back. You alone were providing for the both of you for almost two years and he can't just walk away like that."

"He can and he did," was Nina's simple reply. "I want absolutely nothing from Anton." She promptly signed the papers.

The next morning, Nina woke up in a cheerful mood for the first time in months. She felt as if a heavy burden had been lifted from her shoulders. Even an unexpected conversation in the elevator that morning had not dampened her mood. She had run into one of her older clients. The woman had bluntly asked Nina, "So he finally left you, that handsome husband of yours. Is that right?"

"Yes," Nina answered in a dispassionate voice.

"What can you expect, Nina? He's a computer programmer, a professional, while you're a simple hairdresser. You should find a man of your own stature. For example, my nephew... a wonderful man. He's a plumber so you would have much more in common with him. He just recently divorced his wife. That bitch of a woman just packed her things and left him. Can you believe it?"

"Why did she leave him if he was so wonderful?" Nina inquired.

The woman did not perceive the subtle mockery in Nina's seemingly innocent question and replied, "He was drinking a lot, but only because of his wife. She was such a nag! He needs a good woman, like you. I'm sure that with you, he would stop drinking. So, can I give him your phone number?"

"I don't think I'm ready for a new relationship just yet," Nina replied with restrained politeness. She was relieved when the doors of the elevator finally opened and that conversation was terminated.

Nina was feeling almost content when she arrived to

the opera company that morning. During the rehearsal, for the first time since she had joined the company, she was totally focussed and working to her full capacity. She didn't restrain herself and just let her voice soar naturally. She wanted to probe it in order to measure how much out of shape she really was. Nina was determined that she was not going to lose her greatest asset: her voice.

The reaction of others around her was as pronounced as it was unpredictable. The vocal coach looked at her with genuine surprise, as if he was seeing her for the first time. "What is your name?" he asked.

"Nina Gorchichniy."

"Where did you study, Nina?"

"I'm a graduate of the Moscow Conservatory."

"And where did you work after graduation?"

"At the Bolshoi Theatre, in Moscow."

"It isn't easy from what I've heard to get a position with the Bolshoi."

"I was the winner of an international vocal competition. That helped a lot."

"What was your position with the Bolshoi?"

"Before I quit I had been promoted to soloist."

"So why did you quit, Nina?"

"My husband wanted to emigrate to Canada."

"I see. OK, thank you, everyone." The chorus was dismissed from rehearsal but the coach continued to eye Nina with pronounced admiration.

Later on, one of the other apprentices made an approach to Nina. According to other previous conversations that Nina had overheard, this woman had remained stuck as an apprentice for a long time. Her voice, it was said, just didn't have enough range.

"You know, Nina, I was wondering why you've been so aloof. Now I know; you were simply waiting for an opportunity to show off."

"I'm sorry," Nina politely replied, "my English is not

so good. What does it mean *aloof*?"

"Unfriendly. Stand-offish. Having a decent voice doesn't make you something special you know! If you think this is going to get you a full-time position before one of the more established apprentices like me, you are just plain wrong."

Now it was Nina's turn to be surprised. "For two weeks I was trying to start a conversation with you and others in the group and for two weeks I was being ignored. Today, I had a good class. For the first time in two years, I had a good class. Does this make me aloof?"

The woman did not respond; she just turned her back and walked away.

When Nina was about to leave the premises, she was stopped by the Artistic Director. "Nina," he said, "I gave you a chance, hoping that you would try to fit into the company. I've been informed that you have acted very untoward, quite rudely in fact with one of your colleagues. Please make sure that this is the last time I hear anybody complaining about you."

"Yes, sir. I'm sorry, sir," Nina replied, not knowing what she should be sorry for. After that episode, she quickly left the premises and walked to the subway.

Nina went directly to see Boris and Larissa and recounted the events of the day. "I can't understand this society," Nina was saying. "I really can't understand their definitions of politeness, friendliness, and their ethics. That horrid woman who stole my husband considered it ethical to treat a guest who was in her house for the first time as a mere servant; and furthermore, to order my husband around in my presence. I was his wife, after all. Being an absolute stranger to me, she spoke openly about the most intimate aspects of my life. She called me '*rude and ignorant*' too. It seems to me it was really the other way around.

"And now, for these past two weeks I've been

completely ignored by everyone in the company. Several times I tried to start conversations or ask questions and I was snubbed, again and again. So today, because the coach noticed my singing, I'm accused of being '*rude*' and '*aloof*'. It seems I just don't fit into this society. I can't understand it at all," Nina repeated in frustration.

"Nina, please calm down," Larissa said compassionately, trying to reassure her friend. "It's not all Canadian society that behaves like that. You just encountered several unpleasant and ignorant individuals. Believe me, there are a lot of good, well-meaning and friendly people around. You should continue to attend the company and stop that silly hairstyling business of yours. For that matter, you would be better off to sing in a restaurant, to give vocal lessons, or to do anything else connected with music and singing. Nina, you are so talented! You really must arrange to go to the auditions in New York too, just as you had planned."

Nina shook her head in resignation. "No, Larissa. My voice is really out of shape. I can't go to any auditions right now. Not only that, I'm always feeling tired and weak. I don't know why, but I'm not recovering as quickly as the doctor said I would. In addition, I am always thinking about Anton. I don't even know if I still love him. It's just that I constantly feel that heartache, that feeling of loss of something very beautiful and rare. I am so unhappy right now that I can't even imagine how a person could feel worse than I do."

Indeed, life was about to test Nina's words. The next day she started to hemorrhage and had to be rushed to the hospital again. When she eventually returned home, Nina was too weak to resume her hairstyling work. Larissa cancelled all her appointments for the next several weeks so that Nina could rest and recover her strength.

Return to Moscow

Boris and Larissa proved to be genuine and caring friends, as always. They insisted that Nina stay in bed and brought her nicely prepared meals. And they spent all their free time with her to keep her company and to cheer her up as best as they could. After a couple of weeks had passed, Nina felt strong enough to move about and go for short walks, even though she had lost a lot of weight and still looked pale and fragile.

One afternoon, Boris and Larissa came to discuss Nina's future with her again. Larissa, as always, was brimming with fresh ideas. Boris was more cautious and realistic. Nina sat on the sofa with her legs tucked under her thighs and listened to the bickering between her friends, knowing that both were sincerely concerned about her best interests. Nina didn't enter into the conversation, having a strange feeling that this back and forth dialogue between Larissa and Boris ultimately would have no relevance to the direction of her actual life and future.

The phone rang and Boris took it. He listened for a minute and then looked intently at Nina and said, "She's here, Ekaterina Vasilievna. Yes, I will let her know. Thank you for calling us. Yes, of course she will come."

He set down the phone and said, "Nina that was your former neighbour in Moscow."

"What's wrong?" an alarmed Nina asked. "Aunt Katya has never called me before."

"Your mother is seriously ill. Ekaterina Vasilievna suggested you to come to Moscow as soon as possible."

At this moment, all of Nina's other problems seemed trivial and insignificant. She had always been close to her mother, but for the last several months Nina had been so absorbed with her pregnancy, and then the miscarriage and her crumbling marriage, that she hadn't even called Moscow. Now, in addition to feeling deeply concerned, she felt guilty and despondent.

"Is your Soviet passport in order? Is it still valid?" Larissa asked.

"Yes, it's alright. But I don't have any money to buy a ticket."

"Don't worry, Nina. We'll give you the money and you'll return it whenever you can."

Boris immediately called the Toronto office of Aeroflot, engaged in a lengthy conversation with the airline representative and secured a ticket for Nina for the late-evening flight. Larissa helped Nina to pack and just two hours later Boris was driving Nina to the airport.

Everything had happened so fast that only after the plane had taken off, Nina fully realized that she was going home to Moscow and that soon she would be seeing her mother again. Canada and her problems with Anton, her career, and those unfamiliar ways of Canadian society were all left behind...at least for now. During the entire flight, Nina was praying for her mother and earnestly hoping that she would not come too late.

Ω

At the same time when a frantic Nina was getting ready for her flight with the help of her friends, Anton had been entertaining a guest in his basement flat.

That Friday, he had invited Carol for dinner, and to her surprise, drove her to his apartment instead of to a restaurant. While Carol was sitting gingerly on the edge of a rickety chair, Anton was expertly opening a bottle of red wine.

"Tony, this place is such a dump! How could you live here?" Carol asked him incredulously.

"Would you prefer if I still lived in my old apartment with my wife?"

"Of course not, but…"

"Then don't complain, Carol." Anton put the bottle down, quickly approached Carol and took her into his arms. After that, Carol did not complain any further.

Much later in the evening, when two sated lovers were lying on Anton's old mattress (but on clean linen), Carol said, "You know, Tony, you will have to resign from your job. We can't keep working together."

This was an unexpected turn of events and Anton became visibly upset.

"Carol, even this dump costs money and I have to eat from time to time. I can't just quit."

"Please pass me the phone," Carol instructed, and when Anton did so she promptly dialed and said, "Hi, Robert, how have you been? How's the insurance industry? And how's your project? Do you need more people? … Yes, of course, he's good. I wouldn't recommend you hire anybody who wasn't top notch… Yes, he's working for me now… Well, it would be better if we worked separately. Yes, Robert, you assume correctly. He's very important to me… No, he doesn't know *PowerBuilder* software specifically but surely you could train him. He's very coachable… Yes, Robert, Monday afternoon would be just fine… Let me spell it for you: G-o-r-c-h-i-c-h-n-i-y… Thank you so much, Robert." And with that, Carol hung up the phone.

"You have an interview on Monday. You know, Tony, you have a horrible last name. It's difficult to spell or even to pronounce. Have you considered changing it?" Carol asked.

"Yes, as a matter of fact I have."

"What do you have in mind?"

"*Walker*. Walker sounds suitable, don't you think?" Anton was looking intently at Carol for a response.

"Get your divorce first, stud!" Carol answered,

laughing heartily.

"Oh, I will, Carol, I will," Anton asserted as he drew her close to him again.

Ω

The next morning, following her arrival in Moscow, Nina left the airport in a taxi and as they were driving towards the center of the city she was looking around, utterly engrossed by the sights she hadn't seen in a long while. She was back in Moscow! It seemed uncanny to hear familiar language, and to understand perfectly what people were saying. Except for the occasional new, shiny foreign car, most of the cars on the road were shabbier than in Canada and the streets and buildings, mostly apartment buildings, appeared distinctly more gray and dreary. But soon they passed through the suburbs and reached the old part of Moscow. Nina observed with a sense of pride the beautiful architecture of the city center, the old but still stately buildings intermixed with modern shops that had sprung up since her emigration. She was home and much the happier for it.

The taxi stopped near her mother's apartment building. Nina paid the driver and quickly hurried inside. She could hardly wait to see her mother after such a long absence. But when she opened the door with her old key and went to the bedroom, she stopped abruptly in the doorway and looked in shock at the old and frail woman lying in the bed.

"Mama!" Nina cried out as she rushed towards her mother and knelt at the side of the bed. Mother and daughter cried in each other's arms, so happy and grateful to see and embrace each other again.

Nina had flown from Canada to comfort and care for her sick mother. The last thing Nina wanted to do was to sadden her mother or to burden her with her Canadian problems. She had been planning to assure her mother that everything was fine in her life. But instead, Nina spontaneously poured her heart out. She told her mother everything: about her unsuccessful singing career and her substitute home business, about her failed pregnancy, and lastly, about her disastrous marriage and breakup. Nina's mother comforted and consoled her daughter, gently stroking her head and arms. Just as though she was a little girl, Nina felt that now everything was going to be fine.

For three days, Nina stayed close to her mother's bedside, cooking and feeding her, and administering the required medications. Nina's brother came to visit them daily too. His wife had recently given birth to a second daughter and so he could only stay for a short while each visit. He was happy to see his sister again, and grateful that now she could share the responsibility of looking after their ailing mother.

But on the fourth morning when Nina awoke and went to tend to her mother, she discovered to her horror that she was the sole living person in the apartment. Her mother had passed away peacefully during the night. Nina's grief was immeasurable. For just a moment she wanted to simply end her own seemingly useless and hopeless life, but then she looked intently at the body of her mother and thought of how much this woman, who had never remarried, had sacrificed to raise her. Her mother had dedicated her life to ensure her daughter's future happiness. *I must live for my mother's sake,* a grieving Nina resolved.

It was easier said than done. In those first days after her mother's passing, Nina could barely function. Her brother organized the funeral and proposed to hold a wake afterwards in his family's apartment. He attended to all the necessary details. Nina just sat near the coffin and politely responded to the words of condolence from attending friends and acquaintances of her mother, not really seeing or recognizing any of the people that came to pay their last respects to Galina Georgievna.

Nina cried when it was time to go to the cemetery and she cried during the interment; she cried when they were driving back to her brother's place and she cried all the while during the wake.

Finally, the guests all departed and it was time for Nina to return to her mother's now-vacant apartment.

"I will walk you to the metro station," her brother suggested. Nina kissed her sister-in-law and her nieces good-bye and then accompanied her brother.

"Nina," he carefully began, "how long are you planning to stay in Moscow?"

"I haven't decided yet. Why do you ask?"

"Well," her brother said, "I don't want you to misunderstand me, Nina. I am as upset about mama's death as you are. It's just that I want to move into her apartment eventually. As you very well know, I left our place when I got married. Tanya's parents gave us a room and it was great. But now it's very hard for us. Tanya's parents live in one room, her younger sister is in another room, and the four of us are occupying the third room. To say the least it's quite over-crowded, as you can imagine."

"I haven't been in Moscow for two years," Nina responded. "I would like to stay here for a couple of weeks. Then I'll be leaving, so don't worry."

"Nina, please stay as long as you want. I'm so happy to see you again."

"But you wanted to be certain that I am planning to go back to Canada, right?"

"Yes," he admitted with some hesitation, "I guess you're right about that."

"In two weeks the apartment is yours," Nina assured her brother. They arrived to the metro station, kissed one-another and said good-bye.

Nina took her train and started to count the familiar

stops, but when she heard the voice of the announcer saying *Teatralnaya* (Theatre Station), Nina spontaneously rose from her seat as if in a trance and disembarked from the train, taking the long escalator flight up to the ground level and exited the station.

And there it was, just across the street: the Bolshoi Theatre, the place of her life-long dream, and the place of her previous employment. She crossed the street, came to one of the trees growing near Theatre Square and leaned against it. A cold October wind was blowing Nina's unkempt hair; she was dressed much too lightly for Moscow's autumn chills but she didn't even feel the cold. She remained there, staring at that magnificent building for a very long time. Tears were rolling down her cheeks, but Nina wasn't even aware that she was crying. And then, some inner calm and resolution came over her and she whispered as if in prayer, *"This is my country. I'm not going anywhere. I will stay in Moscow and I will rebuild my life. I am done with crying and feeling sorry for myself. One day, I will work here again. I don't know where I'll live or what I'll do tomorrow, but I do know that I will sing and one day I will sing on the Bolshoi Theatre stage once more."* She was barely conscious of the fact that she was whispering audibly.

"Nina?" She heard a nearby familiar voice. The inquiring voice sounded surprised and Nina slowly turned her head in the direction that the sound of the voice seemed to be coming from.

"Nina?" Now the voice sounded closer and more astounded. "Nina!"

"Tolya!" Nina exclaimed, and with uncontrolled sobs of joy she collapsed into the open arms of her dear old school friend.

BOOK II

The Good Life of Tony Walker

It was a perfect October morning when forty-two-year-old Tony emerged from his house, entering his spacious backyard. It was quite early and his family was still sleeping. He regarded his stately house, located in the prestigious Bonavista Lake Estates in Calgary, with the admiration, pride and measured concern of a homeowner. *The grass has to be cut again and the bushes should be trimmed*, Tony reflected, as he was going through his usual routine of morning stretches.

He loved this early time of each new day: peaceful, beautiful and quiet. The waters of the man-made pond shimmered like a glass surface, while the air was crisp, clean and a little bit chilly, just as Tony liked. He couldn't understand why Carol preferred to exercise in their basement on the treadmill or to do her videotape routines. How could you compare working out on a basement treadmill to jogging outside in the fresh air?

But on this particular morning, Tony was glad to be alone. Today was the fifteenth anniversary of the day he had moved in with Carol. It was not their wedding date. They had not gotten married until the spring of 1989, and so this October day was not officially celebrated as their anniversary, but for Tony it was one of the most important and memorable dates of the year. Again and again he congratulated himself over the best decision of his life: leaving Nina and marrying Carol.

Tony finished his stretches, opened the gates of the backyard and jogged down the street past his driveway. He glanced at their two cars in passing and thought to himself that his BMW SUV was much more practical than Carol's Toyota Lexus sports car.

Tony was relieved that Tom's car wasn't being parked on their driveway any longer. Tony and Tom, Carol's son, were certainly not enemies nor did they dislike each other, but they had never really bonded and had spent all these years living in one house as polite and civil strangers. Tom was now studying at the University of British Columbia. *Well,* Tony thought, *it'll take him at least four years and then who knows? It's unlikely that he would return to his mother's house or even to Calgary.* That suited Tony just fine.

He ran his usual route, nodding to the neighbours from time to time and extending a brief greeting to the other regular joggers that he encountered along the way. That's what Tony liked most about his life: the predictability and the security. He knew the people that he encountered during his morning routine, and he knew what would happen during the day and what he would do in the evening. He was living the organized life of a Canadian, upper-middle-class man with a wife, a daughter and a secure job. Frankly, Tony felt his job was not as exciting and interesting as he might wish for, but it was a good job nonetheless.

Tony and Carol had moved to Calgary fourteen years ago, just before his beloved Megan was born. Carol had picked the timing just right: selling when the real estate prices in Toronto were high and buying at a time when Calgary real estate prices hadn't started escalating yet. That astute move had allowed them to buy their prized lakefront mansion. Now his house was worth seven figures!

Smart move, Carol. His ever-efficient wife made a good career for herself in Calgary too. Her education, experience, brains, no-nonsense attitude and her connections helped her become the Vice President of Information Technology for one of the major oil companies based in Calgary.

Tony never made a real career for himself in the information technology field. Soon after he started in the industry, he realized that he didn't have the aptitude to excel in this line of work. He did learn the primary

programming language of the mainframe computer –
COBOL, at college and later, the most popular database
software of that time, *DB2.* He even learned
PowerBuilder, a so-called fourth generation language,
but then he became tired of perpetually running the
proverbial IT marathon.

He was observing the IT professionals in his midst:
the technology was changing every year. As soon as a
person became proficient in some programming
language or some new database, puff! It's obsolete!
Object-oriented programming became commonplace,
mainframes were replaced by servers, and Internet
development replaced pretty much everything else. The
behemoth enterprise systems, such as *SAP* and *Oracle*,
caused many of the IT programmers, who used to
develop home-grown systems, to become redundant.
His colleagues were constantly training, retraining, and
retraining again - just to stay abreast of the newly-
emerging technologies. The inevitable result was that
sooner or later, most of them became burned out and
quit the IT rat race on their own or were otherwise
eventually terminated by their unfeeling employers in
the name of corporate productivity.

A long time ago, Tony had decided to position
himself into some protected, secure corner of the IT
world – a sea of calm, so to speak, and to let the
dynamics of the technology storm rage around him.
Carol's brother, Jeff, helped him secure a position as a
project leader of a small, 'home-grown' PowerBuilder
system. The system was integral to the business of this
company. A recently implemented enterprise system
had replaced ninety percent of the company's old
systems but didn't directly touch Tony's ancillary
system. There was talk about eventually rewriting this
antiquated (by modern standards) system, but Tony
understood very well that it would remain only idle talk
for a very long time. The company had just invested

millions of dollars on their large implementation and wouldn't be in any rush to waste money by replacing something that already worked reliably for its intended purpose.

And so, Tony and his team of three programmers supported that old technology and did some enhancements time from time to keep their system abreast of any new business requirements. Tony was hoping that nobody from higher levels in the corporate echelon would pay attention to or consider touching his system for the next ten years or so.

Tony's job was exactly that: a job and nothing more. It was something to securely occupy him from nine to five during the weekdays. It was something that allowed him to regularly bring his pay-check home to supplement Carol's much larger income.

His real life would start after five in the afternoons, and carry on throughout the weekends. Three times a week he was playing squash in the winter and tennis in the summer. He became a proficient skier, and in the winter the Walker family spent almost all their weekends on the slopes of nearby Banff National Park. Summer brought with it camping and barbeque parties. Once or twice a year they would travel to all-inclusive resorts in the Caribbean Islands or in Mexico. It was a *very* good life indeed.

Tony loved his family, and especially his Megan. She had inherited her father's good looks and her mother's brains. Tony was certain that Megan would enjoy a great future. He even wanted to have more children but Carol was quite content with her son and their own daughter.

Tony loved his wife, or at least he was confident of that in his own mind. It was not the romantic and passionate love that he had experienced with Nina at the beginning of their relationship, but who needed it? He and Carol shared the love and respect of two mature and compatible adults.

Tony didn't make a habit of cheating on his wife. Well... he almost never cheated. He remembered what had happened to his predecessor and so he was extremely careful and discrete. But a couple of times when he had been sent on training sessions to other cities, the opportunity had presented itself, so why not? No big deal.

Tony reflected on his last trip to Toronto. When was it? Eight years ago? Something like that. On that occasion he had decided to try to locate Nina, just for old time's sake. He was curious what had happened to her. Did she get married again?

Frankly, he didn't think so. She had loved him far too much to be with another man. Did she sing in restaurants or still have her hairstyling business? Tony intended to find out and maybe, just maybe, invite Nina out and spend an evening with her. Why not?

He was quite confident that she would be happy to see him and he was even prepared to comfort her. He rang their old phone number but the line had been disconnected. He looked in the phone book but couldn't find a listing for Nina. Then he called Boris. Tony had lost contact with Boris after his divorce (courtesy of that bitch, Larissa), but he called him anyway. Tony was lucky that Boris picked up the phone, although his voice sounded cold and distant. Upon Tony's inquiry, Boris simply asserted that he wouldn't give out any of Nina's personal information, quickly excused himself and hung up the phone. There was something very irritating in Boris's tone of voice, as if he found Tony's inquiry perversely amusing. But Tony didn't have much time to dwell on it; there was this pretty little lady staying in the same hotel as him and she was quite accommodating. They had a good time. Tony never called Boris again.

Tony was glad that they had moved away from Toronto, away from the Russian immigrant community. Of course there were quite a few Russians living in

Calgary too, but Tony didn't associate with any of them. Carol didn't care for Russians and considered their science and technology skills to be behind the times and inferior to the modern technologies that were well-established in North America. As far as Russian culture, literature, and the arts were concerned, Carol didn't give any of them too much credit. She had tried to read a couple of translated Russian classics and found them boring and tedious. She didn't care much for Russian music either.

Carol had declared to Tony that in general, Russians were rude and pushy and way too forward with their inter-personal directness. Once, during the time when Tony and Carol had just started to date, he took her on a Saturday evening to a Russian restaurant-nightclub. She sat in virtual silence for an hour with her eyes wide open, hardly eating anything, and then asked Tony to take her away from that place. She declared the women's clothes gaudy, the music too loud and primitive, and the behaviour of the patrons much too boisterous. "*It was a zoo,*" she had hotly declared, and Tony had no intention of contradicting her. That was their one and only experience with Russian clubs.

Carol took pains to 'civilize' Tony. She referred to the process as 'the taming of her Russian bear'. She instructed him never to talk about religion and politics during social gatherings. She taught him which topics were safe territory and which should be avoided in mixed company. She sometimes encouraged him to play the piano for guests, but not very often, and even then, not too much at a time. Moderation was the watchword of Carol's behavioural standards.

"Don't ever forget," she told him, "you are a host, not an entertainer."

Tony found her so-called training antics to be amusing but certainly not worth making an issue of them.

Soon his piano playing ceased to be an issue in any event. In the beginning, Tony tried not to show how really skilled a musician he actually was. Then he just stopped being good. He knew it, even if his guests did not. Playing the piano made him feel sad and even somewhat depressed, so eventually he stopped playing altogether. Carol didn't think that it was necessary to spend time and money on the children's musical education, and so the piano was left standing in the corner as just another piece of furniture gathering dust.

His morning workout by now finished, Tony returned home. His women were having breakfast already. He quickly kissed his wife and daughter and ran to the shower.

"Tony," he could hear his wife's voice, "aren't you tired of your business-casual outfits? Why don't you put on a nice suit today? You look so handsome in your suits."

"Carol," Tony replied with a touch of impatience, "nobody wears suits to the office anymore."

"Daddy, just for today... I haven't seen you in a suit for hundreds of years. When you pick me up after my jazz class, all the girls will be so jealous that I have the most handsome father," Megan insisted.

"Fine, but only today," Tony agreed with a chuckle. Nothing was going to spoil his good frame of mind today.

Another ordinary but very pleasant day in Tony Walker's life had begun.

To Russia With Love

Tony's day, however, turned out to be full of surprises and was anything but ordinary. As soon as he arrived at his office and switched on his computer, he found an e-mail from the assistant to the VP of Marketing. He was invited to a meeting at nine o'clock in the morning. Tony immediately called Carol's brother Jeff. Jeff was working in the marketing department and would know what was going on. He, Tony, had never had any dealings with that department before. But Jeff wasn't at his desk and so Tony went to the meeting not knowing why he, a low-level project leader of an old, so-called legacy system, had been invited to see the VP of Marketing. *They are starting the development of a new system and they want to get me involved,* he decided. He became excited and a bit apprehensive at the same time. Did he still have it in him to adapt to a new technology?

The meeting was being conducted in a large conference room and all the top brass of the company were seated in the front row. Tony felt somewhat intimidated and looked for a place in the second row, but William Parker motioned him to a vacant seat beside him. Tony felt somewhat relieved; Bill was an old friend of Jeff and his teammate. Tony had had quite a few beers with Bill at different social gatherings and was glad to be seated close to somebody he knew.

Jeff was presiding. He opened the meeting and quickly outlined the agenda. The company was considering expanding its horizons by entering the vast and rapidly growing Russian market. Tony felt very proud of his brother-in-law on this occasion. It was the first time that Tony had seen him in action. Jeff was talking about Russian demographics, explaining that the giant country was on the move and undergoing a construction boom, and that there was a constant demand for modern construction materials. He addressed different strategies that their company could adopt, ranging from the shipment of ready products into Russia, to building a factory on Russian soil and establishing the domestic manufacture of some of the products there. He presented an analysis of the cost of labour in both countries and talked about taxes, standards, licensing fees, as well as the overhead and risks associated with operating in an unfamiliar jurisdiction.

Following Jeff's thoroughly detailed presentation, the discussion and debates began in earnest. The executive participants were exchanging different points of view and at times the discussion became quite heated. There was one thing Tony understood: the fundamental decision to go after the lucrative Russian market had already been made and that was not what was being deliberated. The arguments centered on different start-up and market penetration strategies.

In the end, a decision was taken to send a small marketing team to Moscow to meet with their Russian business counterparts, with the objective of signing an initial contract for exporting the company's products to Russia. Once their products achieved a degree of penetration by capturing a meaningful segment of the domestic market, the establishment of manufacturing facilities within Russia would be undertaken as the second phase of the project.

Jeff rose once again and explained, "We've heard from quite a number of people who have tried before us to get their foot in the door of the Russian market that the main challenge lies in understanding Russian mentality. Russians think, act and negotiate quite differently than we do. Usually, foreign businessmen hire Russian interpreters, but these people impassively translate literally without conveying the nuances of the discussion or the emotions and the real mood during the negotiations. I would like to introduce you to our *secret weapon*: my brother-in-law, Tony Walker. Tony has been with the company for over thirteen years. He understands the culture and philosophy of our company (*I do?* Tony wondered), and most importantly, Tony is of Russian origin and his mother language is, in fact, Russian. He was born and raised in St. Petersburg but then studied at the Moscow University and therefore knows Moscow very well. I propose that we include Mr. Walker in our Russian delegation.

"Hey, old boy," Bill said, tapping Tony on the shoulder, "you must be tired of looking at the same programs for years. It's time for new scenery. Or should I say old scenery?" and Bill laughed at his own, rather forced humour.

The VP of Marketing turned towards Tony and seriously asked, "What do you think, Mr. Walker? Are you interested in joining the Marketing Department? How do you feel about visiting your native country?"

"That sounds very interesting, sir. I'm really excited and I feel honoured. However, I would like to consult with my wife. It's a big step and it will affect our family, so..."

Jeff interrupted Tony in mid-sentence. "Who do you think suggested your participation in the first place? Carol's all for it."

"Then I'm going," Tony cheerfully announced. The nature of the family conspiracy between his daughter and his wife and their insistence that he wear a proper suit on this one particular day by now had become patently obvious.

"Fine," the VP said, "so this is what we're going to do. Tony, I will talk to your boss and arrange for your temporary transfer to my department. Go with Bill and Jeff to Moscow and let's see how it works out. Assuming the negotiations are successful and you prove to be a good addition to the team, we can discuss the opportunity for your permanent transfer to Marketing after your return."

For some reason, Tony suddenly thought about his parents whom he hadn't seen for over seventeen years. Tony and Carol had been planning to visit Russia for ages, but every time something else had come up - the cruise with their friends, the house renovation, or something else that would cause that travel idea to be deferred to some future time.

Tony had invited his parents to come to visit them in Canada too, and Carol had generously suggested that they would cover all the expenses of his parents while they were in Canada, and would even pay half of the cost of their flight tickets. *"Their visit will cost us three to five thousand dollars,"* Carol had calculated. *"If they want to see you and their granddaughter, at least they could spend a thousand dollars."* His parents never raised any objections to this proposed arrangement for a visit to Canada, but they never took Tony up on this open offer either.

Over the years, a consistent pattern of communication had been established: Tony wrote a letter to his parents once a month, called several times a year, and sent them money in lieu of presents on their birthdays and for Christmas. They in turn wrote to him regularly and sent nice presents for Tony, Carol and Megan once a year.

Now, it was all about to change: he would see his parents, his sister and her family! He remembered his niece as a cute kid and by this time she was a married woman. He also had a nephew whom he had never met. At that moment, Tony felt an unexpected yearning to return to his homeland, back to Mother Russia.

Ω

Tony didn't go back to his desk after that momentous meeting. He just couldn't. He was too excited. He attended another meeting, this time with his new partners, Jeff and Bill. They discussed their plans and their strategy extensively. They all agreed that it would be better to work the first half-day in Russia using an official interpreter and for Tony to remain silent. Two advantages, Jeff pointed out. The first advantage was that Tony would have the opportunity to observe how Jeff and Bill operated and become familiar with their style of negotiating. The second probable advantage was that the Russians might respond more openly if they thought that nobody on the Canadian delegation spoke or understood Russian. Tony would watch and listen, and then pass on his observations to Jeff and Bill so they could evaluate their situation and make appropriate adjustments to their negotiating tactics.

They decided to fly to Toronto on the upcoming Sunday morning, and from there to fly directly to Moscow. It would bring them to Moscow on Monday afternoon and they would have some time to relax and recover from the jet-lag before the first meeting on Tuesday morning. They would have four working days to negotiate the contract. Then Jeff and Bill would spend the weekend exploring Moscow while Tony would fly to St. Petersburg (the city name had reverted from Leningrad back to its original form after the fall of the Soviet Union) to visit his family. Tony had wanted to arrange to fly from Moscow to St. Petersburg on Friday evening, right after the last scheduled meeting with their Russian counterparts, but his associates had convinced him to postpone his intended flight until Saturday morning.

"Hey, buddy," Bill said, "this'll be our only

opportunity to experience Moscow's famous nightlife and you, Tony, are going to show us the town. We will be in need of an interpreter and guide on Friday evening, even more so than during the meetings!" Thus the plan was settled and the three men laughed heartily.

Tony was handed a set of working documents to become familiar with in advance of the trip and was dispatched home from the office early that day.

He was treated like a hero at home. Carol prepared a festive dinner and invited Jeff and Bill, together with their spouses. Tony exhibited mock indignation towards Carol for not even hinting what had been in store for him that day.

Megan playfully jumped about, proudly proclaiming, "I knew about it too, Daddy! I was a part of the conspiracy."

After the guests left, Carol inundated Tony with numerous instructions and advices: how to behave during the meetings, what to say and what not to say, how to behave socially, and so on and so on. "And don't forget," she cautioned, "your associates will tell their wives about everything that you say and do and then half of Calgary will know all about it too. Take them to the nightclub or whatever if they insist, but please, Tony, behave yourself."

"Of course, Carol. Whatever you say, dear. You shouldn't worry, Carol. You know me; I would never do anything inappropriate. Have I ever?"

Carol ignored that rhetorical question and pressed on. "Darling, I want to discuss your priorities with you."

"What are you talking about?" Tony asked, somewhat impatiently. He was growing rather tired of Carol's overbearing and persistent nagging.

"I realize that you have not seen your parents for a long time, so you would be inclined to shower them with presents and I'm all for it. After all, they *are* your parents, even though they have obviously been unwilling to come to meet Megan and me for all these years. However, we have a lot of unusually heavy expenses before us, so don't go crazy with the gifts."

"What sort of expenses?"

"Megan needs braces for her teeth and you know we've been planning to change the windows this year."

"I remember," Tony grumbled.

"Good, so just make sure that you don't lose sight of your priorities when you are in St. Petersburg," Carol concluded.

Tony was feeling rather relieved when he finally boarded the plane and at last was out of sight of his watchful wife.

Tony – The Marketing Man

The flight itself was uneventful but Moscow was promising to be as exciting as they had anticipated. The city was now very different from Tony's distant memory of it. He never saw so many cars on Moscow streets as he did now. Calgary and even Toronto streets seemed to be virtually deserted in comparison to Moscow's perpetual traffic jams.

"How do they manage to squeeze eight cars into a road with five lanes?" an amused Jeff asked while observing the drivers manoeuvring the heavy traffic from the window of their taxi. "I just don't know why they bother to mark the lanes at all. Nobody's paying any attention to the dividers anyway."

"Oh my goodness," Bill exclaimed, "did you see what that car just did? Are they all training to be stuntmen or something?"

Tony was preoccupied absorbing the city's noises, smells and views. How could he have stayed away from this city for so long? From a distance, tranquil Calgary now seemed very small and provincial. In the last fifteen years Moscow had grown to become one of the most important capitals of the world and Tony could see why. The city had grown bigger, brighter, more prosperous, and more exhilarating than ever.

The taxi stopped near a five-star hotel, and again Tony was impressed by the opulence of the hotel and the excellence of the service. Yes, Moscow had certainly changed; there weren't any hotels like this in Soviet times.

Tony proudly ascended several stairs leading to the lobby. He felt that he had returned as a winner, as a successful business representative of a large Canadian company. Yes, sir! He had made it!

The following morning, Tony and his marketing team-mates had an early breakfast, discussed the strategy for the first day of meetings, and went to the lobby to wait for their interpreter. Tony glanced at their collective image in a grandiose wall mirror and decided that they made a remarkably commanding team. He noticed with pleasure that other people milling about the lobby were turning their heads to take a second look at their little group.

Tony was quite right in his self-evaluation of the Canadian delegation. All three men were tall, athletically built and good-looking. Bill and Jeff were both dark-haired, while the blonde-headed Tony added an eye-catching contrasting accent. He was observing the casual and confident manner of his partners and sought to replicate it. He had little doubt that they would prevail in the business meeting proceedings and felt supremely confident that by the very same afternoon the contract would be signed on favourable terms.

Ω

Tony's initial confidence evaporated within the first hour of the meeting. The representatives of the Russian company were smooth operators.

On the surface, it appeared as though the Russians were agreeing with the Canadian proposals, and everyone in their group was nodding their heads approvingly, or so it seemed. But when Tony heard the word '*lokhi*", he knew that something must be done immediately. He recognized the deprecating tone associated with that slang word which he himself had used back in his youth to describe those people whom he didn't respect. *They're going to walk all over us, and Bill and Jeff won't even realize it*, Tony thought. He continued listening attentively to the negotiations and only when he grasped the trap that his Canadian colleagues were about to fall into, in clear Russian without any hint of a foreign accent, he spoke up for the first time and said assertively, "Let me just recount your proposition."

The Russian team was totally taken aback. They hadn't realized that *Tony Walker* was Russian by birth and understood the language perfectly well. There was an awkward moment of silence as the members of the Russian team recounted in their heads the conversation that had transpired, recalling the numerous uncomplimentary words they had spoken about their Canadian business counterparts. The Russians tried to recall if they'd revealed any sensitive information that would put them at any negotiating disadvantage.

If Jeff and Bill were surprised that Tony had spoken up, seemingly out of turn, they didn't even blink. However, after Tony reiterated the terms of proposal made by the Russian group, first in Russian and then in English, Jeff started to nervously drum his fingers on the table. Bill was all smiles facing their Russian counterparts, but Tony detected him cursing under his breath. Jeff and Bill were astute enough to surmise that they had almost been 'taken to the cleaners'.

From that moment on, the atmosphere of the meeting changed dramatically. Tony didn't quite know what had come over him, but he took charge of the proceedings and steered the discussion as he thought appropriate. An hour later, he was becoming more confident that he and his group had regained some level of respect and that the contract outcome could be salvaged on an acceptable basis.

During lunch-break, Bill asked him, "Tony, what the hell was going on in there? Why did you jump in and take over? I thought we were doing fine without any help from..." Bill hesitated, looking for an appropriate word.

Tony finished the sentence for him, "From the raw rookie."

"Something like that," Bill replied curtly.

Jeff then intervened. "Bill, let's not jump all over Tony. When he spoke up, I immediately had the distinct feeling that maybe we weren't doing as well as we thought. Tony, would you please explain it to us?"

"Guys, I had to intervene when I did. There was no choice. One Russian said *"They are lokhi,"* and the others agreed with him. I'd never allow anybody to call me or my friends a *lokh*."

"What does that mean?" Jeff asked.

"It's not so easy to explain. You won't find this word in any Russian dictionary. It's slang. A *lokh* is a weakling, a 'mark' to be taken advantage of easily, a naïve person," Tony explained. "You know the expression 'I wasn't born yesterday'? Well, a *lokh* was born yesterday."

"We get the picture," Bill gruffly muttered. "That's a first for me! Nobody ever took me for a *lokh* before."

"Bill, it's nothing against you personally. Russian society is polarized in the extreme, much like it was in America a hundred or more years ago. It's raw capitalism at its worst.

"Russian society is sharply divided these days between a minority of the very rich and a majority of the very poor; between the highly successful new Russian businessmen – the oligarchs - and the rest of the nation. The ones that have not 'made it' from the point of view of the New Russians, are the losers, the *lokhi*. Everyone is judged and placed into one of two categories: either *krutie* or *lokhi*.

"*Krutie* people are considered to be cool, successful, witty, and clever, all taken together. You show a bit of weakness and you're a *lokh,* ready to be taken for a ride, so to speak. You guys were too civilized, too polite and too straightforward for them."

"In that case obviously *lokhi*," Jeff concluded. Then he asked, "How do you know so much about modern

Russian society, Tony? I wasn't aware that you were all that interested in your former motherland."

Tony wasn't too happy about Jeff's assessment of his intelligence and replied curtly, "Jeff, I do keep abreast of the Russian news."

Jeff took that slight snub well enough and nodded his head in agreement, "OK, Tony, we'll play it your way. Obviously you understand the mentality of these people much better than we do. You lead and we'll follow. We'll provide you with all the support that you need. But remember, the stakes are high. The future prosperity of our company, our reputation, and not to mention your own future, are all on the line. And don't lose sight of those very lucrative bonuses that we don't want to miss out on."

"Yeah, Tony," Bill added, "no pressure, eh."

For the rest of the series of business meetings that week, Tony could do no wrong. He intuitively felt all the crosscurrents and turbulences during the proceedings. He was weaving through the negotiations and astutely avoiding all the potential traps. He managed to ingratiate himself as a 'buddy' with the Russian team and thus they addressed and negotiated exclusively with him. Jeff and Bill withdrew to the background and for the most part were just left to observe Tony's wheeling and dealing. But they were there for him with the required documents or necessary pieces of information, as the need arose.

The meetings were continuing all day long and extended through dinner. Afterwards, the Canadian team was meeting alone until late into the night to review the outcomes of the day and to plan the agenda for the next day. There was absolutely no time to explore Moscow or to experience any of Moscow's famous attractions. They might just as well have been isolated in some remote God-forsaken rural village; it would have made no difference.

Finally, on Friday around mid-day, all the wrinkles were finally ironed out and the contract had been signed, faxed to Canada for executive signatures and then faxed back, fully executed.

The three-man Canadian team emerged by mid-afternoon from the office, feeling like victors. The mission was accomplished! They decided to go for an early dinner, to relax a bit, and to discuss plans for the evening. A bottle of Armenian brandy was ordered and poured. Jeff rose to his feet and said, "I want to propose a toast to the success of our team: Jeff Walker, Bill Parker and Tony Walker. Tony, you have really proven yourself this week. Welcome to our team. This one's for Tony!"

"For Tony!" Bill repeated. "You did well, man. Without you in the lead, those sharks would have eaten us alive."

"They're not really sharks, and actually, quite nice people when you get to know them," Tony commented. "They were just probing us at the beginning, like any other good businessmen would have done. But hey, I wouldn't have been able to accomplish anything without you guys. You provided me with outstanding support. You are great mentors and I learned so much this week. I want to thank you for giving me this opportunity and to say that it's an honour for me to be part of your team. Here's to you, guys," Tony said humbly as he raised his glass.

"For us!" and three self-proclaimed heroes downed their third shot of brandy. Jeff and Bill continued to lavish praise on Tony and his ability to negotiate skilfully, telling him that he was *a natural* and asking how he, such a talented man, could spend years in the background, merely supporting the same old system. Tony was inclined to agree with them, knowing now that never again would he be able to be satisfied performing the mundane duties of a project leader and programmer

- not after he had succeeded to such a degree in the high-powered world of international commerce.

Once the formal part of the dinner was finished, the men started to eagerly discuss their social plans for the evening. Tony showed them a list of some casinos and nightclubs that the Russian group had suggested to him and they settled on several of the most enticing places.

By the time the 'three amigos' left the restaurant, they were not drunk but they were certainly feeling a slight and pleasant buzz. It was an auspicious start to the evening. "Tony," an enthusiastic Jeff asked, "where's the Kremlin? We've been in Moscow for five days but still haven't seen it. Can you take us there?"

They took a taxi to downtown Moscow and then walked a short distance towards the Kremlin and Red Square. Tony, as a proud host, showed them the granite mausoleum of Lenin, the magnificent St. Basil's Cathedral, and finally the Kremlin. His Canadian mates were visibly impressed. They were walking towards the famous GUM department store when Bill asked, "What is that grand looking, rounded building on the opposite side in that big open square?"

"Oh, that's the Bolshoi Theatre," Tony replied casually.

"You mean the world-famous Bolshoi Theatre? It's quite a landmark. Let's get closer."

At that point, throwing caution to the wind, Tony started to describe the history of the building, and spoke about the many famous personalities associated with the theatre, and about the opera and ballet companies that the theatre hosted.

"You're quite the theatre buff," Jeff commented.

"I lived in Moscow for years so I've been here lots of times," Tony said modestly.

"Well, I've never been here," Bill replied, and then he spontaneously proposed, "let's go to see a performance."

"Oh come on, guys," a suddenly alarmed Tony reacted. "What about our plans? The casinos and the clubs are waiting for us."

"I'm with Bill," Jeff chimed in. "I've been to the casinos in Atlantic City, in Vegas and even in Monte Carlo. But I've certainly never been in the Bolshoi Theatre to see a performance. When I tell my wife about this she will be so impressed and incredibly jealous too! Let's do it. What time is the performance over? Ten-thirty? Eleven? That's still early enough to accomplish everything else that we planned. After all, sleep is overrated."

La Traviata

Tony examined the announcement board and deprecatingly commented, "But its *La Traviata* tonight. How many times can a person listen to the same old Verdi score? Tra-la-la-la-la," Tony was humming the beginning of the overture from that famous opera.

Both men stood still and looked at Tony with undisguised curiosity. "Wow!" Bill exclaimed, "do you know this opera by heart?"

Tony realized that in his enthusiasm he had gone a bit too far and started to back-pedal. "Not the entire opera, just the opening stanzas. As you guys know, I finished music school and we were studying it a bit. In addition, my parents were opera lovers so they took me to *La Traviata* performances several times."

"Well, my parents never did that sort of thing so I never heard this opera. Let's go. We'll still have time for the nightclubs after the performance," Jeff enthused.

"It's always hard to get tickets for a same-day performance," Tony indicated. "We probably won't be able to get any tickets at all for tonight."

"Leave it to me," Bill declared, and he disappeared in the crowd somewhere in the vicinity of the box office. Scarcely ten minutes later he re-appeared, triumphantly waving three tickets in his hand.

"OK, Mr. Music Man, so what's this opera all about?" he asked.

Tony rendered a synopsis of the famous opera. "Well, she's a famous courtesan and he's a nobleman. He loves her and she loves him. His father convinces her to give up her love for his son for the sake of the family and she agrees. Later on, however, they'll be reunited and she will die happily in his arms."

"Are you serious?" Jeff asked.

"Absolutely," Tony confirmed, and with a touch of malice he added, "and they'll be singing in Italian."

Unfazed, Bill proclaimed, "OK, gentlemen, onward to a new experience," as he prompted his friends to enter the theatre.

It felt uncanny for Tony just being inside the Bolshoi again after so many years. While his companions went to buy themselves a drink before the performance, Tony found his seat. He sat down slowly and looked around. He felt overwhelmed by familiar and yet forgotten sensations: the sound of rustling women's dresses and the smell of their perfume; the quiet whispers punctuated by the occasional bout of coughing; and, the sound of the string instruments being tuned by the musicians in the orchestra pit. To his surprise, Tony suddenly realized how much he had missed this ambience and this pre-performance routine.

Before long, Jeff and Bill arrived and took their seats. Soon the lights started to dim and the theatre became quiet. The overture began and Tony's practised ear absorbed the musical strains with the acute awareness of a professional. Long ago, back at the Conservatory, he had been obliged to take a mandatory conductor's class. Tony conducted the *Le Traviata* overture as a part of his exam. Why was he remembering it so vividly now? He concentrated on the music and decided that the orchestra sounded very good. He examined the program and in the dim light read the name of the conductor: Anatoly Kuznetsov. The name sounded very familiar but Tony couldn't immediately recall where or when he had come across it. *Kuznetsov... he would be called Tolya Kuznetsov... he's very good. Where have I heard this name before?* Tony pondered in frustration.

The overture came to a conclusion, the curtain rose and the scene on the stage was that of the salon of the famous Parisian courtesan, Violetta Valery. Violetta was celebrating her recovery from a recent illness and throwing a big party. Tony looked intently at Violetta and his heart started to pound. *It can't be. It just can't be,* he thought incredulously, and then Violeta began to sing and he forgot about everything else. His reaction to this rapturous and enchanting voice was as strong as it had been twenty years earlier. For a moment, he ceased breathing and then realized that he was covered in perspiration.

Tony seized the program again and studied the cast listing - *Violetta*: Nina Kuznetsova. Now he remembered where he had heard the name of Tolya Kuznetsov. He immediately recalled that nondescript boy who had also brought flowers for Nina on that memorable day of the annual recital. He recalled their trip to Tolya's dacha, and Nina's assurance that Tolya was simply a long-time good friend. Now that *boy* was the conductor of the Bolshoi Theatre orchestra and Nina was singing the leading role of *Violetta*! Oh, such irony!

Tony examined the program closely once again and noticed the designation beside both names: *People's Artist of Russia.* This was the highest artistic designation, only awarded by the state to the most distinguished and highly recognized actors, musicians, singers and dancers in Russia.

By now Tony was feeling dizzy and disoriented. Nina was a major star. He fought the desire to get up and to go backstage to see her at the intermission. What would he do? Give her another bouquet of flowers? Tony glanced at his companions. They were both thoroughly mesmerized by the opera and in particular by Nina's performance. They couldn't take their eyes off her. She looked absolutely stunning, more beautiful in Tony's eyes than she had ever been before. *It's only stage make-up and lighting,* Tony sought to convince himself, but for the second time in his life he was falling under the spell of the tall, slender woman who was captivating the entire theatre audience.

When Nina ceased singing at the conclusion of the first act, the theatre erupted in thunderous applause and there were shouts of "*bravo*" coming from all directions on the main orchestra floor and cascading down from the tiers above.

"That was incredible!" Jeff exclaimed almost breathlessly, and Bill extolled, "I didn't know that women of such beauty and talent like that even existed in this day and age. She's no mere mortal; I think she must be some kind of goddess!"

"Let's go for a drink," Tony suggested when the intermission had been announced and his friends agreed. He needed a drink...*badly*.

There was a long line-up of thirsty patrons and the Canadian trio joined it. While they were waiting, Bill and Jeff continued to praise the first act of the performance and had an array of questions for Tony. "You told us that you'd heard this opera a number of times before. Is it always as powerful as it is today? Is the singing of that Nina woman a typical performance? Do all the leading singers sound as good as her, or is she something really special?"

Before Tony had an opportunity to respond, an elderly lady that was standing in the line ahead of them turned her head, and with a kind smile and in very decent English said, "There's nothing typical or ordinary about our Ninochka. She is quite unique. Her voice is recognized and praised throughout the world."

"We're from Calgary, Canada," Jeff said, almost apologetically, "and the Bolshoi Theatre's Opera Company hasn't visited us on a tour yet."

"In that case, consider yourself lucky to be here today," the lady replied. "Today is the premiere of the season. As far as I'm concerned, Nina is singing at the top of her form today." Nina's husband, Anatoly Kuznetsov, is such a wonderful conductor too.

"Do you know them personally?" Bill asked with considerable curiosity. "You speak about them as if they were your friends or at least your acquaintances."

The old woman laughed profusely and then replied, "The entire country knows of them, although I am a huge fan. I always try to see them after each performance and to get an autograph for my grandchildren."

"Hey, guys, I have an idea," Bill exclaimed, "let's go and try to get a couple of pictures taken with the Russian stars after the performance. My wife will die from jealousy when she sees me with such a woman. How can we find them?"

And while the lady was explaining to Bill and Jeff where to find the famous couple near the stage door, Tony was contemplating what excuse he could drum up to disappear right after the performance.

Nina's acting was as strong as her singing (if that was possible), and when Violetta died, Tony noticed that Jeff and Bill looked overwhelmed with emotion and there were even tears in Bill's eyes. Tony was absorbed with an unspeakable feeling himself, and so instead of leaving right after the performance, he was now resolved that he had to see Nina, up-close, one more time. Subconsciously, he wanted to rationalize that her beauty was really only skin-deep due to the ornate costume and her make-up. Realistically, there seemed to be no way that a woman of forty-two could look that spectacular.

Tony could still remember Nina as he had seen her for the last time in Canada. She had been sitting in a chair in that pathetic apartment, looking very small, frail and pitiful. At that time, her eyes were red and puffed up with tears, she was grotesquely skinny, and she had unattractive short-cropped, highlighted hair. No, Tony rationalized, Nina's striking appearance was all just a stage illusion.

So, after the conclusion of the performance, he

followed his companions to the stage-door exit to observe Nina up-close and to satisfy his curiosity.

Ω

There was already quite a crowd gathered around the stage-door exit and Bill and Jeff tried to ease their way through the crowd to get as close to the doorway as possible. Tony decided to remain discretely in the background. The last thing he wanted was for Nina to see him this evening.

Finally, Anatoly and Nina emerged through the door from backstage and the enthusiastic crowd of admirers eagerly milled around them. Nina was dressed in a simple but elegant, long dark gown with an open neck. Her long light hair was gathered in a bun, revealing her smooth, sculptured forehead and graceful neck. A single strand of large white pearls and matching earrings accentuated her natural beauty. She had removed all of her stage make-up and wore only a light, pink lipstick. Tony was compelled to admit to himself that she looked radiant and much younger than her age.

"Valentino, she's wearing a Valentino!" someone called out, nearby to where Tony was standing.

"Oh yes," another woman's voice in the crowd concurred. "I like this dress even more than last year's Chanel."

Tony was by now scrutinizing Anatoly, who was still wearing his tuxedo and confidently and benevolently smiling at his adoring fans. With a pang of jealousy, Tony had to acknowledge that the conductor looked quite handsome.

Suddenly, the crowd dutifully parted, allowing an older, nicely groomed and bountifully endowed lady to pass through. She was holding the hand of an adorable little blonde girl, about three years old. Trailing behind them were a tall boy and another slim, older girl. The boy was about eleven years old and had inherited his mother's light hair but his father's facial features. The eight-year-old girl looked the spitting image of her mother, and even at this tender age she looked decidedly beautiful.

Tony felt new sensations of shock from this latest revelation - *Nina has children. How is this possible?*

Meanwhile, the older woman approached Anatoly and in the critical voice of a mother, said, "You were quite adequate today, Anatoly."

"What do you mean adequate, grandma? Dad was phenomenal! And Mama was outstanding too!" the boy proclaimed in a proud voice.

"Mama, I want to sing the aria of *Violetta*! When can we start rehearsing it?" the older girl asked.

With a chuckle, Anatoly patted his older daughter affectionately on the head and then scooped up the little girl. Nina smiled and fondly kissed all three children. She whispered something into the ear of her older daughter, straightened the boy's tie, and smoothed the hair of her little girl. A chauffeur-driven, black 'stretch' limo pulled up near the stage door, whereupon Anatoly opened two of the vehicle doors and ushered his family inside.

"Mama," Anatoly said, "please put the kids to bed. We'll be home soon." Several older ladies, evidently friends of Anatoly's mother, joined them as passengers in the car too, and then it pulled away from the side-street adjoining the theatre. Anatoly and Nina waved good-bye to the children and then turned to mingle with the boisterous crowd of adoring fans.

The Celebration at the Dacha

Bill approached Nina, taking momentary advantage of a vacuum in the space around her.

"Hello," he said boldly, "my name is William Parker and I'm a Canadian businessman visiting Moscow. Mrs. Kuznetsov, I just heard you for the first time today, but from now on I'm your biggest fan. May I ask you to have your photo taken with myself and then with my colleagues? Without a doubt this would be the most memorable souvenir from Moscow for us."

"Yes of course," Nina agreed with an affable smile as she stood posing near Bill. Jeff quickly took the photo with his camera and then asked Anatoly to move closer so he could take a photo of the three of them together. A moment later, Jeff was changing places with Bill for another photo-op.

An imposing gentleman in a tuxedo and wearing a white bow-tie approached Anatoly and asked in British-accented English, "Should we wait for you, Mr. Kuznetsov, or should we go ahead and meet you at the dacha?"

"Go on ahead, Mr. O'Connor. We'll be there soon. I'm sure that a hundred people or so are already well on the way and will be arriving before long," Anatoly instructed informally in fluent English.

A not-so-subtle Bill exclaimed, "A party of Russian celebrities! In a Russian dacha! What an incredible event that must be!"

Anatoly caught the essence of the hint and graciously responded, "We always host a party after the season premiere and there are always a lot of fans and friends attending. If you wish, please join us. Quite a few cars are heading that way so somebody would certainly be able to offer you a ride."

"Splendid!" Bill effused.

Jeff chimed in, "We would gladly come. Thank you for the kind invitation. But there are three of us." He looked around. "Where's Tony? Oh, there he is!" Jeff located his brother-in-law standing apart behind the rest of the assembled crowd and motioned for him to approach.

Reluctantly, Tony stepped forward and Jeff made the introduction, "My colleague and brother-in-law, Tony Walker."

"Hello, Anton," Anatoly said coldly.

"Hello, Anton," Nina repeated in a non-descript tone of voice.

"Nina... Anatoly," Anton tensely nodded his head as he returned their cryptic salutations.

"Hey, Tony, do you actually know them? Why didn't you tell us anything?"

"There wasn't the opportunity," Tony replied bleakly and evasively.

"So, are we invited then?" Bill asked, looking from Tony back to the Kuznetsovs with heightened curiosity.

"Yes, of course," Anatoly said in a slightly amused voice, while Nina shrugged her shoulders indifferently.

"Gentlemen," Tony protested, "you go ahead. I should be getting back to hotel to get ready for my flight tomorrow."

"Oh, come on, Tony, don't be a spoil sport! You can sleep on the plane," Jeff implored him.

Anatoly motioned to one of his friends, said something confidentially to him, and then, before Tony quite realized what was happening, he was sitting in a car that was speeding toward Anatoly's dacha.

This is folly, Tony thought, *it's madness. Why am I doing this?* And then he realized that indeed he very much wanted to go. He very much wanted to find an opportunity to talk with Nina. He needed to know if she married Anatoly out of desperation or if she had truly grown to love him. And most importantly, did she still care in any way about him?

At this late evening hour, the traffic had receded and the auto was moving along quite fast. Bill was seated in the front beside the driver and was trying in an animated fashion to communicate with him, while the driver in turn was trying with limited success to respond in his very broken English.

Jeff was sharing the back seat with Tony and he turned toward him and in a straightforward manner asked, "Were you interested in Nina when you were living in Moscow all those years ago? I'm not blind, Tony. From the first moment you first saw her on the stage, your demeanour changed completely. It's written all over your face, buddy."

Tony nodded his head, ever so slightly.

"Well, I thought so. No surprise there!

"If I had met a woman like that when I was young, I would have been after her too, big-time! But don't worry, Tony. I won't say anything to my wife that might get back to Carol."

Bill, who evidently overheard the conversation from the front seat, turned his head and added, "What can you expect, Tony? She's a singer. She's a star, a celebrity. And who are you? You are an ordinary computer programmer, like thousands of others. Even if you were a marketing guy now, there are still thousands of us to go around as well. Kuznetsov, however, is a musician, a conductor, and there are only a few of his profession and obviously he is an accomplished one at that! It's no reflection on you that she chose him. Take it easy, buddy. You already have a very good woman."

"You're right, Bill," Tony concurred, "I have a very good wife and I love her very much." But deep inside he was still torn with anguish. *She didn't choose him. She chose me, and now she's back with him on the rebound.*

In no time at all they were out of Moscow and before

long they turned onto the winding rural road that led to
the dacha. When the Kuznetsovs' dacha came into view,
there was yet-another surprise waiting for Tony. In
place of the small cottage that he remembered, there
was now a big, modern mansion, brightly lit.

"Wow," Jeff whistled. "These Russian stars are
living in style, just like in Hollywood."

"Nina should live like a movie star because she *is* a
movie star, along with being a star of the opera stage,"
their driver said with strong conviction.

An astounded Tony was having a hard time to
absorb this additional gem of information and so he
asked, "Did you say movie star? What do you mean by
that?"

"Didn't you know?" the driver asked, genuinely
surprised. "Nina has already performed in three
movies. Their friend, a movie producer, asked her to
play a small role in one movie that required a good
singer. Nina was so impressive that she landed two
principal roles in other movies. She's a great actress."

Upon hearing this latest revelation, Tony fell into a
brooding silence.

There were dozens of cars parked in the huge
parking lot and the party was already in full swing. The
three Canadians thanked their driver and offered him a
small gratuity. "No money," he said firmly. "You are the
guests of Anatoly and he's a good friend of mine." Then
he led them closer to the center of the activities.

Someone thrust a glass of wine into Tony's hand and
someone else handed him a plate with a grilled shish-
kebab and some veggies.

Tony soon became separated from his two
companions and started to stroll slowly around the
expansive grounds on his own. He observed a cheery
campfire glowing in the center courtyard (just as there
had been so many years ago). In addition, the outside
patio area was ablaze with numerous, glowing electric

lights of various colours mounted on high light standards. It was definitely a grand party atmosphere.

Tony didn't want to be spotted by any of his old friends and acquaintances so he drifted away from the bright circle to the darker periphery of the grounds. He hadn't yet caught sight of Nina or Anatoly anywhere. He paused to stand behind a large tree, yet even there he wasn't alone. Several older ladies were sitting nearby with Anatoly's mother in the middle of their circle. Nevertheless, Tony's position seemed safe enough because they hadn't noticed him and were just carrying on with their conversation.

"You are so lucky, Lena," one of the ladies said to Anatoly's mother. "You have such a wonderful son. With him, you don't have to rely on your pension and you can live very comfortably."

"You're right, Tanya. I have nothing to complain about. My pension alone wouldn't even cover two weeks' worth of food. I don't know how you manage, Tanya."

"Thank God I have a kind niece in the United States. She faithfully sends me three hundred dollars every month. Without that extra allowance from my relative, I would starve."

"You wouldn't starve, Tanya, you would just learn to live very modestly like I do," another lady commented.

"Do you call it a life, Masha? I really can't understand why your children can't help you more than they do. You shouldn't be working as a nursemaid at your age. After all, you used to be such a good doctor."

"They have their own needs and their own problems. Besides, you know my son-in-law. I'd rather starve than ask him for anything."

Old biddies, Tony thought. *They always find something to complain about,* and with that thought he slipped away to continue his solitary walk.

Tony noticed several men standing in a separate group who were laughing amongst themselves. He recognized all of them as he came closer. They were his old schoolmates from the Conservatory and they were busily discussing rehearsals, upcoming recitals and recent tours. They didn't notice Tony lurking in the shadows behind them, listening in on their conversation.

Tony's heart started to ache. He wanted so much to be part of that group. All of a sudden he realized how much he had suppressed his longing for music and for the life of a musician. The life he had denied to himself so long ago now returned to haunt him.

He reluctantly drifted away and moved cautiously towards yet-another group. This group was engaged in a discussion about modern Russian politics in the context of Russian history. Someone began talking about the renewed interest in religion in Russia. Religion and politics - two topics banned by Carol because she said they never mixed well in strange company. *Why should they be banned?* Tony pondered with growing agitation. *Nothing is as important and nothing defines a person's perspective on life as much as his or her views and attitudes towards these two topics. These people are vigorously exchanging and debating their views but they're not becoming enemies because of it. More than likely they're actually reinforcing their friendship,* Tony reflected.

Tony then resumed his prowl around the grounds of the dacha, while continuing to observe and take in all the activities of the party goers from a distance. Here was somebody playing a guitar with a group of people sitting around the musician and singing along; over there was someone reciting poetry to another group of attentive listeners.

Again Tony felt from within a welling mixture of anger and resentment. Why had he allowed Carol to put down the immigrant Russians and their society? Why had he let her judge Russian culture based solely on one visit to a boisterous nightclub in Toronto? As one who had absorbed the Russian music and culture from childhood; and as one who had been taken to see his first ballet and opera performances at the age of five - how could he have permitted anyone, even his spouse, to speak about his fellow Russians and the rich Russian culture so derisively?

Suddenly there was a loud commotion near the campfire and Tony could see that Nina and Anatoly had finally joined their guests. Someone was enthusiastically imploring both of them to join in the party activity. Eventually, Anatoly took a guitar in his hands and sat down near the fire. Nina positioned herself comfortably very close to him.

Tony cast his eyes intently on Nina. She was dressed in tight jeans and a button-down shirt. She had let her long hair down and from where he was standing she looked very much like a young girl - beautiful and highly desirable.

Anatoly started to play a Russian folk song and Nina sang about a young girl and her unrequited love. The connotations of this simple old tune were more than Tony could bear. He turned and walked away towards the lake where he sat down on a huge, moss-covered rock. He was trying to recall if this was the rock where he, as the young Anton, had taken Nina's hand in his for the very first time. It didn't matter anymore. Right now he was seeking nothing more than silence and personal privacy - he just wanted to be left alone with his thoughts.

But Nina's powerful voice reached out from the distance, even to the shores of the lake. In frustration, Tony made his way back to the party and looked for Bill and Jeff. He found them drinking wine and flirting with two Russian women. Tony was about to join them but at that moment someone called out to him, "Anton? Anton Gorchichniy?"

Tony was startled and turned about quickly, finding himself face-to-face with an elderly, grey-haired man. With heightened curiosity, Tony stared intently at the man's wrinkled face with its intense, intelligent dark eyes, also observing the gentleman's straight back and proud stance. All at once Tony recognized the gentleman.

"Professor!" Tony exclaimed, as he hastily took several steps back. He didn't want to take the chance that Bill and Jeff might overhear his conversation with his old teacher. The professor followed Tony for a short distance away from the crowd.

"What are you doing here?" the startled teacher asked his former favourite pupil.

"I'm not really sure myself," Tony mumbled. "I'm in Moscow on a business trip," he added vaguely.

"Are you performing, Anton? Are you still playing?" the professor asked in a inquisitive voice.

"No, I am not, Professor. I'm working for the marketing department of a large Canadian corporation," Tony started to explain, but there was so much pity and disappointment in his old teacher's eyes that Tony promptly fell silent.

"Well then, good luck with your business. I must be going," the Professor said and walked away.

"Guys," Tony said, finally re-joining his colleagues, "I'm on my way. As it is, I'll only have enough time to pack my bags and get ready to go to the airport."

"You're right, Tony. We should all be going. I wonder how we can find a ride?" Jeff mused.

"I think Zoya and her husband were about to leave. Let me talk to them," one of the young ladies said as she smiled to Jeff and then strolled off.

"Lyuba, my dear, so we have an agreement, right? I'll call on you tomorrow morning and you'll show me around Moscow." Bill emphatically kissed the hand of the other woman who had remained near him.

"Not too early, William," Bill's new lady-friend replied coyly.

"And please don't forget to bring your friend along too," Jeff added with a telling smile directed at Lyuba.

Finally, Tony led Jeff and Bill towards the parking lot. They stopped along the way to say their good-byes to their hosts.

"Thank you so much for inviting us. We had a spectacular time. Please call us if you're ever in Calgary," Bill said, and then he warmly shook Anatoly's hand and kissed Nina's hand elegantly.

The same routine was repeated by Jeff. Both men handed out their business cards and made some vague provisions for meeting again. Anatoly and Nina were very courteous and indulgently friendly.

"Vladimir and Zoya will drive you to your hotel. Zoya has very good English, so I hope you will not be bored," Nina said. Tony was taken aback by how easily and clearly Nina was speaking in English.

Now it was his turn to say his farewells. Anatoly was hugging Nina's shoulders and Nina was leaning on her husband with such a gesture of intimacy and tenderness that there was no longer any doubt in Tony's mind about where her true feelings lay.

"Good-bye, Nina; good-bye, Anatoly."

"Farewell, Anton," Anatoly replied with barely masked animosity.

"Farewell," Nina repeated in an indifferent tone of voice, as she might casually address any stranger.

It might well have been easier for Tony to bear if Nina had displayed disdain towards him, but that absolute indifference in her manner was so much worse. Tony felt as though he had been slapped in the face by some indignant female stranger.

The Drive Back to Moscow

They piled into the car belonging to Vladimir, an old friend of Anatoly Kuznetsov. Vladimir's wife Zoya sat down next to him, so the three Canadians were sitting together in the back seat. Tony was relieved that he was sitting next to a window.

As the return ride to Moscow began, Jeff, still relishing pleasant memories and emotions, said, "I'm so glad that we were invited. It was an unforgettable evening! And the Kuznetsovs are looking so incredibly happy together. It's very rare these days to see a couple who are so obviously in love with one-another."

"Oh, that Nina! What an incredible woman," Bill enthused. "Sometimes I think that it's simply unfair that God gives so much to one person: talent, voice, beauty, good children, wealth and love. She has it all. We have a saying in my family about such people, that they've been born with a silver spoon in their mouths."

Zoya turned her head from the front seat and started to laugh. "Do you think that Nina was born with a silver spoon? Let me tell you something about her background. Nina's father left them when she was a small girl. She was raised by a single mother and lived more than modestly – barely above the poverty line, actually,

"She knew Tolya from school but she was never in love with him in those days. He loved her but the feeling wasn't mutual. When Nina was still very young she married some loser. I never met him because I only met Nina after I married Volodya, but other people have told me that he was a very handsome man and a talented musician. Like Nina, he graduated from the Moscow Conservatory and everybody was predicting a bright future for him. But in reality he was nothing but just another loser because he was too vain, greedy and impatient to honestly commit to work for his success.

"He wanted everything out of life immediately: you know - career, success, money, and whatever else that money could buy. As soon as he realized that he would have to work hard for some years before he'd get ahead in the music field, he convinced Nina to emigrate and whisked her away to Canada."

"Are you saying that Nina lived for a time in Canada?" Jeff asked incredulously. "Why didn't I ever hear about her?"

"Why would you?" Zoya responded rhetorically. "She didn't sing in Canada. Her husband asked *her* to support *him* until he got established. He insisted that Nina work as a simple hairstylist! Can you imagine? Our Nina working as a hairstylist!"

"Yes, that's hard to believe," Jeff said thoughtfully, while looking at Tony as though he wanted to ask him some penetrating question.

Tony fidgeted under Jeff's inquisitive stare. Jeff knew that Tony had been married to a hairdresser before he met Carol, and of course by now he was aware of Tony's extensive knowledge of music. Jeff was not a stupid fellow and surely could connect the dots.

Meanwhile, Zoya carried on relentlessly with her story. "Anyway, that loser of a husband soon found out that the life of a musician in Canada was no easier than in Russia, so he enrolled in some course and became a programmer or something like that. Then, as soon as he got a job, he dumped Nina and married his boss. Boom! Instant gratification: a house, cars, money, and a new wife with a good income. Everything that he had yearned for but could never earn honestly on his own!

"Nina never talks about him but we gradually found out all about her two years in Toronto in bits and pieces from Tolya's mother. One thing is for certain: she returned to Moscow on her own, absolutely devastated.

At that time Nina was physically not well and totally depressed mentally."

Tony glanced briefly at Jeff and Bill and could see that they were staring at him with obvious disdain, in much the same way they would look aghast at something very unpleasant that they accidentally stepped on in the street.

Tony defiantly glared back at them in silence and then turned his head away to stare out the window. From that moment he knew that he would never be part of Jeff and Bill's team again. *So what*, he thought, *I have a good job*. But even the thought of going back to his old job made him feel nauseated. *I'm good at marketing; I know that now. Carol will help me to get a good new job in a different company.* But then Tony considered how the events of the evening would inevitably be presented to proud and self-righteous Carol by Jeff and Bill and their spouses. His future with Carol suddenly didn't seem terribly secure. He could just imagine her reaction when she was informed that he had married her as means of realizing 'instant gratification'.

He could still hear Zoya's voice, drifting into his consciousness as if cutting through a thick fog. "Nina's mother was very ill and that is why she returned to Moscow, just before her mother passed away.

"Tolya took Nina to his parents' home and his mother nursed her back to health. Tolya practiced with Nina every day for months until she regained her voice, her good form and her confidence. Only then, Nina auditioned with the hope of returning to the Bolshoi Theatre. Before her emigration to Canada, she had been a soloist there. After she returned, she had to start her career again from the beginning. But Tolya was always close by and he believed in her and always encouraged her. You could say she found her strength and her voice again thanks to him.

"You know, I remember that some fourteen years

ago, we came to Tolya's dacha for the first time. It wasn't looking anything like it is now; it was just a small cottage in those days.

"Volodya and I went for a walk and we stumbled upon them sitting on a rock overlooking the lake. They didn't see us, and quite accidently we overheard how Nina asked Anatoly why he hadn't proposed to her. He replied that he had already proposed when they were teenagers and that this proposal still stood. He told Nina that he wanted her to be sure about her feelings and that whenever she was ready, she should propose to him. Imagine that!

"A year later we were invited to their wedding, so evidently Nina proposed," Zoya concluded with an easy laugh.

She fell silent for a moment and then commented, "Nina's story is the story of two men: one selfish and the second, selfless. One man almost destroyed her, while the other made her into the star she was always destined to be. Anatoly is a very accomplished man in his own right too, but he always puts Nina ahead of himself. You should hear how he says *"My Ninochka"*. With such pride and such love! He treats her like a duchess and she behaves like a true duchess. Do you know what I mean?"

Zoya apparently wanted to make certain that the Canadian men fully appreciated the meaning of her words and so she continued. "He only buys her designer clothes. Even when they were poor, he didn't allow Nina to buy anything but the best for herself. I suppose she became a star in three stages: first, she was treated like a star; then she started to dress like a star; and finally, she emerged as a star. It's as if Tolya had placed her on a pedestal and gradually she grew to fit comfortably and securely on top of it."

By now Tony wasn't listening to Zoya's ramblings any longer. He was trying to forget all about this unfortunate evening and concentrate on something positive instead. Megan! He had Megan and nobody would ever take her away; she was her daddy's girl. She was always much closer to him than she was to Carol. But in just a few years, Megan would enter university and it might not necessarily be in Calgary. That alone was a distressing prospect in Tony's mind.

Then Tony re-oriented his thoughts to his parents. They had always loved him unconditionally. But now he was recalling the banter of those old women that he overheard at the dacha. What were they talking about? That they couldn't survive on their pensions? That they needed at least an additional three hundred dollars each month, just to have some semblance of a normal existence? And yet he was sending only three hundred dollars a year to his parents, if that!

At that moment, it became clear to Tony that his proud parents never used a cent of his money for themselves; rather, they spent it all to send back in the form of presents for himself, for his wife, and for his daughter. How were they managing to survive? His sister and her husband were not wealthy people either, so they could not be expected to be of much help to the parents.

His thought process caused Tony to feel deeply ashamed of himself. He had invited his parents to come to visit Canada but had asked them to spend a thousand dollars towards the airfare from their own meagre means. For them a thousand dollars must have seemed more like a million dollars from Tony's perspective. Didn't he realize that? There was no reason to blame Carol either. She had no basis for appreciation of the real situation in Russia, but he certainly did.

Why hadn't he insisted on providing more substantial help to his parents? They had never asked him for anything. They had given up the best years of their lives for their dream - to see their son become a celebrated concert pianist. What did he have to show for all those wasted years? A photo of a house or a car? Or a photo of a woman and a girl that they had never met and probably never would? Nothing of substance or of any real meaning.

They must know about Nina, Tony suddenly thought. They go to the theatre and to the movies and they read the newspapers. But they've never mentioned anything about Nina in their letters.

By this time Tony wasn't looking forward to his trip to St. Petersburg in the slightest. How would he be able to look straight into the eyes of his parents and his sister?

Tony's thought process then gravitated back to Carol. Surely she would understand. She loved him and she would never leave him; he was almost certain of it. Besides, Carol already knew something about Nina anyway. Well, she didn't know that Nina was a singer, but that wasn't terribly relevant; and that small white lie about the university as distinct from the conservatory wasn't important any longer either.

Tony tried to imagine Carol as he had seen her for the last time before his departure for the business trip, impeccably dressed in her formal business suit and looking very professional, as always. But then, the image of his wife gradually became hazy and the contours of the suit gradually metamorphized and it became a long, dark, softly flowing gown. The woman that he envisioned in his mind became taller and slimmer, and the dark short hair became lighter and longer, trailing almost to the waist. Finally, Tony had to admit to himself that it was Nina that he was subconsciously thinking about. It was his Nina he was dreaming about now.

He could no longer gather his thoughts rationally or focus on anything. By the time the bright lights of Moscow became visible, there was nothing but emptiness in Tony's soul. This darkness and feeling of distress were so overwhelming that he felt as though he was drowning and couldn't breathe.

He realized that Zoya had stopped talking some while ago, but he couldn't stand the silence in the car any longer and so he asked in a gruff voice, "Could you please turn on the radio?" Anything would be preferable to this overwhelming silence and this feeling of a black void in his soul.

Zoya obligingly switched on the radio and scanned several stations until she found one playing an English song. She looked at her husband and said, "It's their new hit. This is the one that I told you about earlier."

The song was sad but hauntingly beautiful. The female vocalist was singing in a low, throaty voice that was laced with deep emotion. The piano accompaniment could be heard in the background and somehow the music and the voice blended together in perfect harmony. The words and raw emotion of the song caused something to stir inside, and for the first time in years Tony wanted to allow himself to cry openly.

"Who's the woman that's singing and what's the name of the band?" Bill asked. "It sounds so beautiful."

"Oh, come now, don't tell me that you don't know!" Zoya exclaimed. "They're so popular! OK, I'll give you three hints: first, it's a Canadian band founded by immigrants from Russia. Second, the husband is playing the piano and the wife is the one who's singing. Third, they won a Grammy award this year for the best R&B hit. Do you know who they are now?"

"I'm not a big fan of R&B," Jeff said apologetically. "But I really like that song. I'd like to buy their CD. What's the name of that band?"

Before Zoya had an opportunity to reply, the song was over and the male host of the radio program announced, "You have been listening to the music of *The Wandering Stars.*"

BOOK III

The Reunion

Parents always ultimately forgive their children, even if they're very angry with them. Tony's parents were no exception. Actually, he stopped being *Tony* as soon as he landed in St. Petersburg. Nobody there knew about that version of his name, and for some reason it was very comforting for Anton to hear the sound of his real name again. Perhaps the fact that he was returning to his childhood home as a humble prodigal son, and not as an arrogant victor, really helped him face his parents and his sister.

His parents had aged considerably. His mother had added several inches to her waistline and his father had lost more than a few of his hairs and those remaining on his head were gray. Anton regarded the lined faces of his parents and felt unexpected tenderness and pity towards them. His sister, Valentina, didn't look much better. She looked thoroughly worn-out and old for her age in her severe, dark brown dress. Was it the same dress that Anton had helped her buy ages ago? Valentina's husband greeted Anton with indifference and went to watch TV. On the other hand, Valentina's children were fascinated to meet their Canadian uncle.

In the evening, Anton, his parents and Valentina had a serious talk. His father didn't beat around the bush and bluntly asked, "How did you manage to lose Nina?"

Before Anton had an opportunity to respond, his mother rushed in with another question, "Why did you stop playing piano?"

Anton was definitely expecting these questions. He had been rehearsing his answers to them during the entire flight to St. Petersburg. But now, confronted by the concerned faces of his parents and sister, he had a hard time finding the right words.

Finally, he said, "It was a mistake to emigrate. I realize that now. Actually, I realized it years ago, but when we just came to Canada I wanted to do my best to succeed and I didn't want to return as a failure and have to admit my grievous mistake. I blew away my chances to become a concert pianist during that ill-fated competition. I hoped to redeem myself and to prove to everyone that I could be a serious pianist in Canada. Unfortunately, Nina fell apart right after our arrival. She never wanted to leave Moscow and the Bolshoi Theatre in the first place, and she couldn't ever forgive me for insisting on our emigration."

Anton stopped speaking at that point and looked for something to drink. His father poured him a shot of vodka and a grateful Anton tossed it down. His mother gave her husband a withering glare and placed a glass of water in front of her son. Anton smiled and continued on with his story.

"I think that subconsciously Nina wanted to punish me, or maybe she was just too depressed to act rationally... I'm not sure. But during her audition for the Canadian Opera Company, she sang so badly that they rejected her. Can you imagine the winner of an international competition flunking a simple audition? After that audition fiasco, Nina became really depressed. I was playing in small theatres, in churches, and for some charity concerts, but I couldn't provide for the two of us just by myself, so Nina started to sing in Russian nightclubs. I don't want to say anything bad about her and it's all ancient history now, but she started to drink and flirt with other men so I had to put my foot down and take her out of that environment."

Anton could see that his family was looking at him with total disbelief and shock. He ruefully smiled and carried on with his version of the story. "I felt guilty, incredibly guilty. I had two choices: to return to Russia or to get another profession. I was too proud to return, so I decided to study for a year and get a profession that would give me a stable income. The plan was that as soon as I started working, Nina would be able to travel to the United States and attend auditions there. I was prepared to move to any place where she would be hired. I hoped that when Nina got settled down, I would be able to start playing again. That was what we had agreed on: her singing career would be our priority, and then I could refocus on my piano career.

"Maybe everything could have worked out in time but there was somebody who was constantly meddling in our affairs, manipulating Nina and setting her against me."

"Who was that?" his father and mother asked in unison.

"Larissa, Borya's wife. That woman has a sweet voice but a cold heart. She's a conniving snake."

"I never liked her," Valentina said, interjecting herself into the conversation in support of her brother.

"By the time I started to work as a programmer our marriage was already in tatters," Anton said. "Nina and I had squabbles and sometimes serious fights almost every day. It became so bad that eventually I had to move out. I rented a small room in the basement of a house, although I was sure that it would only be for a week or two. I kept hoping that Nina would calm down and I would be able to talk to her rationally.

"Maybe that's exactly what might have happened if not for the illness of Nina's mother and her hasty return to Moscow. I didn't even know about it. Several days after I moved out, I called Nina and she wasn't at home. Then I received my divorce papers. Nina never returned to Canada and I lost track of her completely. Boris and Larissa wouldn't even tell me where she was. The only person who was even somewhat close to me in that difficult time was Carol, my manager at work. She was understanding, supportive and helpful. She encouraged me to go ahead with my life and not to dwell on the past.

"Mama, Papa and Valentina, I know that I have disappointed all of you. I know that you're angry with me for leaving Russia in the first place, for losing Nina, and for quitting the piano. You're right of course, a hundred percent right. I made a big mistake, but life goes on. I'm married to a nice woman now and I have a beautiful daughter. Can you please forgive me?"

Valentina and Anton's mother by now were openly crying, feeling genuinely sorry for him and moved by his story. They had never realized how difficult Anton's life in Canada had been. His mother rose from her chair, came to her son and kissed him and hugged him, just as she had when he was a small boy.

The remainder of the evening was spent discussing and comparing life in St. Petersburg and Calgary.

The following day Anton called the airline and changed his tickets for a later departure on Wednesday. He called the hotel where Jeff and Bill were staying and told them about his change of plans. He had a distinct feeling that they were quite relieved not to have to fly together with him. He called Carol too and explained that he would stay in St. Petersburg until the Wednesday, asking her to notify his manager that he would be back in the office only on Thursday. Predictably, Carol was unhappy to say the least about this delay, and she made her displeasure quite obvious.

"Tony," she told him, "this is absolutely unacceptable. Your entire career is on the line. I understand that you helped to secure a good contract for your company, but you can't afford to lose this momentum. You must be in the office on Tuesday when Jeff and Bill are back."

For some reason, her words did not have the intended effect on Anton. Calgary, his career, and even Carol herself all seemed less important and quite remote from St. Petersburg.

"Carol," Anton said in a firm and even tone of voice, "I haven't seen my parents or my sister for over seventeen years. I want to be with them for at least three days. I'll see you on Thursday. Give my love to Megan." He hung up the phone and felt immeasurably proud of himself for standing up to his wife for a change, instead of capitulating to her wishes as he usually did.

Anton took his mother and Valentina for a shopping trip. He bought warm leather winter boots, nice dress shoes, new coats, sweaters and dresses for both of them. Then, together, they selected a new leather jacket for Anton's father and clothes for Valentina's children and her husband. Anton filled his credit card to the maximum but didn't feel guilty about it in the slightest.

The three days passed by very quickly. Each morning Anton walked Valentina to work and they discussed the life of musicians in Russia and Canada. She told him how difficult it was to work as a teacher of music in the new Russia. Whereas in the former Soviet Union the parents of young children considered it prestigious and almost mandatory to give their children a music education, these days, parents preferred to spend their money to teach their offspring about computers, the Internet, and foreign languages.

Anton spent as much time as he could with his parents and the main topic of their conversations was Megan. Anton couldn't stop praising his daughter and perhaps now, for the first time and even from a distance, that teenage Canadian girl felt like a real granddaughter to Anton's parents.

In the afternoons Anton walked the streets of the city where he was born and where he had lived for the first eighteen years of his life. He couldn't stop marvelling at all the changes. The city was busier than ever, and most of the cars had expensive foreign brand names and dwarfed the few remaining Russian Lada and Volga models on the streets. Anton liked this city, its rhythm, its vibrancy, and the harmonious blend of historical grandeur and modernity. From the vantage point of St. Petersburg, his life as a programmer in far-away Calgary seemed detached and almost surreal.

When the time came to leave, it was with strong regrets and some dark premonitions that Anton said goodbye to his family and departed St. Petersburg. He took the short flight to Moscow, followed by the much longer fight to Toronto, and finally, an overnight flight home to Calgary.

The Homecoming

Anton's flight landed in Calgary early on Thursday morning. He quickly retrieved his luggage and made his way out of the airport. He looked around for Carol's car but didn't see it. He wasn't particularly surprised or worried; after all, it was a weekday. He hailed a taxi, told the driver his address and instructed him to drive there as fast as possible. For some inexplicable reason, Anton couldn't wait to be at home. *Quick shower*, he thought, *and then small breakfast and off to the office*. After all, it was he, Anton, who had clinched that contract, and perhaps he had overreacted during the drive from Nina's dacha. On an optimistic note, maybe he was already a designated member of the Marketing team.

Half-an-hour later, Anton paid the taxi driver and quickly ascended the porch steps of his house. There was a large note taped to the front door.

Anton grasped the note and read: "I'm not planning to be the laughing stock of Calgary. You lied to me about your past and I can't live with a liar. We are through. Your clothes are in the shed. You know how to open it. Nothing else in this house belongs to you. I'm going ahead with a divorce. Call my lawyer with your forwarding address and he will send you the separation agreement. Carol.

"P.S. I checked the outstanding balance on our credit card and verified the transactions that had been posted within the last three days. How could you do it, Tony? You spent money that was designated for Megan's braces. You stole from your daughter. That was the last straw! C."

A hot flash of anger took hold of Anton. With trembling hands he attempted to open the door but the lock had been changed. He went around to the backyard, opened the shed using the numeric combination he set up just recently on the digital lock, and retrieved two large suitcases that had been packed by Carol.

Fortunately for Anton, he had taken the keys to his car with him to Russia. He took the suitcases to the car and set them into the trunk. He checked the glove compartment and saw that the registration papers had not been removed from the car, so that was no problem. Anton then returned to the backyard and noticed that one of the windows in an upstairs bedroom was not completely closed. Like a common thief, he managed to climb up and get through the window to enter the house. He hurried downstairs and carefully disabled their home security system (he was well-familiar with the system; after all, he himself selected and helped install it).

Anton went to his bedroom and then to the office, collecting the things that he considered to be rightfully his. Oh no, Carol, he thought, you aren't going to get rid of me this easily. After fifteen years of marriage I'm not going to just disappear into the sunset with two suitcases.

Then he made his way into the kitchen, made himself a pot of coffee and tried to consider his next steps. The coffee calmed him down a bit.

Back in their home office, Anton switched on Carol's computer and to his amazement, he easily accessed her files. *Carol must consider me to be a total idiot not to change the code of the house security system or her computer password*, he thought contemptuously. *Well, it's my own fault – I was always congenial, laid-back, and easy-going with her. Those days are over now.*

He opened the computer files where the well-organized Carol was meticulously maintaining records of family assets and liabilities. The extensive files contained all of their bank account numbers and the recent balances, the policy numbers and coverage details of their insurance policies, a list of stocks and other investment holdings, the name and phone number of their broker, and the appraised value of their house and ski chalet near Lake Louise that Carol had inherited from her parents. Anton printed the contents of all of these files and then, just to be on the safe side, copied them onto a disk and dropped the disk into his pocket.

He took his own, almost brand-new computer, his golf clubs, the tool-set, and his jewellery to the car...all items that Carol so conveniently had forgotten to pack. When everything he wanted was loaded, Anton left by the front door and one more time took a look at the house where he had lived for over fourteen years. Then he drove off.

His first stop was Megan's school. Anton waited until recess and went to look for his daughter. When Megan saw her father, she didn't run to hug him as she usually would, but instead looked at him with a sulky expression while keeping her distance and said accusingly, "Dad, you lied to mom. You lied to all of us. You're not a programmer at all!"

"I finished community college and worked successfully in that job for fifteen years. I believe that qualifies me as a programmer," Anton responded as calmly as he could.

"But you didn't finish the Moscow University; you finished the Moscow Conservatory! You're a musician!"

"Guilty as charged, pumpkin," Anton acceded with a forced smile. "Is it a crime to be a musician? Immigration, Megan, is not an easy thing and you do whatever you have to do just to survive."

"I don't care what you say! I hate you! And mom hates you too!" Megan cried out before running back into the school.

Carol will pay for this big-time, Anton thought. He was seething with anger. It was not even anger any longer, more like a terrible rage. *How could that bitch dare to set my sweet girl against me?*

Anton got back into the car and sat unmoving for several minutes, trying to regain his composure, and then he drove to the office. His telephone was blinking and when he dialled up his phone-mail, the familiar voice of the HR manager was asking him to call the Human Resources office as soon as he arrived.

Anton didn't even bother to turn on his office computer. Instead, he headed immediately to see the HR manager, by now expecting to hear what he was quite sure would be another round of bad news.

Instead, the manager was all smiles when Anton walked in. "Congratulations! I heard about your brilliant performance in Moscow. Well done, Tony, well done indeed. I was asked to initiate your transfer to the Marketing Department. Isn't that great news?"

"That *is* great news," Anton replied, waiting for the catch that he was certain would follow. He was not mistaken.

"Very well, Tony, but I reviewed your file and to my surprise I didn't see a copy of your university diploma. The head of the Marketing Department wants to see it. A simple formality; I hope you understand. Would you be able to bring it in tomorrow?"

This is Jeff and Bill's work. Nobody cared to see my diploma before. It's their doing to undermine me, Anton thought.

"Of course I could," Anton replied pleasantly before pausing momentarily. "However, I came here today to give you my letter of resignation. I received an offer that I simply couldn't refuse. Would you please help me with my letter?"

"Well, yes I can, Tony, if that's what you really want." The manager almost stuttered in response to this unexpected twist in the conversation. "Are you sure about this? Annual bonuses won't be given out until next January and you would have to be an active employee to qualify. You'd forfeit a substantial sum of money if you quit now."

"I realize that," Anton responded. "Nevertheless, I've made my decision and I've decided to terminate my employment here immediately."

Less than half an hour later, suddenly unemployed, homeless and practically single, Anton was driving away. One more box had been added to his collection of earthly possessions: the personal things that he kept in the office. Megan's photographs took up most of the space in that box. He had picked up a large photograph of Carol and had been ready to rip it to shreds, but then he changed his mind and stashed it on the bottom of the box.

Anton's next step was to visit his bank. He withdrew the entire balance of four thousand dollars from their savings account and with that sum of money stuffed in his pocket he felt somewhat better.

Jeff and Bill will pay for this, Anton was thinking. He didn't know how or when, but he pledged to himself that he would make his former colleagues suffer dearly for their betrayal.

But to begin with, he would deal with Carol. From now on, his wife, his brother-in-law, Jeff, and Bill Parker all qualified as his mortal enemies.

Anton decided that he needed a good lawyer. He remembered how one of the men he was working with had complained the prior year that his wife had hired the most ruthless lawyer in Calgary to handle their divorce. "*He's a barracuda*," the chap had said.

The name of this lawyer had remained ingrained in Anton's mind by some co-incidence: Richard Wisotsky. Anton parked his car near the phone-booth, located the lawyer's listing in the phone directory and jotted down the number. He placed a call and speedily arranged an appointment with the secretary.

Anton then realized that he had not yet eaten today

and decided that he had time for a quick lunch. He drove to the closest MacDonald's and ordered a Big Mac and fries. *Carol would frown at this,* Anton thought unashamedly and asked to double-up his order. Only when he was sitting with his lunch and hungrily wolfing it down, Anton thought about the circumstances and events of that morning. Something didn't add up. Sure, he knew that Carol would be angry with him, but to throw him out and to divorce him over events that took place fifteen years ago or over the issue of his education – none of this made any sense. He was missing something, something very important.

Had Carol been thinking about divorcing him before now and had just been waiting for an excuse, for the right moment? But why? He thought that they had a perfect marriage. Perhaps she was tired to be married to a person whom she considered to be beneath her stature and had given him one last chance to redeem himself and he had blown it, at least in her eyes? Well, anyway, it didn't matter any longer.

An hour later Anton was sitting in the office of Richard Wisotsky. He briefly recounted the story of his marriage and the nature of his current problem with Carol (his own sanitized version, of course). When Anton eventually produced the spreadsheet with the details of the Walker family assets and liabilities, Mr. Wisotsky was visibly impressed.

"It's a pleasure to deal with such organized people. So, what do you want by way of a settlement, Mr. Walker?"

"Fifty percent of everything: the house, the cash, the stocks. She has her Lexus; I'll keep my BMW. I'm not a petty man, so she can keep all the furniture and her jewellery too. I want bi-weekly visitation rights and I want to be able to take Megan for vacations at least once a year. We should be able to travel with no restrictions," Anton proclaimed.

"Sounds reasonable," the lawyer mused thoughtfully and then added, "in addition, ask her to cover all your legal expenses and ask for a monthly support allowance. In a way, it's your wife's and her brother's fault that you are currently unemployed. You were married to her for fifteen years, so she must help you maintain the lifestyle that you're accustomed to. She'll refuse these terms of course, Mr. Walker, but we'll use the monthly allowance as our bargaining chip."

By the end of their meeting, Anton and Richard (it was no longer *Mr. Wisotsky*) were quite pleased to be dealing with one-other and parted on very good terms.

Now, after all the logistics had finally been dealt with, Anton felt exhausted and dejected. He drove to some nondescript, inexpensive motel, rented a room, collapsed on the bed fully clothed and fell asleep almost immediately.

$$\Omega$$

After several hours of uneasy sleep, Anton woke up feeling disoriented. He examined his surroundings, registering in his mind the dismal furnishings, dull gray walls and antiquated TV. He silently repeated his pledge, feeling his anger welling up yet again. *Carol will pay dearly for this, and so will Jeff and Bill.*

Anton took a shower, changed and went to look for some food. He found a small Italian restaurant nearby and strode inside. After eating a hearty and delicious meal and drinking a glass of red wine, he felt considerably better. He ordered another glass of wine and looked about the restaurant that was almost unoccupied. There were only two other couples dining at this time. In one dimly-lit corner, Anton noticed an upright piano and suddenly felt an urge to play. He called over the owner and politely asked, "May I play a couple of tunes on your piano?"

"Do you know how?" the owner asked suspiciously. "We originally bought it for my son but he didn't want to study. It's an expensive instrument so I don't want anything to happen to it."

"I know how to play," Anton answered confidently and added, "let me show you."

He crossed the dining room and sat down at the piano. *When was the last time I played?* Anton tried to recall. *Do I remember anything?* He opened the keyboard cover and placed his hands on the keys. Anton sat on the piano bench without making any movement for several minutes and then, at first tentatively, he started to play an easy piece; then another one, and then one more.

Anton couldn't stop himself. All his frustration, his anger, and his longing to perform again were expressed through his passionate playing. The two couples that were dining rose from their tables and gathered near the piano. Anton continued to be absorbed with his music, oblivious to his surroundings and having but one thought. *How could I have stayed away from the piano for so long?*

When he eventually ceased playing, the owner approached him, shook his hand and almost reverently said, "You can come to play here anytime if you need to practice or whatever..."

"I may just take you up on your kind offer," Anton responded enthusiastically.

With his mood vastly improved, Anton walked briskly back to the motel. In the lobby he picked up a daily newspaper and found a quiet spot in the sitting area of the motel lounge. He prepared a cup of tea at the self-serve counter, made himself comfortable on the couch and began scanning the newspaper. What was in the news? The problems in the Middle East, the government deficit, some unimportant local election...the usual. He turned to the entertainment section and noticed a large ad. Two weeks from today, there were going to be auditions for entertainers in Vancouver. The cruise lines were hiring dancers, singers, comedians and piano players.

Anton studied the advertisement again and again while contemplating the possibilities. He ripped the page out of the newspaper and carefully put it into his pocket. He recalled how he and Carol had enjoyed their carefree times on the luxury cruise ships, and how they liked to go to the ship's piano bar, order some cocktails and to have a congenial conversation with other guests in this pleasant and relaxing atmosphere.

The Cruise Entertainer

Anton envisioned himself playing in the piano bar lounge of a luxury cruise ship and decided that it was well worth a try. The idea had a certain appeal. It would be so much better to live on a cruise ship than in this cheap motel. The food would be good and what's more, he would be playing piano and getting paid for doing what he loved to do. He would also have enough time to decide what to do in the future... after he received the substantial settlement from Carol, of course.

But would he be good enough to get hired? Were two weeks sufficient to get ready? Would the owner of the Italian restaurant allow him to practice ten hours a day? Should he apply for a position in the ship's orchestra, or as a solo entertainer in the piano bar? In the latter case, he would also be obliged to sing and Anton was no vocalist by any means. He certainly could carry a tune and the timbre of his voice wasn't entirely unpleasant, but his range was small. *Well,* Anton contemplated, *maybe it would do for a piano bar.* Dozens of frantic thoughts churned through Anton's mind, but nonetheless, now he had a purpose.

The next morning Anton called the agency organizing the auditions and got all the necessary details. He hastily prepared his new resume (without mentioning his programming career) and went to the bank where he was secretly keeping his documents in a safe-deposit box. He withdrew his Conservatory diploma and the transcript of his academic credits, and then he made copies and faxed it all to Vancouver.

For the next two weeks Anton worked as hard as he could at restoring his technique. He knew that he was rusty and that he didn't have enough time to get his playing skills anywhere close to the shape he would have liked, but like a trapped animal, he was now fighting for his survival. He learned several new popular songs and practiced performing them. His playing was gradually improving, although Anton had just one word to describe his own singing, and that was *pathetic*!

Anton allowed himself only two phone calls a day: one to his lawyer and the other to Megan. He always called her around four o'clock in the afternoon when he knew Carol wasn't at home. But with every passing day, Megan became more and more hostile towards her father. Some days she would hang up as soon as she heard his voice, while on other days she would scream into the phone, "How can you do this, Daddy? Why are you robbing mommy and me? You took away the computer and the car that mom promised me, and now we have to sell the house! Where are we supposed to live?"

"I didn't start it, Megan," Anton would say, but his daughter didn't want to hear his excuses.

Several days before the audition, Anton checked out of his motel room, thanked the owner of the Italian restaurant for his kindness and help, and then set out to drive to Vancouver.

There were so many candidates who showed up for the audition that it seemed to Anton that the entire populace of the city had suddenly decided to work as entertainers on cruise ships. Anger and desperation must be powerful motivational triggers, Anton was thinking, since he didn't feel at all nervous. He was adamant that he was going to land this job. He played even better than he had anticipated, unmindful of the presence of the jury or other candidates still waiting for their audition opportunity. Just like in the old days at the Conservatory, there were only himself and the piano in the studio, working in unison. He was asked to sing, and with considerable trepidation Anton performed a song from his very limited repertoire.

After the audition was over, Anton was instructed to proceed to the studio office. There was a skinny young man with long dark hair waiting for him behind an oversize mahogany desk. Anton scrutinized the office and the expensive designer clothes of the agent, concluding that the agency must be quite a profitable business. The man rose from his chair, walked around his desk to shake Anton's hand, smiled and introduced himself, "Tim Harper."

Anton instantly took a liking to this confident and friendly man with his open and kind face and gratefully accepted the agent's invitation to take a seat.

"Anton," Tim began, "your performance today was very impressive. I would like to offer you a contract with the Holland America Line. When can you be available to start?"

"Immediately," Anton hastily responded and then mentally chided himself for appearing over-eager.

The agent nodded his head in satisfaction and said, "In that case, I would like you to sail this Saturday on the *Statendam*. It's a twelve-day cruise from here in Vancouver to Alaska. Upon your return the cruise director will provide his feedback. If it's positive, as I'm sure it will be, then we will sign a longer, nine-month contract with you. It's our usual procedure when we engage a new entertainer."

Ω

On that Saturday afternoon Anton was sitting in the Ocean Bar of the *Statendam*, dressed in a formal suit and playing the recommended 'easy classics' repertoire. He soon became bored with these familiar tunes and injected some more challenging music into the mix. Before long, an attentive crowd had gathered in the bar. The waiters were constantly passing through the room, busily serving drinks, but Anton paid them no heed. He kept on playing and the audience clearly appreciated his music, as was obvious judging by the smiles on their faces and by the constant nodding of heads and whispered comments amongst the passengers. The predictable requests then started to materialize and Anton remembered his instructions: everything you do on the ship is for the pleasure of the passengers. Passengers should never become annoyed or made to feel unhappy.

Anton was happy to oblige. Now, with his future for a foreseeable timeframe being seemingly assured, his lingering inner anger subsided and he felt more content.

During his mid-session break, a middle-aged man approached to introduce himself to Anton. "Marek," he said with a distinctive accent. "I'm a drummer in the ship's band. Is this your first voyage?"

"Yes it is. My name is Anton and it's a pleasure to meet you." Anton smiled politely and then asked, "How long have you been on the high seas, Marek?"

"Seven years. It's not a bad life. Are you hungry? Let's go to eat something."

Soon, two new friends were sitting in the ship's dining room relating their life stories to one-another.

"So, what brought you to the *Statendam*?" Marek inquired.

"My own stupidity and naïveté," Anton began with decided frankness. "I made a decision years ago that it's too hard to make a living by playing piano. I became a computer programmer and married a Canadian woman who was a business executive. I didn't want to have any confrontations that would upset our cozy union, so I played the agreeable husband for fifteen years. Even so, as soon as she got tired of me she discarded me like a pair of old shoes," Anton professed.

"How about yourself, Marek?"

"I am a cheat, a drunkard and a selfish, lazy egotist," Marek confided with a wry smile. "Three wives and four children later, I'm a single guy again with no responsibilities, no regrets and no worries."

"Wow! That's quite an admission! Where are your children?" Anton inquired.

"Two of them are still in Poland; the other two are in the States."

Marek then abruptly changed the subject. "One word of advice, Anton. Be careful with the female passengers. I mean, if you want a little romance, stick to the other crew members. And by the way, there are a lot of pretty young dancers on this voyage. The female passengers are nothing but trouble. You have a little cozy talk with them and the next thing you know they think they're entitled to invite you to their cabin. If you fall for that, then you're stuck with them until the end of the cruise. Who needs it?"

"Are you speaking from personal experience?" Anton asked with a slight smirk on his face.

"Believe me," Marek sighed, "keep your distance from the female guests. Fewer problems."

Ten minutes later Anton was back in the Ocean Bar, working his next shift and having every intention of heeding Marek's advice.

Ω

Anton noticed her almost right away. It was hard not to notice such a woman. She was in her forties (or possibly young-looking fifties), impeccably groomed, and dressed in a dark red gown with a low cut that was guaranteed to attract the attention of the male passengers and crew alike. The large ruby necklace and matching earrings blatantly declared that she was a woman of considerable means. She was exceedingly attractive in a very striking manner, with large anthracite eyes, bright red lips, and fashionably styled, copper-coloured hair.

Anton immediately took a dislike to this woman. Everything about her annoyed him, especially her imperious manner. Despite the differences in appearance and the woman's much less conservative style in apparel, she reminded him of Carol. Anton attributed his instantaneous emotional response to this notable resemblance.

The woman behaved as if the ship belonged to her and the waiters had no other duties but to serve and cater to her every whim. What irritated Anton more than anything else was her obvious interest in him. She sat alone facing the piano, looking intensely at his hands and then at his face. When Anton stopped for a break, the woman approached the piano and introduced herself: "Susan Harper." And then she added, "I like your performance and style at the piano very much. May I invite you for a drink?"

This offer sounded more like a command, Anton thought, but remembering the golden rule that the passengers are always right, he politely responded, "Thank you, ma'am. I do feel a bit thirsty. My name is Anton Walker."

"I know," Susan replied. "Why don't you follow me?"

Remembering Marek's words of caution, Anton replied, "My break is very short. Let's have a drink here."

"Your break is half an hour," Susan contradicted, "and this bar is far too noisy. There are better places on this ship." Without waiting for a reply, she started to walk out of the lounge and Anton obediently followed her, despite the fact he was seething inside.

They reached an elevator at the aft of the ship. Susan inserted her onboard pass-card in the card reader and when the door closed, the elevator started to ascend toward the more exclusive and expensive upper decks of the ship. Anton realized immediately that they were heading for Susan's private suite. This was the last thing that he needed or wanted on his first day of employment.

Susan led him into the living quarters of a spacious suite, picked up the phone and ordered a bottle of champagne and a bowl of strawberries.

"We made the right decision hiring you," Susan began. "I'm the president of the Harper Talent Agency. Tim is my son; he works for me. As I've already mentioned, I am very pleased with your performance and your musical style."

Anton zeroed in on the words *we made the right decision.* He wondered where Susan had been hiding during his audition and when she had found time to discuss his performance with Tim. It was not important where and when; but it became very important to Anton to understand *why* he was hired.

"Whew, frankly I'm relieved that you're not a passenger," Anton said somewhat coolly while looking directly into Susan's eyes. "I've been informed that I have to be exceedingly polite and accommodating with the passengers and I started to worry that I was putting myself in a compromising position by coming to your cabin, Ms. Harper. I'm very glad to know that you are my agent and that this occasion is strictly professional."

Susan's eyes narrowed as she measured Anton up and down and then she let out a chuckle. "Don't worry. My interest in you is, as you said, strictly professional. However, I don't think it's such a good idea to be rude to your agent either, Tony."

"My name is Anton. I would kindly ask you to refrain from using that diminutive form of my name in the future. As you know, Susan, I have to be back in the bar very shortly. Is there something else you wanted to speak about with me?"

"As a matter of fact, yes, Anton. It wasn't clear from your resume where you've been playing for the past fifteen years."

"I haven't played for a while. I took a sabbatical from the piano."

"A fifteen-year sabbatical?" Susan quizzed.

"Apparently I've still retained my form, wouldn't you agree? Otherwise, you wouldn't have hired me."

Before Susan could respond to that provocative remark, there was a knock at the door and a waiter appeared carrying a tray with a bottle of champagne, two glasses, and a bowl of strawberries, just as Susan had requested.

The waiter hurriedly set everything on the table, politely bowed his head and left the suite, closing the door behind him.

Anton got up, apologetically smiled and said, "I really must be getting back to the bar. Please enjoy your champagne."

As he was heading towards the cabin door, Anton heard Susan's confident and compelling voice. "It will stay chilled in the fridge until we have a better opportunity to continue this conversation."

Anton was fuming. The last thing he needed was to get involved with his agent. To his way of thinking, Susan and Carol stood in juxtaposition to one-another. There were too many parallels. In both cases, Anton was hired not for his professional abilities, he was certain of it, but because those ladies were interested in him on a much more personal level. In both cases, Susan and Carol considered themselves superior to him. Susan's imperious manner was quite similar to the demeanour of his estranged executive wife.

Been there; done that, Anton thought to himself. He felt deeply insulted and sullied. He tried to dismiss any further thoughts about the encounter with Susan, but as he started to play again, he thought about the large crowd of hopefuls who had attended the audition and about the considerable number of entertainers working on different cruise lines. A fresh idea was beginning to take shape in Anton's mind.

He felt tired when he finished playing his last set of the evening but Marek was waiting for him. "We're going up to the Crow's Nest lounge. Quite a few ladies are looking forward to meeting you."

"I already met one," Anton smirked and bitterly recounted his early evening encounter.

"You'd better be careful," Marek cautioned. "Susan's quite a tenacious woman and she will not give up that easily. And remember, if you offend her, you can kiss your long-term contract good-bye." Marek looked appraisingly at Anton and added wistfully, "Susan is a remarkable and very attractive woman. I wouldn't mind being in your shoes, but look at me!" He patted his large belly, pointed at his balding head and said, "My days in the limelight are over. You, my friend, should carefully consider how to make the most out of Queen Susan's overtures."

In the Crow's Nest bar, Anton was introduced to a number of the ship's other entertainers. He flirted with several of the attractive young dancers, complimented one of the lead singers and had several drinks, all the while completely ignoring Susan who was sitting alone near a window and observing Anton's antics from a distance.

Some while later, Anton excused himself and made his way to his cabin. On his way out of the bar he waved to Susan and flashed his most charming smile.

Anton had a difficult time falling asleep that first night in his small cabin. He longed to be back at home in his comfortable bed. He had spent only one day working as a cruise entertainer and the initial novelty had worn off almost immediately to the extent that in some respects he loathed it already. He remembered how he used to play years ago to a rapt audience, how nobody dared to get up and leave in the middle of the recital or even to whisper a sound; and he remembered the long and loud applause after his performance of each piece. Here on the ship, his performances were simply pleasant background noise, meant to keep the passengers in a good mood. People were coming and going even while he was playing and for the most part seemed more interested in their drinks and their conversations than in his piano repertoire.

Ω

The following day Susan invited Anton to join her to have lunch in the dining room. Once they were seated, Susan apologized. "I'm sorry, Anton, if I came on too strong yesterday. I didn't mean to offend you. It's just that I'm just genuinely intrigued by you."

"There's nothing terribly intriguing about me, Susan. I emigrated over seventeen years ago and tried to make a living as a piano player but it didn't work out. Then I worked as a programmer for fifteen years until I finally got tired of it. I'm quite happy to be here and playing the piano again."

"I'm sure there's much more to your life than that brief rendition, Anton. For example, there's a trace of a ring on your left hand, but no ring."

"Susan, now you're getting really personal. I could ask you essentially the same question. You have a son, but there's not even a trace of a ring on your left hand."

"Tim's father passed away almost seven years ago. That's been more than enough time for any physical trace to disappear," she explained.

"You're a very attractive woman, Susan. Seven years is a long time. How is it that you're still single?"

"Clearly, you operate according to that expression 'the best defence is a good offense', Anton! Now, you're the one getting personal, but I will answer the question anyway. I love my freedom and my independence, and I do love the thrill of new romantic encounters from time to time."

"Please forgive me, Susan, but I don't for a minute believe a word that you just said. I'm sure that you'd prefer real companionship, lasting friendships and maybe even another marriage. The reason these things aren't attainable for you is that you look at men with the attitude of a conqueror, if I may say so. Maybe you do enjoy the conquest during the heat of the moment but don't you feel lonely and empty afterwards? To be honest, Susan, in spite of the fact that you're a very beautiful woman, I really have no desire to become just another specimen in your prized collection of conquests."

Anton glanced at his watch and said, "If you'll excuse me, please, I have to work. I hope I haven't offended you."

Without waiting for a response, Anton left a now agitated and angry woman to finish her lunch in solitude.

Anton didn't need to psycho-analyze his feelings. He understood within himself why Susan infuriated him to the point that he had a difficult time to control himself and why he had been pointedly rude towards her. In effect, by punishing her he was punishing Carol. He was quite certain that after that abortive lunch Susan would leave him alone, although whether he would still have a job at the end of this cruise was quite another matter.

In any event, he was wrong. Susan put in an appearance for Anton's evening performance in the piano bar and lingered nearby waiting for him to finish. She looked less sure of herself, somehow softer, more feminine. Even her clothes and jewellery were more subtle. Anton was inwardly quite pleased and even felt vindicated by this tell-tale change in Susan's deportment.

That entire night was spent in Susan's suite. Anton frowned at the champagne that was waiting for him and asked if he might have cognac instead. Susan made a call and a bottle of expensive cognac was promptly delivered. Anton silently relished and accepted as his due Susan's attention and her evident desire to please him. After several drinks, they retired to the bedroom. Susan proved to be an experienced and voracious lover, much more innovative than Carol, and Anton found this new experience to be thrilling and very satisfying.

Feeling content the morning after, Susan gave him a peck on the cheek and as she made her way to the shower, rather condescendingly announced, "We'll have breakfast here in my suite, stud!"

When Susan emerged from the shower, Anton was gone.

All that day, Anton ignored Susan and shamelessly flirted with his numerous female fans. No sooner had he finally returned to his cabin in the late evening, the cabin phone was ringing. Anton let it ring for some time before eventually picking it up.

"How dare you treat me like that?" Susan exclaimed in an enraged voice.

"I was planning to ask you the same thing, my dear," Anton calmly retorted. "I don't care to be called *stud*."

"Stop being so sensitive, Anton!"

"I don't call it sensitivity. I call it dignity, Susan."

"Oh, come on, Anton. Come to my suite and I'll demonstrate how respectful I can be to my man," Susan replied coyly.

"I'm quite tired," Anton replied dismissively, trying to get comfortable on his narrow bed. "I'll see you tomorrow."

That was the last time for the duration of the cruise that Anton slept in his own cabin.

Marek couldn't resist commenting on this latest development. "Wow, Anton, congratulations! I've been working for Susan Harper for years but never suspected that she could be so sweet and yielding."

"Elementary, Dr. Watson," Anton smirked. "Here's the recipe: an equal measure of compliments and indifference, add a pinch of jealousy and a heaping spoonful of sex, and voila - the woman is at your feet!"

"I wish that it was really that easy to conquer the ladies," Marek mused wistfully.

"But it is, my friend. The secret is not to feel any emotional attachment towards the subject you're taming and to always act with a cool head," Anton instructed.

"Come on, Anton. She's an unbelievable woman! I've admired her for ages. Don't you feel anything for her? Not even some sort of infatuation?"

"Absolutely nothing."

"And here I thought that I was a selfish pig, but you take the cake. Why are you doing this if you're not even slightly attracted to her?" Marek inquired.

"She has something I want," Anton replied vaguely.

"What's that, if I may ask?"

"The agency."

"Are you planning to rob the *poor* widow and steal her agency?"

"By no means...not at all, Marek. I want her to teach me how to be a top agent. I want to learn everything there is to know, including all the trade secrets of this industry, and then I'll open my own talent placement agency."

"Couldn't you just ask her to hire you instead of playing devious amorous games?"

"Marek, do you really think that she would reveal all her business knowledge and secrets to a mere underling employee? It would take me ages to learn the business that way. I'm simply taking an expedient shortcut."

"Anton, you have my utmost respect and admiration." Marek said as he stood and bowed mockingly. "And the first step your new agency must take is to engage me as an agent!"

Anton burst into laughter. "Now why would I do that?"

Marek became serious and replied, "Because with me you know exactly who you're dealing with. No illusions; no pretence. I'm tired of drumming on the high seas, one cruise after another. I would work my butt off for something that would provide me with a decent income. You're an ambitious son-of-a-bitch and I want to ride this ambition of yours."

"I'll keep that in mind," Anton said and heartily shook Marek's hand.

When Anton woke up in Susan's cabin on the last morning of the voyage, she presented him with a folio. Inside the cover there was a long-term contract with his name inscribed on it.

Instead of signing the contract, Anton motioned to Susan to sit near him and said, "Susan, I don't want this contract. This cruise was a trial period for both of us, but in different ways. The life of a cruise entertainer is not for me."

Clearly disappointed, Susan asked, "What is it then that you really want, Anton?"

"Do you remember that you asked me once about my life story? Let me tell you a little bit more about myself, and most importantly about the most recent one-and-a-half months. Then, I hope, you will understand."

Anton briefly recounted the story of his life (his version, of course) and told Susan about his unfortunate homecoming after the business trip to Russia. That brought him to the punch line. "Susan, what I really want is to work for you. Please engage me as an agent and I'll prove to you that I can be a great asset to your agency. With my contacts I can secure a major contract for the agency in Russia, just like I did for my former employer. I love the process of negotiating, and apparently I'm pretty good at it. So, what do you think,

Susan? Would you hire me?"

Susan didn't respond specifically to Anton's request - she was concentrating on something else. "Anton, there is something about your story that doesn't make sense. No woman would kick her husband out after fifteen years of apparently good marriage, simply based on somebody else's hearsay. Besides, why would she be so concerned now about events that happened so long ago? You were working as a programmer for the past fifteen years, so why would your wife suddenly care about your previous education? Or about your first wife for that matter? Something is definitely missing from this picture."

"Funny, I was thinking the very same thing. Of course Carol is a very proud woman. She'd hate to be the laughing stock of all her friends."

"Trust me, Anton, she'd hate being single much more. She was divorced before, right? There's no way Carol would want to go through that experience again, unless there was a serious reason."

"Susan, to be frank, I was under her heel. As people are saying, *whipped*, although I admit I only came to fully realize it quite recently. Maybe she was afraid that after my success in Moscow, I wouldn't be so agreeable and easy to get along with...something like that, perhaps."

"No, I don't buy that either. More likely than not, your wife had somebody else in her life and used her brother's story as an excuse for the breakup with you."

That possibility had never occurred to Anton and his first impulse was to dismiss it completely. "No way. Carol really loved me; she would never cheat on me!"

Susan didn't say anything in response to that but looked intently at Anton with a slight, condescending smile. *This won't do*, Anton thought to himself. He was not about to sacrifice his hard-won superiority in his relationship with Susan.

He shrugged his shoulders and said, "Even if you're right, Susan, Carol will be sorry that she ever crossed me. It'll cost her plenty."

"I don't care about your Carol. What I care about, darling, is you and our relationship. Still," Susan mused, "Carol might have overestimated the marital intentions of her lover. It's one thing to have a casual affair with a married woman but it's quite another thing if that woman is ready to leave her husband for you. It means responsibility and men usually don't like that word. If I'm right in my supposition, Carol will be after you again before long, Anton. You have a teenage daughter too, so most likely you would return to your wife and daughter and to your comfortable, boring life."

"Is that what's bothering you, Susan? Perish the thought; I would never return to Carol. That part of my life is over and done with."

Adroitly changing the subject, Anton then said, "Let's talk about business. Here's what I propose. I can recognize real talent in music, dancing, singing and acting, and I can certainly distinguish between a genuine artist and an impostor. Russia and the other countries of the former Soviet Union have a long history of excellence in music, ballet and theatre. I can go there and find talented people for you – artists who'd be eager to work in the West and you can be sure they'd gladly work for a substantially lower wage than their American and Canadian counterparts."

"The problem with the artists from those countries is obtaining a work visa. It's not as simple as you think," Susan said thoughtfully.

"I'll find the right contacts," Anton replied confidently.

"Well, maybe, but why don't we first start here in North America? I have several meetings scheduled with young performers for the next week and I have an upcoming audition in California. Actually, it's not too difficult to find good performers. It's much more difficult to place them. It took me years to establish a good relationship with several cruise lines. There are quite a few other agencies and the competition is fierce. Anyway, I agree and let's see how it goes. I assume you will stay with me. I have a large house and Tim lives separately."

"Thanks very much, Susan. I'm certainly looking forward to working with you and I'm sure it will prove beneficial for both of us. I hope to start making some serious money soon and to be able to rent my own apartment. But for now, I will gladly accept your hospitality." At that point, the pact with Susan being sealed, Anton hugged her affectionately.

Ω

For the next four months, Anton was keeping extremely busy learning the talent agency business. Susan was very pleased with the performance of her new hire. He could readily detect the difference between a genuine artistic performer and a *wannabe* applicant. Anton was very kind and understanding when he wanted to be and he could drive a hard bargain when necessary as well.

As it turned out, Susan was right about Anton's marital situation with Carol. In due course she called Anton and sounded loving and apologetic. "Tony, where did you go? Why did you disappear like that?" she started. "I'm sorry that I overreacted when Jeff told me about your meeting with your first wife. You never told me that she was an opera singer."

"She wasn't in Canada, Carol."

"Tony, I never intended to divorce you but I overreacted. I hope you realize that. Why don't we meet and discuss this misunderstanding?" Carol pleaded.

For Anton, this was a call from a different lifetime

and a different planet. He felt no remaining attachment whatsoever towards Carol and had no inclination at all to return to his former life. He had different plans now and Carol was not a part of them – pure and simple.

Anton replied coldly but courteously, "Carol, I didn't start it, you did. Furthermore, your gesture of dumping the suitcases in the garden shed demonstrated your true feelings towards me very clearly. I'm going to proceed with the divorce. Say hello to Megan from me. I hope to see her soon." He then hung up the phone without giving Carol any opportunity to respond.

Susan, who happened to be nearby when Carol called, had listened attentively to the conversation and while she refrained from comment, she nodded her head almost imperceptibly in quiet satisfaction.

The Birth of a New Talent Agency

Susan considered her personal relationship with Anton to be ideal in the present circumstances and was furtively hoping that it would lead to a more permanent relationship, perhaps eventually to marriage. In the agency Anton was attentive and diligent; at home - loving and romantic. Susan felt as though she was the happiest woman in the world. Even her son Tim had warmed up to Anton, especially after the two men had a serious talk.

"Tim," Anton said, "I'm the best thing that could happen to your mother and to you. Your mother needs a man, a partner and a friend. I like your mother very much and respect her greatly. However, I have no intention to marry again and I have no desire to take over your business. So you see, I'm not a threat, Tim, I'm a friend."

Anton looked directly into Tim's eyes and there was so much honesty and consideration conveyed in that look that Tim was convinced of Anton's sincerity.

But secretly Anton was counting the days until he could start his own agency and be his own boss. He prompted Susan to organize an audition in Russia and suggested conducting it in St. Petersburg. Anton assured her that he had more connections there and that the cost would be less. In addition, artists in St. Petersburg were easier to deal with than their counterparts in Moscow.

It was the end of February when Anton and Susan arrived in St. Petersburg. This was Susan's first visit to Russia and she immediately disliked the cold, windy and damp weather. The majestic city looked gray and uninviting at this time of the year. It suited Anton just fine, because he hoped that it would be Susan's first and last visit to Russia. He was impatiently looking forward to the day when he would be working without her constant supervision.

Susan checked into one of the best hotels in St. Petersburg but Anton decided to stay with his parents. He explained to Susan that his parents were very old-fashioned, and under the circumstances she was agreeable to those arrangements.

Quite a number of prospects showed up for the audition. The majority of the applicants were young people, recent graduates from Russia's best ballet schools or from the premier music conservatories.

Susan was very critical in her appraisal of each of the candidates. There were many more hopefuls than positions, so she could afford to be choosy.

Anton kept his own independent list and his own ratings of each candidate. He noticed that Susan rejected all the applicants without fluent English, yet among those candidates there were a number of quite talented performers. Susan rejected all 'unpolished' or 'raw' talent as well. She selected only those artists that she could potentially place effortlessly right away.

Three days later, Susan flew back to Vancouver while Anton remained behind to organize visas for the selected performers.

Ω

The first thing that Anton did after Susan's departure was to have a serious conversation with his parents and his sister.

He needed their moral support, their help and their understanding. Anton knew very well that they were quite upset about his second divorce and his decision to change his profession yet again, and that they were deeply concerned about his future. Nevertheless, he was quite certain that despite their past disappointments, his parents now wanted him to remain in Russia.

"Papa," he said, "I want to organize a talent agency for young, budding performers. I know how difficult it is to start out in show business. I know all the obstacles that they'll face and I know that nobody is genuinely interested in developing new talent. Most everyone in this business is only interested in 'ready product'. I want to help those young people. Maybe if somebody had been seriously interested in promoting my career when I started, I'd be an established pianist today just as I dreamt, but I had no help to guide and support me. Not here; not in Canada. I made many mistakes along the way and eventually I just gave up. I didn't succeed as I expected, although I did learn some valuable lessons from my experiences, and so now I want to help other talented young people to succeed and avoid the disappointments that I endured."

Anton could see that his mother's and his sister's eyes were glistening with tears. He continued. "In addition to the talent agency, I want to organize a school, an image consulting school. Do you know what I mean? I want to help people to identify their unique and ideal image, to polish their talents, and to help them find their niche in show business. For example, there are dancers that have the body and personality more suited for modern dance, for jazz, or maybe even hip-hop; but instead they insist on dancing classical ballet and always wind up in the back row of the corps de ballet if they make it at all.

"Similarly, there are singers with the voice for classical Russian romance songs, yet they insist on singing rap or hard rock, and then they fail too.

There are also many potential performers who simply don't know how to dress on the stage, or what hairdo to wear, or how best to present themselves in an audition. They have the God-given talent but absolutely no defining image that makes them stand out from the crowd. We would help them at the school that I envisage."

"Anton," Valentina timidly inquired, "aren't you trying to accomplish too much all at once? Aren't you worried about the possibility of failing again?"

"Sure I am, sis, but you will help me, won't you? I want you to be the director of the school. I'll concentrate on the agency and you'll hire a vocal coach, a dance instructor, an image consultant, and a pianist to accompany the singers. We'll rent a small place, just several rooms. We'll work together and you will see that together we will succeed."

Valentina's eyes by now were alight with growing excitement. She had just been offered not simply a new job, but a meaningful role in a new business with her brother. She'd been offered the opportunity for a new life and a better future.

"Papa," Anton said, "there is one other matter I want to discuss with you. I don't like the last name that I'm using now. I'm not *Walker*."

"I agree with you on that subject," his father grumbled.

"Fine, but Americans and Canadians don't like long and complicated given or last names either. They abbreviate their first names to a minimum. That's why they have so many people named Ben, Len, Joe, or Tom. And if the last name is complicated, they have to ask you to spell it. By the time you finish spelling your surname, they've lost interest in doing business with you. I'm serious, Papa. I'm proud of our family name so please don't misunderstand, but I can't use it to operate an international business."

His father was frowning now. Finally, he asked, "So, what do you suggest?"

"Please, Papa, allow me to adopt mama's maiden name. It's short, crisp and easy to spell or to pronounce:

Zubov."

Anton's mother had been sitting quietly until this point but now interjected herself into the discussion. "Matvei, please don't make a big deal out of this. We have to help Anton, not put obstacles in his way."

Grudgingly, Matvei Ivanovich Gorchichniy nodded his head in agreement.

The following day, Anton applied for a change of his surname. Then he proceeded to register two new businesses: the *Pinnacle Talent Agency* and the *Pinnacle School for the Performing Arts.*

Valentina located a building where the first floor was available for rent. Anton wasn't too happy about the location (it wasn't one of the better parts of the city) and he wasn't thrilled about the condition of the premises either, but the rent was relatively low and so he went ahead with the rental arrangement. He was in business!

Anton sent an e-mail to Marek, informing him about his new business venture and offering him a position in his newly-founded agency.

With Valentina's help, Anton began to make some useful contacts. It was easier than he had anticipated organizing visas for the performers selected by Susan and so before long, those applications were successfully processed and the lucky performers were on their way.

However, Anton still wasn't yet ready to return to Canada. He called a number of the candidates that Susan had rejected but whom he had considered to be quite talented and invited them to a meeting at his agency office.

$$\Omega$$

Nine young people made an appearance for the meeting: two male singers, three female singers, a piano player, a drummer and two dancers: a man and a woman. Anton, Valentina, and the newly-hired employees of the *Pinnacle School for the Performing Arts* warmly greeted the young prospects. Anton briefly made the necessary introductions and then proceeded to explain his plan to the group.

Anton's short presentation was very straightforward. "You've been invited here because you have talent and the potential to succeed in show business. However, your talent is raw and unpolished. You haven't established the right image for yourselves. As it stands now, you're not marketable and no other agency is going to sign you up.

"In spite of your obvious talent, you failed the audition and my associate, Susan Harper, has no interest in you for her agency. She selected other entertainers and they're already on their way to their first assignments," Anton explained.

He looked at the now visibly dejected and downcast young people and continued with his proposition. "As I said, nobody else will sign you up, but I have good news for you - I will.

"Here are my conditions. You'll be enrolled in our school where you will work with a vocal coach, along with music and dance instructors. You'll have an interview with our image consultant and he'll develop for each of you the image that best suits your talent and personality. You will have three months to graduate. After that, I will find employment for all of you. Of course, if any of you don't work hard, or if you prove incapable of following instructions and directions, I will have the right to terminate our arrangement.

"If you graduate successfully, as I believe each of you is capable of doing, you will sign an exclusive contract with my agency for three years. You won't have to pay anything up-front for the school instruction or the image consultancy. I'll deduct the cost of your education from your future income. After three years, you will have the option to re-sign with me, or you will be free to sign with any other agency. Do you have any questions?"

One of the young female singers frowned, then smirked and provocatively posed a question. "So, your so-called image consultants and school instructors would decide how I should dress, what I'm supposed to sing, and how to behave on the stage. Is that it? I won't have any choice in any of these matters. Have I understood you correctly?"

Anton carefully and deliberately measured up this young lady. He remembered her very well. She had the best voice among the three female singers that came to the audition. He had expected some hesitation and resistance but he was, frankly, sorry that it was this girl that he was about to lose. There was so much sarcasm in her tone of voice that Anton understood that he just had to forget about trying to convince her to alter her attitude and would have to concentrate on the others.

"Yes, you understood me correctly. There's no choice whatsoever, young lady. You had your choice up until now but apparently it didn't bring about a positive result for either of us. You have a pleasant voice but your stage manners are appalling, your clothes are hideous, your hairstyle is unbecoming, and the song that you chose for the audition wasn't even suitable for your voice."

The girl jumped from her chair and exclaimed, "That's your opinion and you can keep it to yourself! I'll become successful without your stupid school and your proposed terms which are little better than slavery!"

She turned around and with her head held high, pompously strode briskly out of the office.

Anton regarded the rest of the candidates who had remained quiet during the verbal skirmish with the female singer. He smiled warmly and then apologetically said, "I'm very sorry for her outburst but that was her right. We're living in a democratic country now and everyone is free to choose his or her own road to success. Let us all wish her the best of luck. She made her own personal choice."

After pausing a suitable few moments to allow the other attendees to digest the events of the past several minutes and his calming comments, Anton then asked, "Now then, what about the rest of you?"

One of the male singers shrugged his shoulders and spoke up. "That girl is stupid. I understand that I need to take training classes but I have no money for them. And here's somebody offering to teach me to improve my skills for free and then get me a job – I would be a complete idiot to refuse such an offer. Where do I sign?"

All of the other seven prospects then promptly fell into line as well.

The following day, the first eight students of the *Pinnacle School for the Performing Arts* began their studies and Anton considered his next steps. He knew that he needed to find some means to make money and make it quickly. The rent for the premises and the salary for his employees would eat up his own funds within a month. Furthermore, he didn't have any idea where he would find employment for his students in three months.

After such a long absence, he had no viable contacts in show business in Russia and his only contact in Canada was Susan. He went to the bank, but without any collateral or any credit history in Russia, his application for a business loan was declined. By now Anton was becoming gravely concerned that he had made a mistake by starting the business before his settlement with Carol was finalized. To make matters worse, his Canadian lawyer was tactfully asking him for a retainer too.

Ω

Anton badly needed a breakthrough and surprisingly, he found the answer to his problem in the

St. Petersburg metro. As far as he was concerned, it was not simply an answer - it was a miracle.

He was visiting a downtown store looking for some supplies for the school (another expense!) and his travels took him into the Gostinny Dvor metro station. There, inside the station, he noticed a string quartet. Four tall, beautiful, blonde girls were playing classical music for the passers-by and trying to earn a few rubles. Anton stopped to listen and he was instantly enthralled with their obvious talent. It was apparent to his practiced ear that these young ladies must have been students or even graduates of a conservatory. Indeed, these were talented musicians in need of a meaningful job and Anton concluded that they would be a great find for any cruise line.

He approached the quartet as they were preparing to play their next selection and asked in English, "Does any one of you speak English?"

One of the girls replied in heavily accented English, "We all speak a little bit. Why do you ask?"

Anton responded, but this time in Russian. "Would you like to work on a cruise ship? You'll obviously enjoy much better working conditions than in this metro and I'm sure the pay-scale would be much better too." He smiled and added, "The food is good and you would be able to see the world."

The girls regarded Anton warily and with obvious scepticism.

"My name is Anton Zubov and I am the president of the *Pinnacle Talent Agency*. I'm looking for entertainers for cruise ships and I very much like what I heard from your group. If you're interested, please come to my agency and we'll make a video audition clip. It would also be a good idea if you would get dressed as you would for a major recital...no jeans or sneakers."

"We know how to dress," the same girl replied somewhat indignantly. "Let us think about it."

"By all means... here's my business card."

Anton was so excited about finding the string quartet that for the remainder of the day he travelled from one metro station to another, seeking out more musicians or other artists with talent.

Indeed, the next positive encounter for Anton took place at Vladimirskaya station. There he found a young man surrounded by quite a large crowd of transit patrons. Anton found himself a comfortable spot and attentively watched the solo performance. The boy was a mime, a juggler, a magician and a comedian all put together. Anton observed the laughing and cheering crowd and decided that this young man could successfully perform a one-man 'headliner' show on a cruise ship. Anton tried to restrain his enthusiasm and after the performance, as calmly as he could, he invited the multi-talented young man to pay a visit to his agency office.

The next day, the four ladies of the string quartet appeared at the agency office, dressed in long, black gowns and carrying their instruments. With full make-up and properly attired, all four looked glamorous and truly sensational.

Anton recorded the performance video clip by himself. When the young ladies learned that Anton was a graduate of the Moscow Conservatory, their lingering scepticism faded away and they warmed up towards him considerably.

The mime also showed up at the agency office, accompanied by his girlfriend. They were both graduates of the Moscow Circus School and had brought their own audition tapes with them. The girl was a talented dancer and an acrobat as well.

Now Anton was quite ready to fly to Canada.

Ω

Susan welcomed Anton home with a lavish dinner and a bottle of his favourite French cognac. By now, she knew that Anton could not stomach champagne and preferred his cognac to any other liqueur. Susan was a bit apprehensive that her lover had spent such a long time in St. Petersburg - this man and his native Russia were both an enigma to her. She had missed Anton more than she was willing to admit, even to herself. She certainly didn't want to lose him and wasn't prepared to even contemplate such a possibility.

They had a passionate reunion that night and with that, Anton dispelled all her fears. He was as ardent and hungry for her as she was for him.

In the morning while Susan was still in her bathrobe and he was sitting up in bed, Anton initiated a business discussion, despite her protestations that it was too early in the morning.

"Susan, the artists you've selected have their visas, as you know. Opportunities to find other great performers are almost limitless in Russia. However, there's one sort of problem, Susan. That problem is our relationship."

"Do you want to dump me?" an alarmed Susan asked bluntly.

"Essentially, the continuation of our relationship is up to you, my dear. Please try to understand me. The inequality between us is killing me. I can't be with a woman who is superior to me in social standing. I tried it with Carol – you know the result. I've been thinking seriously about you and our relationship and I've come to the conclusion that I can't love a woman and work for her at the same time. When I'm with a woman, I need to be on a par with her – to be her equal, and certainly not a dependant employee."

"What are you getting at, Anton?"

"I've opened my own agency in St. Petersburg."

Susan's reaction was predictably spontaneous. "What? How could you? I taught you all the tricks of the trade and you decided to use this knowledge to become my competitor? That's vile and sneaky, Anton."

Anton got up from the bed and without saying another word, began to get dressed.

Suddenly, Susan realized that she was on the verge of losing not only a valuable employee but also the man with whom she was passionately in love.

"Anton, stop. Don't you dare walk away from me like that! Talk to me."

"I tried, Susan. I thought that I was dealing with both a friend and a loving companion but it seems I was wrong. Apparently all you really care about is your agency. I'm just another boy-toy for you, just like so many others before I came along.

"I should be going, Susan. Please send my commission to my St. Petersburg address." Anton calmly placed his new business card for the *Pinnacle Talent Agency* on the table and was clearly about to leave.

"Please wait, Anton. What is it that you really want?" Susan started to sob in distress.

"I want to be your partner, not your employee, Susan. If I find an entertainer in Russia and you place him, our commission should be divided equally. When you have a request from a cruise line and can't fill it suitably from your database, I would hope that you'd notify me and I would find the right candidate. In this case, again we would equally share the commission. That would be fair. I want to build a strong and prosperous relationship with your agency as an equal partner. However, my Russian agency should be allowed to operate as an independent entity. I wouldn't directly approach any cruise lines that you're already working with, but I need to feel at liberty to approach other companies."

"You're such a bastard, Anton," Susan said, half sobbing and half laughing, "but I love you anyway."

Anton sat down near Susan, hugged her, and gently kissed her on her forehead. He felt quite pleased with himself: Susan was afraid to lose him and that was good. After all, she was still an important and necessary stepping stone in his ambitious plans.

The next day, Anton went for an appointment with the Princess Cruise Line, which was not presently one of Susan's clients. It wasn't easy to organize this meeting and he was granted just fifteen minutes to make his sales pitch.

As soon as he was ushered into the office of the cruise line representative, Anton removed a videotape from his briefcase and asked for a video player.

"I really appreciate this opportunity," he said, "and I don't want to impose on your valuable time, so why don't we look at these three video clips I've brought to show you."

They watched the clip of the lady-acrobat first. Then they watched and listened to the classical music rendition by the string quartet. When Anton made a motion to pause it in the middle of the clip (as though his time was running short), the representative raised his hand and motioned to him that he should not interrupt the video. Then he picked up a phone and invited some of his colleagues to join them.

Anton ultimately remained in that office for over two hours. In the end, he signed up all of his candidates: the mime, the acrobat and the string quartet. Before that highly productive meeting concluded, they discussed other additional entertainer resources that the cruise line was looking for. The *Pinnacle Talent Agency* was in business...big-time!

Anton spent a lovely weekend with Susan before returning to St. Petersburg and promised her to be back in Canada as soon as he could.

Before leaving for the airport, Anton called Megan. This time, Megan didn't sound hostile but she certainly sounded sad. "Daddy, I've missed you so much. Without you, everything is different around here. Mom's so snappy and she's always seems to be angry with me. I saw her crying one evening. Can't you come back home, Daddy? Then everything will be the way it was before."

"Pumpkin, it can never be the way it was before. Your mother chose to break up our family and we have to live with her decision. However, I would like to take you to Russia for at least a month during your summer holidays. I want to introduce you to your grandparents and to your aunt and uncle. I promise that you'll have the best time of your life. Would you like that?"

"Yeah, I suppose, if mom lets me go. I was invited to spend the summer at Uncle Jeff's cottage, but I'd rather spend time with you. What would I do in Russia?"

For the next ten minutes Anton was telling Megan about St. Petersburg and about all the fascinating things they would do together. He could tell by her reaction on the phone that she had become really enthused about this opportunity.

"OK, Daddy, I really want to go! Please try to convince mom that I can go. I've missed you, Daddy."

The next day after an overnight flight, Anton was back in St. Petersburg and busier than ever. He couldn't imagine how he could have lived as a low-level employee for fifteen years, working nine-to-five and going through the same boring routine day after day, or how he could have withstood such a predictable and dull life for so many years. These days in his self-employed capacity, he was working twelve to fourteen hours a day, seven days a week, but enjoying it so much more. He made new contacts, interviewed potential clients, and worked with the students at his school. He also travelled to Moscow and had a serious chat with one of the Conservatory professors, his old classmate, Konstantin Sorokin. Needless to say, Sorokin was quite happy to establish a new employment opportunity for his graduating students.

In April Marek began working for the agency. He was charged with the task of organizing auditions in Poland and the Czech Republic.

The time passed quickly and after just a couple of months, Anton indicated, to Susan's delight, that he was ready to travel back to Canada again.

Victoria

Near the end of May a new performer knocked on Anton's office door, unannounced. When Anton eyed the young lady standing at the entrance, his heart raced. He had never seen anybody as lovely as this tall girl with golden hair cascading to her shoulders and intense, violet eyes. He was confident that by now he was immune to feminine beauty, but his immediate reaction to this girl was incredibly strong – just as powerful and overwhelming as his reaction had been towards Nina the first time he had seen her. But how could he even compare Nina to this girl? In Anton's eyes, this young lady was a hundred, no, even a thousand times more beautiful and glamorous than Nina ever was. *Glamorous.* Anton liked that word. It was the only word to adequately describe this gorgeous creature.

The girl stood looking at Anton without speaking for several long moments, at first with anticipation and then with seeming confusion.

Anton finally gathered his scattered wits and said, "Please, come in and sit down. May I look at your CV?" He was startled by how hoarse his voice sounded. He studied the short, one-page resume for a longer time than he really needed. What he needed was the time to calm himself down.

Anton made note of the girl's name: Victoria Savelyeva. Victoria...he would call her Vika, Anton decided. Twenty-two years old; studied piano at a music school; took some vocal lessons and some drama lessons; also did some modeling, but nothing serious. Anton was surprised because with such a compelling face and figure, he would have expected her to be a movie star or perhaps a super-model by now.

The silence between them eventually became

oppressive and so Anton asked, "You graduated from the St. Petersburg music school; did you ever apply to the Conservatory?"

"No, I didn't," the girl replied. The haunting tone of her low, melodic voice sent shivers down Anton's spine.

"My father was ill for a long time. My mother was looking after him and I had to help her to provide for our family. I have two younger sisters," Victoria explained.

"How is your father now?" Anton asked as compassionately as he could.

"He passed away half-a-year ago. My mother has a job and one of my sisters is working now too. So, I am free to pursue my own career aspirations. I would like to apply to your school."

"Excellent! So, what are your career aspirations?"

"I would like to be a singer...an actress..."

"Victoria, please make up your mind," Anton smiled and asked, "do you want to sing or do you want to act?"

"Can't I do both?" the girl asked timidly.

"Hmm... Are we talking musical theatre here? Do you have with you your audition tape?"

"Yes, I certainly do." Victoria smiled, and now seemed much more relaxed after the initial tension of their meeting encounter had passed.

For the next ten minutes or so, Anton listened to Victoria's singing and watched her acting. The tape was an excerpt from some amateur production of Kalman's operetta, *Countess Maritza*. Her voice wasn't bad, Anton thought. Definitely it wasn't Nina's voice; it was lacking the strength and the depth, but then again, Nina's voice was unique.

Victoria could certainly sing in some rock band, Anton mused, but then he envisioned the members of that imaginary band and their fans pawing Victoria and felt nauseated. *She certainly could act too. I could secure a role in movies for her*. Anton continued thinking through the possibilities but then dismissed that idea as well. The truth was, Anton had to admit, he didn't want Victoria to be on a stage at all; he didn't want to share her with anybody else. He wanted...no...he *needed* her to be his woman, his wife, and the mother of his future children.

Anton was frantically considering how to secure Victoria's personal attention and to keep her close to him until ultimately, he could win her love. He considered his words very carefully. He needed to dissuade Victoria from trying to develop a career in show business, but without frustrating her to such an extreme that she would get up and leave his office. Anton decided to compliment her first, before rejecting her, at least on the surface, but then also to find some way to see her on a daily basis so he would have an opportunity to woo her.

"Victoria, you are a talented young lady. Talented and beautiful. I'm sure you've heard compliments about your good looks numerous times from others, so let's talk about your talent instead. May I be honest and straightforward with you?"

"Yes, of course," Victoria replied earnestly.

"Good. Then I'll be totally frank. You have more beauty than talent and that's a dangerous combination. People might offer you a role in a movie or a theatre production and hint that you owe them a special favour, if you know what I mean. You'd never know if some agent hired you because of your suitability for a role, or because he expected some additional 'service' from you. You don't have enough talent, my dear, to be a major star and at best you'd always be relegated to playing secondary roles. Quite honestly, Victoria, a rather bleak future is before you as far as acting is concerned, and probably with constant dependency on some greedy, immoral men. I'm truly sorry, dear; do you understand what I'm saying?"

"I suppose you're hinting that I have to perform

some favours for you in order to be admitted to your school, is that right?" Victoria responded in an agitated voice as she rose from her chair.

"That's not the case at all, Victoria. Please, sit back down. What I'm saying is that I wouldn't admit you to my school or sign you with my agency even if you offered me such favours. I do like you and I admire you very much, Victoria. It takes a special kind of person to sacrifice some of the best years of her life to help her family. You are a caring, generous person and I don't want anything bad to happen to you. Show business, unfortunately, can be very cruel, especially to such a beautiful and good person as you."

Anton continued. "I sincerely do want to help you, so I would like to offer you a position as my personal assistant. I'm swamped with applicants, with interviews, and with the administration of the agency and the school. I miss some very important meetings; I anger people vital to my business because of double-booking of appointments or simply forgetting about them. So, as you can imagine, I'm very much in need of a competent personal assistant.

"Victoria, I'm going to let you in on some personal information. Many years ago, I graduated from the Moscow Conservatory and dreamt of becoming a concert pianist. Then reality interfered. I didn't succeed. Now I have a burning desire to help others succeed where I fell short. If you would be interested to help me and be a part of my mission, then here's my offer."

Victoria remained silent while Anton quickly scribbled a number on a slip of paper and moved it closer across his desk so that she could see what he had written.

When Victoria saw the amount of salary being offered, her eyes bulged and she reservedly asked, "Is this in rubles or in dollars?"

"It's in American dollars, Victoria. When can you

start?"

All at once a multitude of conflicting emotions overcame Victoria. Does this man sitting across me and patiently waiting for my answer have any idea what his words and his offer really mean to me?

From one side, she realized, it meant the crushing of all her childhood dreams and ambitions. As long as she could remember, she always dreamt of becoming an actress and her parents always encouraged her. Her father would put her on a chair and implore her to sing for their guests ever since she was six years old.

And after her little performance, the guests wold applaud loudly and roundly praise such a beautiful and talented girl. Then came the school theatre with enthusiastic commendations from her teachers. Her vocal coach predicted a bright future for Victoria. She was told by her parents, her teachers, and her school friends that she would enjoy a life of fame and glamour! Glamour indeed...

Her parents had taken it upon themselves long ago to decide on the future professions for their three daughters. Victoria, being the most beautiful and talented, would be an actress. Tamara, with her quick and inquisitive mind – an engineer; and Maya, the smartest and the most studious of the three girls – a medical doctor.

Her father's long and difficult illness had put an end to all their dreams. The money that had been saved for the girls' education was spent on the doctors and for some rare miracle remedies that cost an enormous amount of money and helped very little to alleviate her father's suffering.

Finally, when it became impossible to care for her father at home any longer, her mother placed him in a hospital and secured a job there as an orderly. She was relieved that she managed to 'kill two birds with one stone'. She could earn some money to provide for her family and still remain close to her ailing husband.

After Victoria finished school, her mother helped her to get a job as an orderly in the same hospital. Now, mother and daughter could take shifts looking after their dear patient and raising two younger school-girls.

Tamara completed her high school studies but had to forget about going to college and got a job on an assembly line in a factory. She was still talking about starting some evening courses sometime in the future, but for now money was very tight.

Maya, the youngest of the girls, was still in school and was still dreaming of becoming a doctor, but how realistic was that?

In the recent months, Victoria had visited several agencies in her spare time. At the first agency she visited, the manager told her that it would be very easy to get her into modelling. "*Just a snap,*" the confident woman said, but Victoria didn't hear from her again.

At another agency, a kindly older gentleman who had been highly recommended to Victoria, promised her a part in a movie. He never called...

Then there was a third, and also a fourth agency. In each case the agency representatives were congenial and praised Victoria's good looks and talent. They accepted her CV and promised to be in touch. Nothing happened.

Maybe, Victoria thought, *this man, looking right now at me with such compassion and understanding, is the only honest man I've met. I want to be an actress! So are thousands of other pretty girls. How many of us have a real talent? How many of us will make it? Meanwhile, I have a very attractive offer before me. This money would help my family a great deal; it will allow Maya to have the opportunity to go to college. At least one of us...*

Having patiently waited for a response, Anton rose from his chair and asked Victoria in a kindly voice, "Well then, what have you decided, Ms. Savelyeva?"

"Tomorrow, Mr. Zubov! If that's alright with you. I can start tomorrow. Thank you very much and I promise not to disappoint you. It's very noble of you to help young artists. Other agents can be so ruthless and unfeeling; trust me, I know. Your agency is providing a very worthwhile service and I am gratified that you are letting me be a part of it."

As soon as Victoria took her leave from Anton's office, she ran off to the hospital to begin what would be her last shift.

The next morning, a new desk was in place just outside of Anton's office and Victoria started her duties. Valentina regarded the new hire with more than a little suspicion but she had learned long ago not to contradict or question her brother's motives. Victoria's outgoing and sunny personality helped ease the transition and before long the two women actually became quite good friends.

Ω

The first group of eight students at the school had been studying for almost three months. Whenever Anton was attending their rehearsals, he felt very proud of them. Instead of fumbling, awkward amateurs, they had become poised and confident professionals. But he still didn't have a prospective place of employment for some of the students. He could try to place the dancers and the musicians on cruise lines, but the Russian singers were a problem.

Anton summoned all the students and their instructors and offered them a plan. "What do you think about a tour of Russian cities? You're not ready for Moscow or St. Petersburg yet, but I could organize a tour in Saratov, Ryazan, Tula, Perm, and Irkutsk - cities like that."

He named the cities where he himself had toured

during his humble beginnings.

"Why don't you consider forming a band too?" he suggested.

"You've been working together for a while and it would be a shame to separate you right now. Why don't you start working on preparing a repertoire for a two-hour concert? I know that you don't have your own songs, but that will come. Select some popular songs, except not the latest hits. We don't want any copyright issues. Each singer should have his or her own solo and the dancers should have some numbers of their own as well. In addition, create some duets and choreograph dances for the songs. A good combination of dancing and singing on stage is always an irresistible crowd-pleaser. I'm prepared to give you two months to get your repertoire ready. If you agree, tomorrow Victoria and I will be starting to organize your tour."

"*The Summit!*" one of the female singers exclaimed.

"What?" Anton asked quizzically and everybody else gazed at the girl.

"I propose to name our new band *The Summit*. What do you think? It means almost the same as pinnacle: the peak of a mountain. That's what we want, to be on top, right?"

"I like it! I really like it!" the male singer exclaimed and then everyone was shouting and jumping about and rejoicing about the spontaneous founding of their new band. Anton regarded them with a benevolent smile - they were still a bunch of kids. He hoped that they would be mature enough to withstand the pressure of a tour; and for his part, he hoped that he could actually organize this tour as he had already promised.

One of the students ran to the local wine store and soon the birth of *The Summit* was being celebrated in style.

The next day Anton began the process of promoting the new band. It wasn't easy. He tried to make some arrangements with directors of theatres in some of those distant cities over the phone but he wasn't getting anywhere with those calls. The new band and the new show needed sponsorship too, but Anton didn't know how or where to begin to find it.

He decided to fly to every city on the proposed tour agenda and to meet personally with theatre directors and concert hall owners. Perhaps, Anton thought, he could marshal some local sponsorship as well.

He took his charming and beautiful personal assistant with him on the promotion trip and this certainly proved to be the right strategy. Anton's personal charisma and assertive business approach, combined with Victoria's captivating beauty, and the carefully edited video clips of *The Summit* did the trick. The doors started to open. The outline of the proposed tour started to shape up.

Anton was never pushy or forward with Victoria; he was always infinitely kind, gentle and patient. Victoria felt comfortable and secure with her new boss and before long she found herself always looking for him, wanting to be in his presence constantly. She tried to control her growing feelings and to convince herself that a romance with the boss was too trivial and too banal an affair which she must avoid, but soon she had to admit inwardly that she had fallen head over heels in love with Anton.

The inevitable happened in the middle of July, in Perm. Anton and Victoria had had a successful business meeting with the mayor of the city who wanted to promote art and culture in Perm and was enthusiastic about the upcoming concert of a new but promising band. After the meeting, they were invited for dinner, during which the mayor flirted with Victoria shamelessly, despite the presence of his wife. Victoria was in a carefree mood; she had a couple of drinks and found the antics of the mayor simply hilarious. She tried to be polite and even flirted in return a bit. After all, tomorrow they'd be leaving the city and she would never see that silly man again.

On their way back to the hotel, Anton was in a dark and gloomy mood in spite of the success of the day and Victoria sensed that it was somehow her fault. She started to apologize for her behaviour but Anton interrupted her, "Don't, Vika. Please, don't apologize. You're a free woman and you are at liberty to encourage the attention and affection of any man you choose. It's not your fault that I, an old fool, have fallen..."

He stopped in mid-sentence, but Victoria encouraged him to go on. "Anton, what were you about to say?"

"It doesn't matter, Vika. You're working for me and I don't want to complicate our relationship. We need to keep it strictly professional."

"We can't, Anton. We can't have a strictly professional relationship because ...I love you very much," Vika blurted out.

"You do?" Anton exclaimed joyfully and pulled Victoria closer to him. He cupped her face in his hands, looked intently into her eyes and then began kissing her. That first kiss began gently and only slightly probing, but soon it grew into something more demanding and compellingly passionate.

They found themselves in Anton's room and spent the entire night making love. Early the next morning, Anton cautiously asked Victoria if she was using some form of birth control.

"No, I'm not," she replied, somewhat apologetically. "I had no reason to for a long time. But I'll get a prescription and start as soon as we return to St. Petersburg."

"You don't have to, my love," Anton said. "With me, you have nothing to worry about."

"But you have a daughter, Anton."

"Yes I do, but I know what I'm talking about. Please, just trust me. Don't worry about a thing."

They returned to St. Petersburg triumphantly. The tour was fully organized and *The Summit* was scheduled to launch performances in September.

Nothing was said, but everyone noticed the meaningful change in the relationship between Anton and Victoria.

Valentina undertook to reason with her brother. "Anton, she's twenty years younger than you. Do you realize that? With her looks, she'll be cheating on you, or even worse! She'll leave you eventually for some young punk, you'll see. One way or another, she's going to hurt you one day! This romance is based solely on infatuation and can only end badly."

"Valentina, please, stop being so negative. Try to be happy for me instead. Finally I've found the woman of my dreams. She's perfect, I tell you, absolutely perfect! When I'm with her I forget about everything else. Please be nice to her. I'm depending on you, sis," Anton pleaded.

Valentina tried another approach, "OK, let's suppose for a second that things would work out between the two of you. Anton, Victoria is a young woman; inevitably, sooner or later, she would want to have children but you have a grown-up daughter. Isn't it much too late for you to be starting a new family?"

"I'll worry about that if and when it happens," Anton replied, shrugging his shoulders casually. It was just an act. Anton was not indifferent to the possibility of having more children. In reality, he was passionately determined to become a father again. But how could he explain to his sister that the fact that Nina and Anatoly had three young children was torturing him? It was just not fair that Nina had three children, and he, Anatoly, only had one daughter. Why should that woman enjoy such fame, wealth, and everything she could wish for, while he was only now starting his business career and working so hard for every ruble? Couldn't he at least have the same number of children as Nina?

He didn't reveal such deeply personal thoughts and the nature of his tormenting jealousy to Valentina. Instead, Anton asserted, "Valentina, I always wanted to have a large family but Carol was against it. So, let's see how everything goes."

Marek's perspective regarding this new state of affairs was not focussed on Victoria. "What about Susan, Anton? If it's over between the two of you, I'd like to have a go myself."

This time, Anton's tone of voice was deadly serious and indeed threatening. "Marek, on the same day Susan finds out anything about Victoria, you're not working for me any longer. Do you understand me? Not only that, I'll make sure that you never work in show business again, either in Russia or in the West. Have I made myself clear?"

"Hey, Anton, chill out! Susan is going to find out sooner or later from somebody else, if not from me. It's a small world in show business. You should know that."

"Well then, Marek, you should make every effort to prevent that from happening if you know what's good for you. "

Marek knew perfectly well what was good for him. He hoped that one day Anton would open a branch of the *Pinnacle Talent Agency* in Warsaw with himself acting as manager.

Cruise lines needed a lot of entertainers but it wasn't easy for new agencies to get their foot in the door. Anton was lucky in that regard; Susan opened those doors for him. Marek regarded his friend and boss as something of an unstoppable tank that makes its way over any rough terrain, sweeping away or crushing any obstacles that might be in its path. He intended to follow along closely behind this human tank and reap whatever riches fell his way. Anton's relationships with women were his own problems, and after this man-to-man talk Marek had no intention whatsoever to rock the boat.

Ω

In August Megan came to St. Petersburg for her summer vacation as she had planned with her father, and loving family members immediately surrounded her. Megan's grandparents and her aunt and uncle were constantly doting on her. Her cousins were eager to introduce Megan to the lively social life of the youth of St. Petersburg. Her father spent every free moment he could find with her and appointed his personal assistant as Megan's chaperone and tour guide.

If Megan had been harbouring some secret hope of persuading her father to return to Calgary, one look at Victoria had dispelled any such idea. She could see how Victoria looked fondly at her father and hear how she was talking about him with thinly veiled affection. Despite Victoria's attempts to present herself as a professional and respectful assistant, Megan could feel the admiration and, as a woman, readily perceive the love revealed in Victoria's eyes. Megan wasn't blind or naive. Her father's furtive looks at Victoria and his affectionate smiles whenever he thought that Megan wasn't watching – these signs all spoke volumes.

At first, Megan deeply resented Victoria. She couldn't help it. In her mind, she was comparing her efficient, disciplined, brisk and rigid mother with the sweet, kind, generous and, what must have been of greatest importance to her father, the very beautiful Victoria. Megan understood very well that her mother didn't have a hope of getting her husband back. It took time, but eventually Victoria's sweet disposition and easy-going manner won over the reticent teenager.

Megan hadn't had an easy year before she came for

this summer's vacation. Her well-established and secure life had crumbled and she was looking for somebody to blame. At first, she was sure that it was entirely her father's fault. Then she became angry with her mother too. Throughout the previous winter, Carol had persistently been agitated and snappy and Megan was on the receiving end of much of Carol's frustration. Now, Megan wanted some stability, some piece of mind, and she wanted someone close to talk with. Quite unexpectedly, she found a trusted friend in Victoria.

It was not that Megan confided personal matters to Victoria or talked to her new friend about her own family's problems. Quite simply, Megan enjoyed Victoria's company. Together they explored the magnificent city of St. Petersburg, its museums, palaces and cathedrals. Megan soon felt relaxed and comfortable in her new surroundings. She liked her relatives and enjoyed the cafés and clubs where her cousins took her. After being subjected to all the rules and regulations imposed upon her by her mother, Megan found life in Russia more easy-going, freer and much more exciting.

But beyond the attractions of the city, the warmth of her new relatives, and the friendship of Victoria, it was her father that held Megan's greatest attention. He had changed. Instead of the agreeable man who was always trying to avoid conflicts and was satisfied with his mundane job, she now saw him as a confident, successful and charismatic businessman. *Why wasn't he like that in Calgary,* Megan wondered? She liked the fact that everyone called him *Anton*, which she regarded as a much more suitable name for him than the anglicised 'Tony'.

When it eventually came time for Megan to return home to Calgary, she pleaded with her father, "Why can't I stay and live with you? I don't want to go back! Mom is impossible now; she's screaming at me all the time. I love it here in Russia."

"Pumpkin," Anton explained, "I can't let you stay here because of all the legal implications. After all, you're only fifteen, so that means you are still legally a minor. However, you can certainly come back here again for your winter holidays, if you would like that."

"Promise?"

"Yes, I promise, Megan. I need to go to Vancouver right away to sort out some business. So I can fly with you via Calgary and take you home. Would you like that?"

"Yes, daddy, that would be great!" Megan rejoiced at the prospect of her father accompanying her all the way home.

Anton was reluctant to leave the agency office when it was so close to the start-date of *The Summit's* Russian tour and he hated the idea of parting even temporarily with Victoria, but he had no choice: he needed to meet with his lawyer in Calgary and he wanted to personally deliver the video clips of his new talent discoveries to Susan. Susan was becoming impatient over his long absence and it would not be a good idea to aggravate her - too much of Anton's business still depended on her.

The first stop was Calgary. They took a taxi from the airport and Anton personally delivered Megan home. He got out of the taxi and retrieved Megan's suitcases from the trunk. When he lifted his head, he could see Carol now standing on the porch.

"Can we talk, Tony?" she asked from a distance.

"No need, Carol," Anton replied dismissively, as he waved his hand to Megan and hastily jumped back into the taxi.

He didn't need any complications. All that Anton wanted from Carol was a divorce and a lucrative settlement.

After a short stop at his lawyer's office, all his business in Calgary was done. During the flight to

Vancouver Anton thought about Susan and about Victoria. He should be honest with Susan, he decided, and let her know about Victoria right away.

But when he strode out of the airport and saw how Susan's face lit up with the joy of seeing him after much anticipation, Anton decided to defer his confession. The poor woman deserved to have some happiness in her life before he brought her dreams crashing down.

The night with Susan was actually quite pleasant. Anton loved to be pampered by her and enjoyed her eager ministrations.

In the morning, they had to attend to business and there was simply no time for a serious talk. A week later, Anton was getting ready to fly back to Russia. His trip had been quite successful. Susan had accepted almost all of the performers suggested by him. Several individuals, whom Anton considered to be the best of the lot, were placed right away with the Princess Cruise Line via the *Pinnacle Talent Agency.*

On his last night in Vancouver, while lying in Susan's bed, Anton was searching desperately for the right words to tell Susan that from now on, their relationship would need to be confined to a strictly professional level only. But with Susan cuddling to him, so happy and so content, Anton just couldn't bring himself to spoil her mood.

After all, he decided, it would not be a gentlemanly deed to spend an intimate week with a woman, conduct business with her, and then break her heart at the very moment before his departure. A gentleman wouldn't do that and he, Anton, considered himself to be a true gentleman. He kissed Susan gently and rather easily fell sound asleep.

The next morning, Anton departed for Russia without saying a word to Susan about his love affair with Victoria.

Anton returned to St. Petersburg in time to join *The*

Summit for the beginning of their tour. Victoria, as might be expected, asked to accompany him. Their reunion was so warm, loving and passionate that all of Anton's thoughts and memories about Susan and his trip to Vancouver were quickly forgotten.

Ω

The tour got underway with an uneasy sense of anxiety, at least from Anton's point of view. Despite extensive advertisements and promotions, ticket sales had been sluggish. Few people had heard of *The Summit* or any of the members of the band.

The day before the first concert, Anton and Victoria went out for dinner alone. Anton was in a very contemplative mood and Victoria didn't want to disturb his thoughts. They ate in virtual silence.

But when desert was eventually served, Anton looked earnestly at Victoria and said with conviction and passion, "Do you understand why I'm doing this? Marek doesn't. He's told me again and again that we should just concentrate on finding ready entertainers for cruise lines, place them, get our commissions and have no worries in the world.

"He's right in a way. It's a whole lot easier to be a booking agent than a real impresario. The money's good and the outcome is predictable. But I had all that, Vika! I've had fifteen years of the good and the predictable. Let me tell you something - it's utterly boring. I'm done with predictability and with mediocrity. I want to become one of the best impresarios in the country; I want the biggest stars of show business to knock on my door. I want it all! Is it wrong of me to have such passionate desire and ambition?"

"Not at all, Anton, and I'm sure that you'll achieve your goal. You have the drive, the charisma, and the desire. You attract good people and people like working with you. I do believe in you, Anton."

Victoria felt silent as she stared back at him with adoring eyes and at that moment she had only one aspiration: to be a permanent part of the life of this incredible man.

They drank to the success of *The Summit* and the *Pinnacle Talent Agency.*

The next evening, the disheartened band found themselves facing a half-empty concert hall. Anton gathered his troops and told them, "I've done my part. But that's only half of the job. The other half is now up to you. Go out there and get them. Perform like you'd perform before a full house. Let the walls shudder from their applause."

The young artists nervously nodded their heads and then, when they were on the stage, performed admirably and even beyond Anton's expectations. At the conclusion of the concert the small audience applauded for so long and so enthusiastically that the group was obliged to perform two additional 'curtain call' songs.

The morning after the highly successful premiere concert, Anton went to the local radio station and to the local newspaper. He wanted to make sure that the city was aware of the prior evening's big success. Nobody could be sure just what had worked best, whether it was Anton's public relations initiatives with the local media or word-of-mouth, but the next evening the hall was at least three-quarters occupied. This performance was even better than on the first night. The young artists were rapidly becoming more confident in front of a larger audience and their spirits were already buoyed by their initial success.

Immediately after that second concert, the manager of the theatre approached Anton and asked him if the band would be willing to perform an unscheduled concert the next day.

"I know that we had arrangements for only two

nights but the public in the city have just discovered *The Summit*. I can guarantee you that tomorrow you'll have a full house. If I give you a substantial discount on tomorrow's rent for the concert hall, would you give one more performance?"

"Let's go and talk to the band," Anton cautiously replied, and so together they went to speak with the members of The *Summit*. Anton needed that extra performance desperately. So far, he was losing money on this tour; ticket sales from the first two performances weren't covering all of his expenses and that additional bonus concert would really help to balance his books.

However, he knew that the artists were drained – both physically and emotionally, and that they would only have two days of rest before their scheduled performance in the next city. He found them still lounging backstage, too spent emotionally and just too tired to move.

"Congratulations! You did it! Only several months ago you were fumbling dreamers and today you're a successful group. However, with big success comes big responsibility. You're invited to perform here again tomorrow. The theatre management guarantees a full house. Let's not disappoint your new-found fans. Success is a capricious thing, so it's not a good idea to turn your back on it."

One after another, the artists nodded their heads in agreement. The third concert was performed before a packed house and was an immense success.

Events unfolded in the second and the third cities similarly, but by the time they arrived in Irkutsk, their fourth stop, advance word had reached the city and attendance was much better, even for the first evening.

Ω

The participants of the tour were in a state of a

constant euphoria; things were going even better than anticipated. And so, Anton was quite surprised one morning when he found Vika quietly crying.

"What's troubling you, my dear?" Anton asked anxiously.

"You told me that I had nothing to worry about but I'm pregnant," the sobbing girl responded.

"I didn't tell you that I couldn't have children. I told you that you had nothing to worry about because I wouldn't let anything bad happen to you," Anton said compassionately. He took hold of Victoria's hand and started to kiss it tenderly.

"Don't you want to have my child? Don't you love me?" he anxiously asked her.

"You know that I do! But we're not married, and..."

'Shhhh..." Anton whispered, while restraining her from talking by pressing a finger gently against her lips. He took a small velvet box from his pocket and presented it to Victoria. "I wanted to give this to you at the end of the tour after our return to St. Petersburg but I suppose now is as good a time as ever."

Victoria took the box and then opened it cautiously. With trembling hands she removed an exquisite diamond ring. She was mesmerized as she examined the unusually large, dazzling stone and she began to cry even harder.

Victoria cuddled up to Anton and buried her head on his chest. He took the ring from her hand, placed it on her finger and said, "Don't cry my beautiful bride. You have to think about our baby."

Victoria returned home alone on the next flight to St. Petersburg, while Anton stayed on with the band for the remainder of the tour.

The next day, Marek called to congratulate Anton. "My best wishes, mate! I don't know how you do it! The most beautiful women are falling down at your feet. One day you'll have to give me some coaching!"

"I don't think you need any lessons from me," Anton chuckled.

"By the way, Anton, where did you find that ring? I saw a similar one in the *Statendam* cruise ship jewellery shop. Do they have the same rings in Irkutsk?"

"I bought it the last time I was in Vancouver," Anton replied casually.

"While seeing Susan? You really are something! But why did you keep it all this time?"

"I wanted to make sure that Victoria was pregnant. There'd be no point in marrying a barren woman, would there?"

"You're the most callous man I have ever met, Anton. You have won my complete admiration," Marek said mockingly.

"You're wrong about me, Marek. I love my Victoria very much. But what can I do? I'm a soft-hearted man and I don't want to break Susan's heart."

"Or your business arrangement!" Marek laughed uproariously.

"Discretion, my friend, discretion," Anton reminded him and they ended the conversation.

Finally, lady luck had smiled upon Anton. Everything was going his way. His divorce was finalized and the satisfactory settlement that he received from Carol was deposited in the bank. He was marrying the most beautiful young woman in the world and she was expecting his child. His parents and sister adored Victoria and Victoria's mother really liked him too. Anton took that as a good omen. Mothers always know. He remembered Nina's mother and how cold the woman had always been towards him. Now everything would be different. Victoria had everything that Nina possessed, except Nina's overpowering ambition. Nina never loved him as much as his Victoria did, Anton concluded with a sense of immense satisfaction.

The growth of the agency and the school had

exceeded even Anton's expectations. After their return home to St. Petersburg, *The Summit* was offered a recording contract. A young but very promising composer (a protégé of Sorokin) started to work on a new repertoire for the band. A well-known producer of music videos had also offered his services. The group was completely booked for the next twelve months.

The success of band was of three-fold benefit to Anton. The *Pinnacle School* gained some recognition and quite a few new hopefuls had enrolled. Most of the new students paid their own way and only a few were picked up and funded by the agency. The school was well on its way to becoming a profitable enterprise.

More and more young, aspiring talents were coming to the agency too. Anton had his pick of future cruise entertainers. He also had started to promote a young woman with a beautiful voice who had good potential of becoming a rock star. Undoubtedly, she required a lot of coaching but Anton had high hopes for her.

The most important aspect of his overall success was the fact that he was now making some serious money.

Anton decided to acquire new, expanded quarters for the school and to move his agency to the cultural center of the city where most of other agencies were located. This time he had no problem obtaining a mortgage for his school. In fact, the director of the bank had invited Anton to his office and encouraged him to seek the services of his bank whenever the need arose. The banker, Georgiy Ivanovich, and Anton discovered that they had a great deal in common, and so after the business part of the visit was over, the two gentlemen decided to continue their conversation over a relaxing lunch.

Before long, Anton and Georgy became good friends, and Anton invited Georgiy and all his family to his wedding with Victoria. Georgiy came with his grown son from his previous marriage, his own young wife, and a small daughter. Now it was obvious what the two men had in common: they were both married to much younger, beautiful women and were starting their new families at the age when most men were becoming 'empty-nesters'.

Anton wanted a small quiet wedding, nothing extravagant, but his employees, friends and relatives had other ideas. The reception for the large group of guests was held in the spacious premises of the new school and the students and agency clients organized an improvised concert. It was an event to remember.

The wedding took place during the winter holidays, and to Anton's great delight, Megan attended the wedding and stayed for another two weeks in Russia. At the end of her visit, Anton flew to Canada with Megan again and then stopped off in Vancouver to conduct some further business with Susan's agency. Somehow, the subject of his new marital status never came up.

Cyprus

In May Victoria delivered a healthy baby boy and they named him Oleg. When Victoria and the baby were discharged from the hospital, a big surprise had been prepared for them by the proud Anton. Instead of returning to their small rented apartment, Anton drove them to his large new condo that was located in the most prestigious neighborhood of St. Petersburg. An emotional Victoria inspected her new home and exclaimed, "I don't know what I did to deserve all of this, and most of all what I did to deserve you, my darling!"

Anton could have purchased this condo with his settlement money, but he astutely decided to leverage his resources and had arranged a mortgage with his banker friend, Georgiy. After the men had concluded their business, Georgiy asked Anton for a favour.

"My son, Peter," Georgiy said, "has just graduated from university. His major was in business and finance. In addition, he took some courses in marketing. He wanted to go to grad school, but I suggested to him that he get a job and continue his education in the evenings.

Anton, would you hire him? I could easily place him in some large corporation, but I would prefer that Peter work in a small, but growing, dynamic and entrepreneurial firm. He's a very bright fellow and he could help you organize your accounting department. What do you think?"

Anton wasn't entirely thrilled with this idea, as he was not sure that he wanted his banker to be privy to all his financial affairs, but he saw no expedient way out - he needed Georgiy and his bank. In a country where the right connections determine the success or the failure of any enterprise, one does not casually say *no* to an important business associate.

Anton slowly nursed his drink, taking his time before giving an answer, and then finally he nodded his head and responded, "Of course, my friend. No problem. To be honest we're a bit too small to have a financial director, but I'm sure my company will grow and Peter will grow with it."

"Splendid!" Georgiy enthused. "One more thing, Anton. I have a house in Cyprus. My wife and my daughter live there on a permanent basis and I visit them whenever I can. Every year I spend a month in the summer there. I'm leaving for Cyprus at the beginning of August. We'd like to invite you and your family to spend August with us. Anton, you're working too hard. You could do with a good vacation."

"Thank you so much, Georgiy, but Megan is coming from Canada to spend August with me," Anton politely declined the offer.

"In my house there's enough space for everybody. Bring Megan with you."

"I've never left the agency for a month before," Anton mused contemplatively.

"Have you ever heard of cell phones and e-mails?" Georgiy insisted.

Anton thought about the Mediterranean Sea, a nice sandy beach, and his beautiful, tanned Victoria lying in the warm sand. He smiled and said, "Thank you again for your generous invitation, my friend. We'll be there."

Ω

The Zubovs fell in love with Cyprus right away. They liked the old city with its cobblestone streets and small cafés, and the contrasting modern district with its fashionable shops. They liked the beaches, the local food, and Georgiy's mansion; but more than anything else, they loved the way quite a few wealthy, ex-patriot

Russians were living there in grand style.

Anton was amazed when he discovered this large and vibrant Russian community in Cyprus. In many cases, the wives and children of prosperous businessmen were living there the entire year, while the husbands conducted their businesses in Russia and elsewhere, coming to visit their families whenever they could. This arrangement seemed eminently suitable for these prosperous *new Russians*. The wives were enjoying lives of luxury and leisure and the children were attending private English schools. The men could concentrate on business, working long hours and knowing that their families were out of harm's way from the turbulent and often dangerous life in Russia.

Georgiy's kind invitation became more explainable when Anton realized that Liza, Georgiy's young wife, was somewhat bored and was craving for compatible female company. Liza and Victoria quickly became close friends. They spent much of their time together, which allowed their husbands time to attend to their business interests, even during their vacation.

Megan loved everything about Cyprus and her carefree life there. She adored her little brother and to Anton's considerable relief, quite liked her stepmother.

Anton's only worry of a sort was Megan's apparent infatuation with Georgiy's son. Peter liked the spunky, easy-going and pretty Canadian girl and the young people spent many hours together swimming, tanning on the beach or exploring the island. Anton wasn't terribly keen about this development. Peter was a grown man of twenty-three, while Megan was just an impressionable teenager of sixteen.

One day, Anton engaged Peter in a game of tennis and when they were alone, he quietly but firmly said, "Peter, you're the son of my good friend and I do like you. However, if you harm my little girl in any way, you're a dead man. Even your influential father won't be able to help you in that event. I do hope you understand what I'm saying."

Peter observed the intensity apparent in Anton's face and believed him. They resumed playing for a while in silence and then when they stopped to take a rest, Peter asked, "Why are you against Megan dating me?"

"I'm not actually against it," Anton replied. "Eventually you might be a good match for her, but for now she's much too young for you."

"Can I take her to the movies, at least?"

Anton looked at the younger man and deliberately said, "Fine. But remember, Peter, she is only sixteen."

With some boundaries established, Anton felt slightly better about this relationship. Nonetheless, he was relieved when August had passed and it was time for him to take Megan back to Canada. Victoria and little Oleg returned to St. Petersburg. The holidays were over.

Ω

Anton and Megan flew via Rome and there, at the Leonardo Da Vinci airport, Anton unexpectedly encountered the Russian businessmen with whom he had negotiated a contract in what by now seemed like another life. They recognized Anton and invited him and Megan to join them for quick meal. Megan preferred to read her book and remained sitting near the gate. Anton followed the men to the bar.

After drinks had been served, one of the Russian men asked, "Are you still working with those chaps Jeff and Bill?"

"No, I left that company. In fact, they played quite a dirty trick on me and I didn't receive any bonus for the deal we made with you."

"Oh yes, *the deal*! Good for Canada; rotten for us."

"Why is that? If I recall correctly, you should be getting enough products to cover all your construction needs and the price was more than fair too."

"That's right, but now they insist on signing a new contract that would allow them to build a manufacturing plant in Russia. At first, they'd be producing raw material only, but after that they could easily expand their facility and replicate whatever we're doing. They could wipe us out in two to three years, that's for sure."

"Then don't sign another contract with them."

"That's easy for you to say, but if we don't have a steady supply of the raw materials we need, then we'd have to stop our construction business right away. Heads they win; tails we lose, as it were."

"Can you stall them for several months?" Anton had a sudden flash of an idea and decided he could use this conversation to his advantage. In fact, he could kill two birds with one stone - make some easy money on the side, and at the same time, at long last, extract his revenge on Jeff and Bill.

"We could do that I suppose, but what would several months change?"

"It would give me enough time to arrange a better contract for you and establish shipment of the materials you need from a different source. I know all their competitors. When we were discussing the deal with you, Jeff and Bill were concerned about the competition and dissected every company that could potentially be interested in the Russian market. I know the names and the players," Anton lied. "Assuming we can come to some agreement on a brokerage fee for my services of course..."

An hour later, Anton and Megan were flying to Canada and Anton was in especially good spirits as he pondered his calculated scheme of revenge against his former colleagues.

After a quick stop in Calgary to deliver Megan, Anton flew on to Vancouver. He spent a day making phone calls and then organized a side-trip to the United

States. Susan decided to accompany Anton and he didn't mind at all having her as a companion for this trip.

Two weeks later Anton re-joined his family in St. Petersburg. He resumed his work at the agency, but was waiting impatiently for a particular phone call. He didn't have to wait for very long.

One afternoon, as Anton was reviewing the video-clips of potential future clients of his agency, his cell phone started to ring. He stopped the video, answered the phone and heard the familiar voice of his former associate Bill, shouting into the phone. "Bastard! Why would you do something like that? Do you have any idea how much money our company invested in that Russian enterprise?"

"Hello, Bill. I missed you too, buddy. I hope you don't mind that I finally collected my bonus," Anton said, calmly and caustically. Then he put his cell phone aside on the desk and proceeded to resume viewing the clips. When he eventually got tired of the yelling and screaming still emanating from the cell phone, Anton just switched it off, as if the brief conversation with Bill had never taken place.

In October Victoria informed Anton that she was expecting another baby and again she was thrilled by Anton's enthusiastic reaction. He kissed and hugged his wife and immediately called his parents to inform them of the wonderful news. Victoria considered herself to be the happiest and luckiest woman in the world.

That year the winter in St. Petersburg was exceptionally harsh, and most days Victoria could not even take little Oleg for a walk outdoors. So, when Georgiy's wife Liza invited Victoria and her son to spend some time in Cyprus, Victoria was happy and grateful to accept the invitation. In any event, Anton was working on several important deals, so he had little time to spend with the family, and Victoria didn't want to distract him from his important business affairs.

Megan again came to St. Petersburg for her winter holidays and to Anton's delight, she insisted on speaking with him in Russian.

"I studied very hard, Daddy," she boasted. "I dropped jazz class to have time to study Russian. Mom is *so* mad at me!"

Anton understood full well that Megan's newly found interest in the Russian language was not for his benefit, but rather for Peter's. Like any father of a teenage girl, Anton came to realize that he had little choice but to accept Peter's attention and apparent affection towards his daughter as an inevitable fact of life.

One day Georgiy invited Anton for lunch and told him about a fabulous house in Cyprus that had just come on the market. The banker suggested that Anton should seriously consider buying it.

Anton smiled at his banker and said, "I'm not in your league yet, my friend! Maybe in three to five years I'll be able to start thinking about a second house, provided that business is still good. But not right now."

"In three to five years there probably won't be such an incredible opportunity. One of the bank's clients is in financial difficulty and must sell his house immediately. Anton, you could buy that house at well below its true market value. Trust me, it's a steal. Prices in Cyprus are going up an up because of the steady influx of new Russians. Think about it as a great investment. Furthermore, there are some additional intangible benefits," Georgiy urged Anton along.

"What sort of intangible benefits?" Anton inquired, his interest now kindled.

"Your wife won't be under your feet. You could work long hours, you could travel, and you could dedicate all your time to developing your business without feeling guilty about coming home late, or about not spending enough time with your family. When you fly to Cyprus, you'll always be a welcome guest. It'll do wonders for your marriage."

The very next day Anton flew to Cyprus, spent several days with his family and in the end bought the house. Victoria loved it. The location was perfect, the ocean view outside of the house was magnificent, and the grand, spacious interior was in excellent condition too. Victoria pointed out that the swimming pool was too small, but this was a very minor drawback. Anton promised her that as soon as he could afford it, the pool would be enlarged. Victoria was overjoyed about the prospects of living in Cyprus instead of St. Petersburg. To be sure, she would miss Anton terribly, but he was an important man with great responsibilities and she rationalized that she had no right to usurp more of his time that he could spare. Liza had explained all of this to Victoria too.

Soon after that, Victoria delivered a second baby boy and Anton moved his family to Cyprus. Victoria's mother moved with them so that she could help Vika with the children. Her second daughter, Tamara, just recently got married; the youngest, Maya, was studying in the university and living in the dormitory. The girls could do without their mother for a year or two. After being in the presence of sick people for a long time, and working long and arduous shifts in the hospital, the woman was very much looking forward to her new life in Cyprus.

Meanwhile, Anton became quite the international traveler. He was constantly on the go. He opened a branch of his agency in Warsaw, Poland, and an overjoyed Marek took up the management of that office, just as he had always hoped. However, knowing something about Marek's character traits, Anton made frequent visits to Warsaw to make sure the office was running smoothly.

He traveled often to international talent

competitions to scout for young entertainment prospects. Sometimes he accompanied his client performers during their tours as well. He also visited Canada several times a year, and of course, despite all his travels, he spent as much time as he could in Cyprus with his beloved wife and his two sons.

Carina

One day a new, young hopeful appeared at Anton's office. By now he had several other employees to conduct initial screening interviews, and never got involved unless the prospective client was already approved for his consideration. However, this young lady was very insistent and somehow managed to bypass all the obstacles to an audience in his office.

Anton scrutinized the girl carefully. She was pretty enough, even if a bit too exotic for his taste. His quick mind assessed the young woman standing before him with her fancy hairdo, large dark eyes accentuated by heavy make-up, and high cheekbones. She was dressed in an expensive designer suit, wore a stunning pair of alligator shoes and held a genuine Prada handbag. The countenance on her face was blatantly haughty and demanding.

Anton became angry with his secretary. The last thing he needed in his busy schedule was to deal with this evidently spoiled, rich-bitch girl. Nevertheless, more out of curiosity than anything else, he invited her to sit down, asked for her CV and politely inquired if she had an audition DVD with her.

He looked at the name: Carina Sukhmanova. The name was unfamiliar. He turned on the player and started the DVD. The girl's voice was at best mediocre, and her performance was atrocious. She had very limited talent and was obviously unschooled and outrageously arrogant.

No reason to beat around the bush, Anton decided. He looked directly at Carina and said, "I'm afraid, dear, that you're not suitable for our agency. Because the performing arts are a very subjective matter, I recommend you try somewhere else."

The girl didn't seem to be the least bit upset or surprised by Anton's negative verdict. She didn't jump from her chair or start crying, as so many other applicants might have done. Instead, she nodded her head in seemingly petulant acceptance and asked, "How about your school then? I don't mind studying and I can afford the tuition."

"I'm sorry, Carina. The school is completely full right now and we won't be accepting new applicants until next year."

He got up as if to demonstrate to the girl that the interview was over and opened the office door for her to leave.

When Anton returned to his chair he was fuming. What a waste of time! He buzzed his secretary, ready to scold her, but instead of his secretary a very distinguished gentleman entered the room.

The man smiled to Anton as if to an old friend and casually asked, "So, Anton, you've rejected Carina. Does my daughter have any sort of talent?"

"I'm sorry, sir," Anton said, taken aback by the man's familiarity, "I haven't had the pleasure of meeting you."

"Oh, I'm so sorry. I was sure that Carina would have introduced herself."

The man presented Anton with his business card and sat down comfortably in a chair. He projected an air of infinite confidence and authority.

Anton scrutinized the name on the card and hastily got up from his chair but then just as quickly sat down again and looked at his visitor in utter shock and dismay. Anton knew this name. The entire country knew the name of Vladimir Alekseevich Sukhmanov, the industrialist, the owner of numerous factories and plants, an oligarch, and one of the richest men in Russia.

Finally, Anton stammered, "I'm sorry Vladimir Alekseevich, I didn't make the connection. I didn't realize that Carina was your daughter."

Sukhmanov regarded the fidgeting Anton and calmly asked, "Would your answer to Carina have been any different if you had known that she was my daughter?"

Anton thought about that leading question for a moment and honestly answered, "No, quite frankly it wouldn't. You have a lovely daughter, Vladimir Alekseevich, but…"

"But absolutely devoid of any form of talent," Sukhmanov completed the sentence for Anton.

Anton smiled apologetically, sighed and silently nodded his head in reluctant acquiescence.

"It's her mother's fault," Sukhmanov confided. "Ever since Carina was a toddler, she loved jumping around and singing. As far as I was concerned, she was screeching, but my wife insisted that this was Carina's way of expressing herself and that the girl was destined to become a rock star. And now my daughter actually believes that folly and desires nothing else but to become a rock star."

"Well, Vladimir Alekseevich, I understand you're in a difficult position. I have a young daughter myself and I know how difficult it is to deny her anything, but…"

Again, Anton was interrupted. "If I may correct you, Anton, we are both in a difficult position. You see, I'm not used denying my daughter anything that she wants and especially not her lifelong dream.

"However, I believe that we can be of tremendous help to each other. I could help you with your difficult position and at the same time you could help me with mine."

"I don't think that my position is that difficult," a somewhat bewildered Anton replied.

"Permit me to disagree with you, dear Mr. Zubov. You've overextended yourself, Anton, really overextended. Let me think… the large mortgage on the school building, the expensive office and a large staff of employees. And then of course there's the mortgage on your luxury condo in St. Petersburg. Whatever was left from your settlement from the generous Mrs. Walker has been spent on your house in Cyprus and that's left you without any financial reserve. It must be expensive to keep up two households. The house in Cyprus was a mistake, Anton. A folly."

"It was a good investment. The prices in Cyprus are going up," Anton stuttered, appalled that Sukhmanov knew so much about his personal life and his finances.

"Well, those were exactly the thoughts of the previous owner of your house. But what would happen, if you, like him, faced some overwhelming financial challenges? After all, Anton, your income depends on several good performers and the goodwill of Ms. Harper. But a couple of unsuccessful concerts, God forbid, or if your new lady singer, you know - the one you've invested in so heavily, becomes pregnant or depressed, and then you, Anton, are in for major trouble."

Anton became pale. In his mind, all these horrendous prospects were already becoming a pressing concern, and with growing apprehension he looked at Carina's father, seeking some indication of the prospective solution to his predicament.

Sukhmanov smiled encouragingly and said, "But I want you to know that I'm willing to help you. From now on, your problems are my problems. On the day my Carina wins the Jurmala Young Pop Singer Competition, the mortgage on your condo will be paid off in full. When my Carina is invited and performs during the New Year's Concert and the Songs of the Year Gala, the school building is mortgage-free as well. Do we have an agreement, Anton?"

"I do have to think about it and consult my employees," Anton hedged. May I give you an answer tomorrow?"

"Of course you can, my friend. I can guarantee you that if nothing else Carina is very determined and will work very hard. If you need to hire additional staff to coach her, that wouldn't be an issue. You'll have access to any resources you need, but in one year my Carina must be an established rock star."

Sukhmanov rose from the chair, curtly nodded to Anton and made his own way out of the office.

Anton remained sitting, unmoving, contemplating how he could politely say *no* to Sukhmanov without the risk of destroying his business and his future.

Moments later, his phone rang. Anton wanted to ignore it but noticed that it was his Cyprus number. Victoria phoned his office very rarely, so Anton picked up the phone, slightly alarmed.

Victoria sounded jubilant, "Thank you, Anton! Thank you so much, darling. It's so considerate and generous of you to decide to enlarge the pool right now."

Anton's hands started to tremble. Very cautiously, he asked, "Did the workers show up already?"

"Yes, darling. They were working all morning. They've excavated the existing pool and left a very large hole. Are they going to come tomorrow to start construction? I hope it won't take too much time. The backyard is a complete mess and I can't allow the boys to play there when it's in such a state. I tried to find out from the workers when they were coming back but I didn't understand a word of what they said. I suppose I'll have to start learning some everyday Greek."

Anton wasn't listening to Victoria's chatter any longer. He had made up his mind. In fact, although he had no way of knowing it at the time, his mind had been made up for him that very morning when the unexpected workers had come to excavate his old pool. He interrupted Victoria and calmly said, "I'm not sure, Vika, if the workers will come tomorrow, but I can guarantee you that by the day after tomorrow they'll resume their work and the pool renovation will be completed in no time at all."

He finished the conversation with his wife and called his secretary's line. "Please invite Valentina and all the senior staff of the school to my office. I need them here as soon as possible. Tell them that it's an emergency meeting."

When everyone had gathered in Anton's office, he played Carina's DVD. He could hear the snickers but ignored them. When the short audition video ceased, Anton asked his collective staff, "What can we do with her?"

The vocal coach was first to respond, promptly and definitively, "Not one thing."

The image consultant then volunteered his opinion. "We can use this DVD video during our classes to clearly demonstrate what *not* to do."

The dance instructor was less congenial than the others and bluntly asked, "Is this a joke or a test? Anton, you know how busy we all are. Why do you waste our time with this nonsense?"

Only Valentina noticed how serious and preoccupied Anton appeared to be and asked, "What do you actually want us to do with this girl? You know as well as we do that she has a mediocre voice, her stage manners are atrocious, and her ability to act is non-existent, at least based on this clip."

"I want her, and in fact I need her to win the next Jurmala Young Pop Singer Competition. In addition, I want her to be invited to perform in the New Year's Concert and the Songs of the Year Gala," Anton solemnly explained.

With that, everyone, including Valentina, burst into raucous laughter. Soon, however, the staff observed that Anton retained the same melancholy expression and one after another they stopped laughing and looked questioningly at their boss.

Finally, the vocal coach guessed what the problem was and gloomily asked, "Whose daughter is she?"

"Sukhmanov's. We have no choice. If we don't deliver and don't make Carina into a super-star, we're doomed," Anton replied despondently. "At least I am. As far as you're concerned, you'll simply lose your jobs, no big deal," Anton concluded, impassively.

"We need Artemov," the image consultant said. "He's the best in our field. This task is far too much for me alone."

"Fair enough," Anton said. "Money, as you may surmise, is no object. I want a list of all the professional teachers and tutors that we need to engage, no matter what the cost. I need all your ideas and I need a plan of action by tomorrow morning. Make Carina Sukhmanova your top priority."

The next morning, Anton placed a call to Sukhmanov's office.

In a crisp rehearsed voice, the oligarch's secretary responded, "Vladimir Alekseevich is busy just now. Would you like to leave a message?"

"Yes, I would. Please tell Mr. Sukhmanov that Anton Matveevich Zubov called from the Pinnacle Talent Agency. Please inform your boss that we are prepared to enrol his daughter in our school and that we have qualified staff available and ready to commence Carina's lessons and intensive training."

In a markedly different tone of voice, the secretary courteously invited Anton to wait for a moment and almost immediately Sukhmanov himself came on the line.

"When can Carina get started?" he asked briskly.

"Tomorrow morning, first-thing," Anton answered, equally laconically, but then added, "there are only ten months left before Jurmala so we have no time to lose."

"Thank you, Anton. You won't be sorry that you're helping me with this predicament. You'll find me very grateful."

The following morning, Carina was seated on a chair in the middle of the large dance studio while a dozen pairs of eyes studied her scrupulously. All four walls of the room were lined with floor-to-ceiling mirrors and Carina could see her own reflection and the reflection of all those critically appraising eyes from every angle. It was evident from her expression that the girl felt intimidated and uncomfortable, perhaps for the first time in her sheltered life. Then she was asked to stand up, to walk, to raise her hand, to turn around, to jump, and finally, to sing a few lyrics.

Carina was then excused to take a break and the debate started in earnest amongst the staff.

"We have to play to her looks," someone suggested. "That's all we have."

"We can't make her look too sexy or vulgar - nothing too explicit. Otherwise her papa would ruin all of us," Anton advised the staff of his school and their newly-summoned advisers.

"Unpredictable and constantly changing, rather like a chameleon, that'll be her image," the expensive and sought-after Artemov announced. "One day she'll perform as a demure young girl and the next day she'll look like a sex-bomb. Well, almost a sex-bomb. Trust me; I'll make her look sexy and desirable to millions of men without the necessity for any vulgar or excessively revealing clothes. Let the public always guess who the real Carina may be and which flavour of Carina is going to perform in the next concert. Yes indeed, Carina will become the mysterious *Ms. Unpredictable*."

"That all sounds good, but what about her singing?" the newly-hired female vocal coach inquired pessimistically. The lady herself had just retired from a long and successful career as a singer and knew very well how overwhelming and practically impossible her new assignment was destined to be. For the moment, the question was left unresolved.

When Anton returned to his office late in the afternoon, there was a voicemail message waiting for him from his wife. "*The workers are here and they're making great progress.*"

The intensive training of Carina began the following day. Secretly, the teachers and professional advisors called the project '*Mission Impossible*'. Carina was required to spend ten-to-twelve hours, six days a week in the school. She had to forget everything that she knew or thought she knew about singing and about stage behaviour, and then to re-learn every aspect all over again from scratch.

The best people in show business were employed to work with Carina. A composer was hired to create a new repertoire for the girl that would best suit the limited range of her voice and what was to be her new image. Anton didn't sit on the sidelines either. He helped Carina to learn her new repertoire, practicing with her for hours on end. To his distinct surprise, she was working hard, listening to advice and following instructions, and actually making noticeable progress.

This pattern continued for a month, until one day Carina disappeared without explanation. Anton was frantic but all the other teachers rejoiced.

"Maybe she finally realized that she's not made for the stage," Artemov said philosophically.

Valentina added, "Anton, it's for the best. At least now, Carina's failure will not be our fault."

"I wish it could be that simple!" Anton groaned.

He had a difficult time concentrating on the business of the agency and he stopped sleeping. Finally, three days after the girl's disappearance, Anton called her father. He was not connected to the great man himself, but Sukhmanov's secretary said lightly, "Carinochka flew to Canary Islands for a vacation with her mother. She should be back in a week or two."

A week later, Carina innocently strolled into the school and announced that she was ready to resume her training. Anton was summoned and he asked the secretary to escort Carina into his office.

"Why are you wasting our time and your father's money if you aren't serious about your career?" Anton asked sternly.

"I worked way too hard last month. I needed a rest," she responded haughtily and unapologetically.

"So, any time you decide that you're tired, you'll just disappear, is that it?" an enraged Anton asked with growing impatience.

"If I want to go for vacation, I will," Carina replied unperturbed. "You still have to make me a star one way or another or you'll have to deal with my father."

"Just how do you envision that, Carina? Before each of your performances, let's say there'd be an announcement: "Presenting Carina Sukhmanova! She can't sing and she can't move on the stage for the life of her, but you must listen to her and you must watch and applaud her performance, or you'll have to deal with her father!"

Carina shrugged her shoulders defiantly and this gesture angered Anton even more.

"Your father can buy you the best teachers. He can bribe the jurors during the competition and you might even win it. None of that will make you a singer. A singer performs for a paying audience and only the public will decide if you're really a singer or not; they will decide whether to buy your CD's and videos or not, and whether or not they will pay good money to attend your concerts. Your father can't bribe or browbeat the entire country. It doesn't work that way, dear. So, I want to hear right now whether you are prepared to resume working hard without any further interruptions. Yes or no?"

Carina was not used to being spoken to in such a

stern tone of voice and was about to lash back in defiance. Then she reconsidered and answered dispassionately, "Fine, I'll work."

The lessons resumed in earnest and Carina kept her word. The entire team was working to the point of exhaustion and eventually they could perceive some visible results. Carina started to sing better and move about on the stage properly. Anton even dared to hold out some hope for her, but that was only until Carina unexpectedly disappeared again. This time her father called Anton and informed him of his daughter's badly needed vacation, which on this occasion was a Bahamas getaway.

"Anton, the poor girl is worn out. She needs a bit of a rest. Besides, Carina claims that she's ready for competition and for the big stage. Do you agree with her?"

"There's only one way to find out, Vladimir Alekseevich," Anton replied deferentially. "There'll be a regional competition in Saratov next month. I think Carina should compete. It would give her a better understanding of the process. She'd have the opportunity meet and interact with her competitors, so she'd have a better understanding of what to expect in Jurmala."

"Excellent idea, Anton," Sukhmanov enthused. "A dress rehearsal before the real battle."

When Anton communicated his plan before his team, everyone was aghast.

"She's not ready!" Valentina exclaimed.

"You're playing with fire," Artemov added, matter-of-factly.

The vocal coach was on the verge of tears of frustration. "I'm not used to being humiliated. It will be a total disaster."

"You're absolutely right, all of you," Anton replied gloomily. "It *will* be a disaster and a humiliation. But it's better to fail in Saratov than in Jurmala. Carina has to come to grips with reality, as does her doting father."

Carina returned from the Bahamas looking fresh and well-tanned. She calmly listened to the news of the upcoming regional competition and responded, "No problem, I'm ready."

"If you don't mind, dear, I'd like you to sing under some pretty pseudonym. Let's not reveal your identity just yet. How about *Alenushka*? Just this time, OK?"

"I don't care. *Alenushka* sounds fine to me."

Ω

Carina's smugness quickly vaporized when she was standing backstage and waiting for her turn to perform at the Saratov competition. One after another, young, talented singers took to the stage and demonstrated their prowess before the judges and the full auditorium audience.

Another young girl from the *Pinnacle School* received a standing ovation and Carina could hear numerous 'bravos'. Finally, it was her turn to perform. In the middle of her song somebody in the audience whistled with the sound of a catcall. Then, another patron began to laugh loudly. Red-faced and humiliated, Carina ran from the stage without finishing her performance.

"I hate you," she exclaimed angrily, facing her team of coaches. "I hate all of you! My father will destroy you!"

"There's still more than half-a-year before Jurmala," Anton said dispassionately, trying not to reveal his true emotions. "Carina, you can quit now, if you wish. You made some progress, but as you can tell it's not anywhere near enough. How serious are you about singing live on the stage? You are a Sukhmanova. The Sukhmanovs are not known to be quitters."

Anton was actually terrified. If Carina quit now after

this public humiliation, her father would never forgive him. At least Anton had been smart enough to have her sing under a pseudonym. Nobody connected this unfortunate contestant with the Sukhmanov name, but still...Anton found himself waiting anxiously for Carina's decision; the entire team was waiting for her decision.

"I'll continue my studies," the girl said defiantly, and there was the ferocious gleam of a true Sukhmanov in her eyes.

When the day of the Jurmala competition finally arrived, Anton was a nervous wreck. He was more worried and anxious than even the debutante herself, and more than the rest of the team put together. Only he understood what was really at stake. But, in the end, there was no reason to worry. The hard work of Carina and her dedicated coaching team had finally paid off. She was ready and she performed splendidly. Anton was astounded and ecstatic.

Carina won the public with her charm and beauty, and she won the judges with her professionalism and impeccable training.

When she demonstrated her gold medal to her happy entourage, it was difficult to determine who was happiest: the newly minted singer, her father, or her agent and his team of coaches.

Ω

The very next day after the competition, Anton received an anticipated and very welcome message from Georgiy: the remaining mortgage on his St. Petersburg condo had been paid off.

From that moment on, Carina was unstoppable. She was invited to the most prestigious concerts; song-writers were creating original compositions just for her to sing; and, her performance-time was completely booked for the next full year. Of course there were singers with a much better voice than hers. But Carina's combined strengths were her on-stage movements, her dancing, the control of her voice, and her perpetually shifting and unpredictable image, all of which added to the mystique of the phenomenon called Carina. Almost overnight she had become a true super-star.

After Carina's stunning performance in the most prestigious gala of the year, the Songs of the Year, Anton's large mortgage on the school building was promptly discharged.

The combined income from Carina's performances and the royalties from her CD's was far greater than all the income Anton was generating from a dozen of his other good clients.

Predictably, Carina became a very demanding and high-maintenance client, and so inevitably the majority of Anton's time was now taken up in promoting and managing her career.

One night after a highly successful concert, Carina showed up unannounced at Anton's hotel room and without speaking a word, calmly began to disrobe. Anton, being the gentleman that he was, considered that it would have been rude to say *no* to a lady.

The next morning, almost like clockwork Sukhmanov called Anton and bluntly asked, "So, did Carina finally get her way with you?"

The startled Anton began to apologize profusely but he was interrupted by her father.

"I have an untamed daughter and she always gets whatever she wants," Sukhmanov said, matter-of-factly. "But her wild days are almost over. She's had her fling with fame and it's time for her to settle down. In a year or so, Carina will be married and she'll be leaving the stage for good. In the meantime, enjoy and be nice to Carina, but remember that it won't last forever."

Her father was right. Anton's affair with Carina did

not last for long. For her there were many other more exciting conquests to be had besides her aging business agent.

One year later, Carina was indeed married to a very successful businessman and quit the stage.

Anton was sincerely sorry to see her go, not to mention the income he was losing, but his hands were full with other projects and more importantly, with plans for his own daughter's wedding.

Stars of Russia

After she graduated from high school in Calgary, Megan decided to enrol in the St. Petersburg University, in spite of Carol's many bitter protests and violent outbursts. And so, Megan came to Russia and moved in with her father and his family. Of course Anton was happy to be re-united with his daughter, but he knew very well that it wasn't himself or the university that was the real magnet in St. Petersburg. Megan and Peter were dating openly now and spent all of their leisure time together.

When Megan broached the subject of her moving in with Peter, Anton reacted firmly, "Not until you're married."

"I can't believe you, Dad! You are so old-fashioned," Megan protested. She was confident that Peter would support her wishes, but the last thing Peter wanted to do was to aggravate his boss and prospective father-in-law.

And so, nineteen-year-old Megan and twenty-six-year-old Peter announced their engagement and the family started preparations for the upcoming wedding. Anton couldn't have been happier. Megan's marriage to Peter ensured that she'd be staying in Russia. Peter was playing an important part in the agency and Anton was glad that the vital position of the financial director would be held by his son-in-law. The close connection with the bank through Peter's father couldn't harm the agency either.

But Carol went berserk. She accused Anton of orchestrating the whole thing, of stealing not only her money but also her daughter. Anton was surprised and amused. Until now he didn't even know that certain profane words existed in Carol's vocabulary, or that she could scream so loudly over the telephone.

The wedding took place in April of 2008 in St. Petersburg. It was a very beautiful white wedding followed by a fantastic reception. The food was fabulous, the entertainment first rate (as was to be expected), and the newlyweds were radiant. Everyone was happy, except the mother of the bride. Carol had come to Russia alone; her brother and the rest of her family had chosen not to attend the wedding. Carol was ice-cold with Peter, barely civil with his parents, completely ignored Anton and his family, and glared fiercely at Victoria and the children at every opportunity.

Everybody was immensely relieved when Carol left the reception early.

As Anton reflected after the wedding, it was a splendid affair.

He purchased a new car and a two-week cruise around the Mediterranean for the newlyweds. Peter's parents bought them a new condo in one of the better districts of St. Petersburg. Megan was starting her adult married life in style.

Ω

After Peter and Megan departed for their honeymoon, Anton accompanied Victoria and the children to Cyprus. Victoria had recently delivered their third child, this time a beautiful baby girl, and once again this made Anton a happy and proud man. He loved his wife more than ever. The three children didn't ruin her figure in the slightest; rather, they just made it a little bit shapelier and more feminine. At the age of twenty-seven Victoria was more gorgeous than ever. Motherhood and the life of leisure and luxury on Cyprus certainly agreed with her.

A local artist offered to paint Anton's portrait. He had already painted portraits of some of Anton's neighbours and Anton liked his work. The Russian residents of Cyprus had a lot of fun with these portraits and dressed up to pose for the artist in a variety of outlandish costumes.

Anton posed for his portrait as a Russian Tsar. He loved coming to Cyprus and seeing the large painting of 'Tsar Anton' surveying his realm. Yes indeed, the house on Cyprus had become his castle, his citadel, and his family was his court. From her designer crib, the newborn princess smiled so innocently and sweetly whenever her father came into view.

In spite of all that he had to be thankful for, Anton was not content. Consuming copious amounts of fine French cognac poured from antique crystal decanters, he fought frequent bouts of depression. He knew the reason why.

The *Pinnacle Talent Agency* was stagnating. And Anton was well aware that in the show-business industry stagnation was equivalent to decline. His agency was still almost entirely dependent on cruise line entertainers and second-rate artists. He hadn't found any new big name stars since the departure of Carina. In fact, being stuck with Carina throughout her heyday had hurt the agency in the long run.

Compounding Anton's troubles, *The Summit* band had become very demanding, fussy and too independent. They constantly complained that he didn't pay them enough attention, didn't promote them sufficiently, and made all the decisions for them, even though they weren't fumbling novices any longer. Their litany of complaints was too long to keep track of. In the end, they didn't re-sign with Anton's agency (ungrateful jerks). The lady singer that his school had trained long and hard, and whose career he had personally nurtured, followed the band's example by signing with another agency. Sure, quite a few of the artists with average talent had re-signed with his agency, but Anton couldn't come close to offsetting the loss of his two prime cash earners.

Why couldn't he attract or retain any genuine stars? Anton enviously observed that some other agencies had no more than a handful of clients, but were making much more money than he was.

And so, Anton started to nurture the idea of buying out another agency with well-established clientele. Such a shortcut – expansion by acquisition - was the best hope to give his business a much-needed boost.

He began to pay close attention to the *Stars of Russia* agency. It was one of the first talent agencies organized in Russia after perestroika and it had been consistently very successful. His former key clients, *The Summit* band and the lady singer, who Anton had hoped would be a big contributor to the future success of his own agency, had both signed on with the *Stars of Russia*.

An older man named Arkady Levitt operated the agency and his name was almost legendary in Russian show business. The *Stars of Russia* handled not only many Russian artists, but also some prominent international stars too. When Anton learned that Levitt's agency was handling all business conducted in Russia by *The Wandering Stars*, he became even more interested in the possibility of acquiring it, provided of course that the owner had any interest in selling his agency, as unlikely as that might be.

After careful consideration as to how to proceed, Anton hired a private detective to find out everything, both public and private information, that could be unearthed about the *Stars of Russia* and its owner.

Two weeks later, Anton had a confidential report on his desk.

Arkady Borisovich Levitt had been married to Faina Grigorievna for almost forty years. They had two grown daughters, both married with children and living in California. On a positive note from Anton's viewpoint,

Faina was spending at least half of her time in California and had been urging her husband to sell the business so that they could also emigrate to the United States.

Arkady had a serious heart condition but so far he apparently had not wanted to think about retirement...that is, until quite recently.

Arkady had just celebrated his sixty-ninth birthday and had promised his wife he'd retire before the end of the year. No one really believed he would follow through with that promise, even though behind the scenes he was currently discussing a possibility of the sale of his agency to the *Allure Agency,* owned by Efim Vernik.

The detective was even able to go as far as finding out the proposed selling price that was being discussed, but he assured Anton that the negotiations were still at a very early stage.

Anton became discouraged when he learned of the premium price under discussion, which was clearly out of his reach. But even so - nothing ventured, nothing gained - he resolved to proceed. And so he went ahead and made an appointment with Arkady Levitt.

Anton's strategy was to approach the celebrated agency owner as a humble supplicant with a less than prosperous competitive agency. He said nothing about his own prospective interest in purchasing the *Stars of Russia* agency; nor did he reveal his knowledge about Levitt's potentially looming retirement.

Instead, Anton deferentially asked for advice. "Arkady Borisovich, I want to understand what I'm doing wrong in running my agency and I would appreciate your advice. Why can't I retain my best clients?"

"It's because you're simply not suited for our business," was the immediate and blunt response.

Levitt then looked Anton in the eye. "You're an arrogant son of a bitch, Anton, and everyone knows it. You'll never attract or retain serious performers. Is that straightforward enough for you?"

"Yes, it certainly is. It's pretty hard to hear that, but thank you anyway." Anton's respectful smile revealed nothing of his chagrin. "I so admire your insight and experience. But please, can you be more specific? If I'm to make some changes for the better I should know what I ought to change. Please, Arkady Borisovich, your valuable opinion is of the utmost importance to me. I hadn't realized that I have such an unfavourable reputation in the industry. People must have told you a lot of uncomplimentary things about my agency and about myself, and that really disturbs me. You're my idol in this industry, you have my greatest respect, and your agency is a model of professionalism for me. So I'm humbly asking for your best advice."

The universal truth is that people are vulnerable to praise and love to receive compliments, no matter how gratuitous the source might be, and in that respect Levitt was no exception. Anton's display of humility and deference, and especially his praise of his competitor, pleased Levitt immensely and caused him to be more forthcoming with Anton.

"Well, maybe you can at least try to change," Levitt conceded without a lot of conviction. "You're still relatively young, Anton. You're dealing with creative people, very sensitive and emotional people who sacrifice their heart and soul during each recording, and especially during every live performance. They have fragile egos. You should nurture them, appeal to their egos, and deal with them as with capricious and demanding children. And what are you doing instead? You work them to exhaustion like a slave driver. You cause them to feel like they have no control whatsoever of their own career or their destiny.

"Your idea to help them with their image is a good one, but you must leave some room for their own creativity, allowing them sufficient freedom for making some decisions. Don't ever tell them what they must do. Instead of that, position your suggestions to them in such a way that they're convinced that these were their own ideas. Let them try to sell it to you. It's called reverse psychology, and it works. Always remember that they are the artists, the stars, and you are only the promoter."

Levitt rambled on for the next ten minutes until he received a call from his secretary. He listened for a moment and then grumpily answered, "Yeah, I remember. I'm on my way." Then he turned towards Anton and said in the same morose tone of voice, "I promised to take my wife for lunch; I have to go now."

Anton stood up and profusely thanked Levitt for his time and his wise counsel. The men left the office together and Anton caught sight of an elegantly dressed young-looking woman waiting for Arkady Borisovich. Anton moved closer to the woman and nodded respectfully.

Levitt had no choice but to make the introductions. "Anton Matveevich Zubov, the owner of the *Pinnacle Talent Agency*; my wife, Faina Grigorievna."

"What a lovely wife you have, Arkady Borisovich," Anton said, putting all his considerable charm into his smile.

"Delighted," Faina Grigorievna said as she smiled back in return.

From up close, Anton realized that the woman wasn't so young after all. *I bet she had plastic surgery done in California,* he thought, *and probably more than once. But the hands of a woman always reveal her real age.* Anton discreetly observed and made mental note of all those minute details.

Several days later, while he was taking a stroll during his lunch-hour, Anton happened to spot Faina Grigorievna, seated alone at a window table of a fashionable restaurant and eating lunch, so he entered the premises and approached her table to say hello.

"How are you today, Faina Grigorievna? Do you remember me? Anton Zubov. We met at your husband's office. Are you waiting for Arkady Borisovich to join you?"

Anton was well aware that Levitt had flown to Moscow the previous day.

"No, my husband left on one of his frequent business trips," the lady replied, in a manner in which Anton detected just a subtle touch of coy intonation.

"I was about to have lunch myself and I really don't care much for eating alone. Would you mind if I joined you?" Anton asked with exquisite politeness.

"Please do, by all means," Faina replied coquettishly. "I don't like to have lunch by myself either but what can I do? My entire family and all my friends live in the States. I'm stuck here in Moscow because of my husband's business, but Arkady never seems to have any time for me."

For the next hour, Anton patiently listened to Faina's complaints about her inattentive husband and her dream of moving to California to be with her daughters and their families. The woman was a nag, Anton decided, but he nodded his head empathetically at all the appropriate moments.

Anton made a deliberate and blatant show of trying to defend Faina's husband by reflecting on the pressure of their demanding business. He suggested that she learn more about some aspects of her husband's business, assuring her that it would help her to feel better about supporting him. Anton callously talked at length about the great responsibility her husband had as a respected leader in their industry, and how the man at the top needs to hold everything in his own hands. Not surprisingly, his appeals and gratuitous advices fell on deaf ears.

Then, for his next scripted move, Anton changed the

subject. He told Faina about his own family and how much he missed his wife and his children. He showed her wallet-size pictures of them, as any proud family man would do. He hinted that he would prefer that his family live in St. Petersburg, but his wife insisted on living in Cyprus. She loved the weather there and she couldn't bear to live without her numerous friends.

Faina nodded her head during his contrived speech and looked at Anton with understanding and telling compassion. What sort of woman could possibly prefer the company of her friends to the company of such a distinguished husband?

Anton thought process drifted briefly to his last conversation with Victoria. She was becoming a bit restless in Cyprus and wanted to come back to Russia and help him with the agency. She was lamenting how much she missed him, how worried she was that he was working too much, and saying that she wanted to be a more meaningful part of his life again. The usual 'wifely' talk. Maybe one day he would bring his family back to St. Petersburg, but not now...definitely not now.

In any event, that conversation was none of Faina's business.

At the conclusion of their extended lunch, Anton offered to accompany Faina to the premiere of an upcoming ballet performance. Faina indicated that she was very grateful for this gesture. She wanted to see the new production of *La Bayadere at the Marinsky Theater*, but Arkady was too busy as always, and it was unbecoming for a woman of her stature to attend the theatre alone.

Over the course of the next two months, Faina and Anton became good friends...very good friends indeed.

In June, Anton called Faina to say good-bye. He was going to Cyprus for a month. He wished her a pleasant summer and promised to get in touch with her again upon his return to St. Petersburg.

Scarcely a week later when he was back in Cyprus, Anton read in the local Russian newspaper that the well-known impresario Arkady Levitt had passed away suddenly. The cause of death was a heart attack.

Anton discretely waited for several days and then placed a call to the grieving widow. "Faina, my dear, I just found out today about Arkady. I'm so sorry. Please accept my sincere condolences."

"Oh, Anton, I've been waiting to hear from you. I'm so unhappy! I feel so guilty in my memory of Arkady! What if he found out about us and that's why he had a heart attack?"

"Faina, how could he, my dear? We were very discreet. Arkady's heart attack and passing are very sad, but I assure you that we weren't the cause of it."

"I don't know, Anton. His secretary told me that just minutes before his death, Arkady had received a phone call in his office that was obviously very upsetting. He was shouting and swearing on the phone. Then he asked her for a glass of water. When the secretary came with the water for him he was on the phone again with someone else and repeating over and over again, '*You were right, you were so right after all.*' Then he collapsed onto the floor. The secretary called the ambulance immediately but there was nothing that could be done."

"Darling, your husband was working on many business deals, all at the same time. He was in a very competitive and very cut-throat business. Trust me, I know. The pressure is sometimes so great that I feel close to a heart attack myself. Any one of those deals could go sour with dreadful consequences for the business."

"You're right about that, Anton. I told Arkady to quit long ago, but he was so stubborn! One more month...one more month! Even though he had promised to retire, he still had to control everything. He must have known he was pushing himself too hard. He had a history of heart trouble, and now it seems his heart was just not strong enough to continue tolerating all that pressure."

"Poor man," Anton sympathized. "He worked so hard. He deserved to enjoy his retirement."

"Oh, Anton, I feel so miserable! I was an unfaithful and horrible wife. I know that. But it was only because I was so utterly lonely. I wanted him to retire so we could move to California. If he had only listened to me! We had forty wonderful years together. How will I ever live without him?"

For the next hour or so, Faina continued crying on the phone and Anton was patiently consoling the grief-stricken woman.

One week later, Faina herself called Anton and asked him, "Anton, are you interested in buying Arkady's agency? I want to sell it as soon as possible so I can arrange my emigration and move in with one of my daughters in California. I already sold our condo. Nothing is holding me in St. Petersburg now except this accursed agency! And they are like vultures, like vultures, Anton!"

"Who are, Faina?" Anton asked in his most innocent, inquiring tone of voice.

"All those other agents. Everybody wants to buy the *Stars of Russia*. They didn't even wait to let Arkady's body come to rest in his grave! People started to call me the very day after the funeral. And now, everybody is in a frenzy. They're all fighting amongst themselves and one or another of them is calling me every half-an-hour. Don't they have any decency at all? Don't they have any respect for my feelings? I'd much rather deal with you than with any of the rest of them. You're an honourable man and you're my dear friend. If you're interested to buy the agency for a very fair price, Anton, it's yours."

"Faina, my dear, let me be totally honest. With my greatest respect for the memory of Arkady, of course I would like to buy the agency. I'm a businessman like everybody else. But I am not as wealthy as you may think. I'm afraid that the price of the agency would be too high for me. You'd better sell it to Vernik. I'm sure he could pay you a better price than I could."

"Not Vernik! He's the worst of them all. He behaves like the agency is already his. He had the audacity to tell me that I *must* sell it to him. They're all swindlers and crooks. You're the only person I can really trust. I know that you would protect my interests."

"Faina, let me think about your very kind offer. I'll call you back in an hour."

Anton did call back, and during that conversation he made a proposal. "Faina dear, if we are agreed that you will sell the agency to me, I will give you all the cash that I have available right now. I realize that it would only cover about half of the fair value, so in addition, I will pay you every month a percentage of the royalties which the agency receives on each contract. In that way, dear lady, you would have more than enough funds to start your new life right away in California in the style you deserve And then you would have a guaranteed monthly income to keep you in comfort for the rest of your life. As long as the agency remains active and profitable, you would be all set. How does that sound to you, darling?"

Anton also promised to attend to all the legal paperwork and transaction logistics. Faina readily agreed to this generous and thoughtful offer. She had only one more question.

"Will I see you again, Anton?"

"How could you even think otherwise, my dear? I travel to The States on business quite often, as you know. So if you would like me to come to California sometime to see you, I most certainly would do that."

Faina started to cry. "I'm a wicked woman! I just buried my husband and I'm already thinking about you!"

"It's all right, Faina. You aren't wicked at all, just wonderfully alive."

Ω

Everyone connected to the show business community was talking about nothing else but the buyout when the news became public. Pundits called it the 'steal of the century' and 'a coup', but several weeks later, the *Stars of Russia* buyout just as quickly became old news and the gossip had subsided.

Within a few weeks, Anton was sitting in the office of the president of the *Stars of Russia* agency, studying the portfolios of his new (and former) clients. Anton now controlled one of the most well-known and prestigious talent agencies in all of Russia.

He remembered all of Arkady's critique and advice, and even intended to subscribe to at least some of it. But as his first priority, Anton had to re-organize his vastly expanded business. He called Marek and asked him to fly immediately to St. Petersburg from Warsaw. When Marek arrived, Anton held a strategy meeting with his team of Marek, Peter, Megan and Valentina to outline his plans.

"I want to keep the two agencies separate, each with its own identity: the *Pinnacle Talent Agency* will concentrate on young, starting performers and the cruise entertainers, while the *Stars of Russia* will continue to manage established artists," Anton explained.

"You, Valentina, will now have full responsibility for the school. Can you handle it?"

"Of course I can. I've actually been doing it for years anyway, even though you were constantly under my feet," Valentina replied good-naturedly and everyone chuckled.

"Good, then that's settled.

"Peter, I want you to take on the leadership role for the *Pinnacle Talent Agency;* and Megan, you'll be Peter's second in command. For a while, however, you'll need some help.

"Marek, can you please stay in St. Petersburg for a year and take on the responsibility of coaching Peter and Megan? You'll get a nice bonus for your trouble."

Peter and Megan were overjoyed. Marek grumbled a bit, as could be expected, but in the end he agreed to remain in St. Petersburg until Peter and Megan became familiar with all aspects of the business.

With these management arrangements in place, Anton could now focus all his attention on the *Stars of Russia.*

He called Levitt's clients and organized a personal meeting with each of them, during which Anton was at his most charming self. He listened to the requirements and demands of each of the performers and promised to do his best on their behalf. He also met with *The Summit* and apologized for his mistakes. He guaranteed them his unwavering support. After a somewhat awkward and tense beginning, the leader of the band and Anton shook hands and peace between them was re-established.

Then Anton bought an exquisite bouquet of long-stemmed roses and went to visit the lady singer at her home. The reunion was emotional, tearful, and quite difficult for both of them. But in the end, the singer agreed to work with Anton and he promised to make her career his number one priority.

The only significant problem Anton encountered was in contacting Boris and Larissa. He sent e-mails and left phone messages; he wrote a long letter and sent it to them via courier, but all to no avail. *The Wandering Stars* were seemingly unreachable. Anton eventually decided to employ drastic measures. He instructed his assistant to halt all preparations for the upcoming tour of *The Wandering Stars* in Russia.

Two days later he received the predictable phone call from Boris. "Hi, Anton. What's going on with our tour?"

"Hello, Boris. Is that any way to greet your old friend after so many years?" Anton responded with caustic familiarity.

"Anton, we want out. Larissa doesn't want to work with you. We want to sign with another agency."

"I can appreciate that, Borya! If you don't want to work with me, then fine, that's your choice. But for the next four years you won't perform in Russia or anywhere else in Europe and your CD's won't be on the market here...unless of course you choose to pay the early termination penalty as prescribed in your contract."

Boris was about to say something but Anton didn't let him get a word in edgewise and instead tried to reason with him.

"Listen to me for a minute, Borya. I used all my life's savings and still had to get a substantial loan to buy this agency. If I let you go, it would set a bad precedent and eventually I could lose everybody.

I do agree that I was wrong in my treatment of Nina. I was a jerk and your wife has every reason in the world to dislike me. But I've changed, Borya. I learned my lesson. I have a very good wife now and we're very happy together. Frankly, I'm sure that Nina's much happier with Anatoly than she ever was with me and I'm truly happy for her. Let's set aside the distant past and concentrate on today's issue and our future opportunities. Life has many strange and unpredictable twists. Here we are now in the position where you're the star and I'm the agent. Let's find a way to work together."

"Larissa's objections have nothing to do with Nina," Boris confided miserably.

"If not Nina, then what is her problem with me?" the

bewildered Anton asked.

"She thinks that you were somehow responsible for Arkady's death and that you tricked Faina into selling you the agency for a fraction of its real value."

All the warmth in Anton's voice immediately dissipated and he lashed out angrily at Boris.

"Now listen Borya, you've been my friend for a long time but I won't countenance nor forgive such unwarranted accusations from you or anyone else. That's a complete lie and you ought to know it! I was a poor husband to Nina, agreed; but I never had anything to do with anyone's death and I never stole from anyone either. How could Larissa even think such a thing about me?"

"Anton, did you ever sleep with Faina?"

"What? My wife is young and beautiful and I have three wonderful children with her. Have you seen Faina? What utter nonsense," Anton laughed incredulously.

"Then what was going on between you and Faina?"

"Well, if you must know, Faina was very lonely without her family and friends. Arkady never seemed to have time for her. I took her to the theatre several times and we went for the occasional dinner together. That's all there was to it."

Boris sighed. "Arkady called Larissa and asked about you. He was uneasy about that *friendship* between Faina and yourself. It's not that he was terribly jealous...more like he was concerned that you wouldn't be spending your precious time on Faina without some compelling reason. He thought that you were after something."

"That's strange," Anton said contemplatively, "he was always very cordial with me. But that's neither here nor there now. The true reason Faina offered me the agency was that she became angry with all the other prominent agents. They were after her like vultures. She sold it to me as much as anything just to spite them.

"I sincerely believe that the terms of the sale agreement were very fair too. Faina has nothing to complain about. It's me who has to worry about paying her a considerable monthly stipend for the rest of her life, as long as the agency remains in business.

"Borya, please assure Larissa that I'm not a scoundrel. All that I want is to establish a sound working relationship with my clients and to do my best to support them. Would you please work with me, Borya?"

"I have to talk to Larissa. I'll call you later."

Anton silently congratulated himself for handling Boris so deftly. He knew that Boris had no other choice but to agree to work with him. Boris's band was very popular in Russia, and apart from their live performances, a good portion of the band's revenue was derived from the royalties on the sales of their CD's in that market. Furthermore, Arkady's agency handled the business of *The Wandering Stars,* not only in Russia but also throughout the countries of Eastern and Central Europe. Boris couldn't possibly afford to lose this level of income.

An hour later Boris called back. "Anton, I hate all this administrativia and I usually let Larissa to take care of all the logistics. However, we are agreeable to working with you but you'd be dealing directly with me and me alone. If there are any problems or issues, I will expect you to call me on my cell phone. Let's keep Larissa out of it."

"Understood and agreed," Anton reassured his old friend. "Boris, I'll be the best agent that you ever had in your life. I promise to do everything I can for you and then some. What do you need to be done now for your upcoming tour?"

Ω

The tour of *The Wandering Stars* took place as scheduled and was immensely successful, as always. Logistics-wise, everything was executed without a hitch. Boris couldn't have been happier. Larissa took pains to avoid Anton, but after the last performance he stumbled upon her while she was sitting in a corner of the dressing room and covering her face with her hands.

Anton felt tense with this chance encounter but asked as congenially as he could, "Are you okay?"

Larissa lifted her head and Anton could see how much she had aged. Constant travel and the pressures of stardom had prematurely transformed Larissa into a distinctly middle-aged if not older-looking woman. After two hours of singing and performing non-stop in the concert, she looked completely exhausted and emotionally drained. Anton quickly concluded that this was the last time *The Wandering Stars* would be signing a contract with any agency and wondered if they'd even last for the duration of their current contract.

Larissa just scowled. "What do you want?" Without her on-stage smile, Anton found her quite unpleasant to look at.

"Larissa, I just wanted to know if you need anything," Anton reacted in a non-committal voice.

"Nothing from you. Arkady was an old man, Anton. He was a good man, a very good man. Did you have to kill him? I know it was you who called him that day; I don't know what you said, but it upset him enough to trigger a fatal heart attack. Do you want to know how I found out? I called him to discuss the details of our tour. He answered the phone and said, '*You were right about Anton, Larissa, so right.*' Then I heard the phone drop. What did you say to him, Anton? Did you try to blackmail him, or what?"

"As I've already told your husband, I will not take

such accusations lightly so be careful what you say, Larissa." The slight hint of a veiled threat had filtered into Anton's voice.

"You found a way, Anton, that's all I know. You wanted the man's agency so you wanted him dead."

"That's enough! If I hear you're spreading any such malicious rumours I will sue you for slander, Larissa, and meanwhile withhold your payments. Believe me, I will find a way to put a stop to this nonsense. Do you understand me?"

"Go to hell. Just tell me this - was it worth it to destroy your soul? All these additional clients and extra money - do they add up to the life of a good man like Arkady?"

"You're becoming tedious, dear. Stop worrying about my soul and start worrying about your health instead. You look like death warmed over. We wouldn't want anything to happen to you, would we? After all, every time you open that big mouth of yours, I make money. Just remember that and take good care of yourself. For the next four years, you, your husband, and your precious voice belong only to me."

Larissa sat in silence and watched Anton coolly stride away from her dressing room.

Anton located Boris and said apologetically, "I just saw Larissa and tried to be friendly with her, but it didn't work out. Trust me, Borya, I didn't do or say anything to aggravate her."

Boris went to look for his wife and when he found her, Larissa started to relate the testy conversation that had transpired between Anton and herself. "Do you know what your so-called friend just said?"

"No, and I don't want to know. Anton is our agent and let's leave it on that professional level, Larissa."

Anton went home that evening in a very good frame of mind. The next day, he flew to Vancouver to attend to some business and a week later he was back in Cyprus with his family.

Ω

How nicely his children were growing, Anton thought proudly. They were overjoyed to see their father, and Victoria was as lovely and loving as ever. Every time he saw his wife, Anton was enraptured yet again by her beauty and asked himself how he could stay away from her for so long at any one time. He resolved that in the future he would spend more of his time in Cyprus with his family.

While reclining in a comfortable lounge chair near his enlarged swimming pool with gorgeous Victoria at his side, Anton observed his boys playing in the grass and his little daughter trying to take her first steps under the watchful gaze of her nanny. He felt quite content. He had achieved what he had wanted to achieve and he fulfilled the promise that he had made to himself - to exact revenge on all his enemies.

He recalled how furious Bill had been when he stole Bill's prized customer (Jeff had never called, but Anton could just picture his reaction). He also remembered the lonely and unhappy Carol as she behaved during their daughter's wedding, and he thought about the enraged Larissa too. Yes indeed, he had made them all squirm. He was satisfied - well, almost satisfied. There were only two people out of his reach whom he couldn't harm, 'though he still yearned to do so. Those two persons were Nina and her intolerable husband.

Yes, while it was true that it was he, Anton, who had left Nina, her complete indifference towards him now was unbearable. Anton still saw Nina and her snobby husband once in a while during different events and performances. Chance meetings were inevitable; after all, they were circulating among the same crowd. No, Anton corrected himself, he had to admit this wasn't entirely true. The Kuznetsovs belonged to a tighter circle, one to which he had not yet gained admittance.

Although those occasional encounters with Nina and her husband were infrequent and entirely accidental, how conceited and ill-mannered she was! Whenever Nina would see Anton, she would merely nod her head slightly in recognition and then proceed to ignore him, as though he was a total stranger. If nothing else Anatoly was more straightforward - he invariably glared at Anton with obvious hatred, loathing and disgust. Oh, how much Anton wanted to hurt them and to put them both down! But like the gods of Mount Olympus, the Kuznetsovs were unreachable and untouchable. Anton was left to reconcile himself to the lingering thought that there was always a faint hope that maybe one day fate would intervene and deliver them to him.

The Crime...

It happened sooner than Anton could ever have predicted. One day fate landed in Anton's office in the guise of a beautiful, sixteen-year-old girl. Anton had just returned to his office with Marek from the recording studio and was startled when he observed this particular young girl arguing with his secretary. With only a momentary glimpse, Anton instantly knew whose daughter she must be. She had the same green eyes, the same heart-shaped face, and the same long and very light straight hair, and even exhibited the same poise as her mother.

"What seems to be the problem?" Anton inquired.

"Oh, Anton Matveevich, thank God you're here. This young lady insists that she needs to see you and I've been trying to tell her that we don't deal with juvenile artists and that she should go to some other agency."

"That's OK. Let me take over."

"Please," Anton said, nodding to the girl and motioning for her to proceed into his office.

Behind his back, the secretary and Marek exchanged surprised glances, whereupon Marek shrugged his shoulders in a gesture indicating *he's the boss* and then followed Anton and the girl into the office.

Anton sat down behind his desk, invited the girl to take a seat and then innocuously asked, "What is your name?"

"Katya Kuznetsova," the girl answered bravely.

"What's your father's name?" Anton inquired, as if he had no idea.

"Anatoly."

"So, Ekaterina Anatolievna, what has brought you to our agency today?"

The girl, somewhat taken aback by the formal

treatment, sounded less sure of herself when she replied, "I want to sing. I want to participate in this year's Jurmala Young Pop Singer Competition."

"Ekaterina Anatolievna..."

"Please," she interjected, "call me Katya".

"No problem, Katya, but if I'm not mistaken your parents are very much involved in show business. Why didn't you ask them or their own agents to help you?" Anton was presenting himself as patient but authoritative at the same time.

"Oh, how do you know who my parents are?" the now-downcast Katya asked.

"Katya, the entire country knows who your parents are, and I must say you look very much like your mother. But you haven't answered my question.

"I did! They won't listen to me. They insist that I finish school and then the conservatory before I start my career. But by that time I'll be an old woman... ancient! I don't want to waste the best years of my life in the stupid conservatory. Besides, I don't want to be an opera singer. It's so boring! I want to sing pop and rock music. I can also be a jazz singer. I have a very good voice, maybe even better than my mom's. I want to start performing right now!" Katya exclaimed passionately.

"And none of the friends or agents associated with your parents would touch you because they don't want to alienate your parents. Is that about right?"

"Yes, Anton Matveevich, that's true. But can't you help me? Please! You made a big star out of Carina and I have a much better voice than her; and besides, I'm better looking too," Katya asserted.

Anton couldn't help but smile at the arrogance of this teenage girl. Indeed, he thought, apart from the strong physical resemblance, she was very different from Nina. Even when Nina was a recognized soloist of the Bolshoi Theatre and the winner of the most prestigious competition, she was considerably less sure of herself than this upstart daughter of hers. Katya was a conceited and spoiled brat, Anton concluded, but he maintained his smiling countenance. This girl was a potential godsend, as long as he could play his cards right and exploit her properly.

"Katya, your home is in Moscow. What are you doing in St. Petersburg?"

"I'm staying with my uncle this summer. Anton Matveevich, my parents keep me at home almost as if I'm in prison. I had a hard time convincing them just to let me come for a vacation visit with my uncle and cousins. So, this is my only opportunity to escape their clutches and get started in the career that I want more than anything else! Please let me sing for you; I want you to hear what I can do!"

"One more question, Katya. Why did you choose to come to me? Is it because of Carina or are there other reasons?"

Katya shifted uncomfortably on her chair, furtively looked at Anton while appearing downcast and remaining silent.

"Katya," Anton prodded, raising his voice ever so slightly, "if you want me to help you I have to know why you selected my agency. You have to be honest with me or you can leave right now and go to look for somebody else who might be prepared to work with you."

"My papa thought that you were the only agent that would agree to work with me," Katya said quietly.

"I beg your pardon? What did your father tell you about me?"

"Well," Katya confided, "actually he didn't tell me anything, but I had a fight with my parents recently and after they sent me to bed, they were talking between themselves on the porch and I overheard them. My mama said that there was nothing to worry about, that I'm simply going through a stage, and that none of the agents would work with me anyway. Then papa grumbled that if I went to somebody like *"your Anton Zubov"* – that's how he referred to you - then anything might happen. That's how I heard about you and now here I am."

Katya looked on at Anton miserably, waiting for his reaction.

Anton thought for a moment and then said, "I wasn't aware that your father apparently dislikes me but that's not important.

"Let's talk about you, Katya, and I have to be straight with you. I will have to think carefully about your request before making a decision one way or the other – it's a delicate situation for you and especially so for me.

"Here's what we're going to do. Prepare several songs and come back here on Thursday around six in the afternoon. I'll invite several of my associates to listen to you and then we'll talk again."

"Oh, thank you, Anton Matveevich. Thank you very much!"

"Don't get your hopes up too high, Katya. I haven't promised you anything yet."

"That's OK! I'll see you on Thursday," Katya exclaimed, as she said her good-byes and virtually ran from the office in a state of excitement.

"Are you out of your mind, Anton?" Marek asked, after having kept silent for the entire duration of Anton's conversation with Katya. "What are you going to do with that conceited pip-squeak? The last thing you want is to make the Kuznetsovs your enemies. They're much too influential and they'd undoubtedly find a way to destroy you!"

"Marek, don't you worry. All that I'm actually planning to do is to call the Kuznetsovs and ask them to deal with their rogue daughter."

"Good man!" Marek agreed with Anton's decision and the subject was dropped as they moved on to discuss other, more pressing agency business.

But after Marek left, Anton could think about nothing but Katya's visit. He truly believed that it was fate that had intervened in such a way that he finally had before him both the means and the opportunity to take his revenge on the indifferent Nina and her snooty husband.

He briefly considered calling them but quickly discarded that idea. How would it sound? *Your daughter has asked me to make a rock star out of her. What are your instructions?*

He just could hear Nina's dispassionate voice - *Thank you, Anton. We'll deal with her.*

Or Anatoly's sarcastic voice, - *It's just too kind of you to inform us.*

Then they would whisk Katya back to Moscow and that would be the end of that. Not very much revenge to be had in this scenario.

All that evening and for the next two days, Anton devised any number of possible schemes to exploit the girl to his advantage in order to bring her parents down a notch, but eventually he discarded every one of them. He became increasingly agitated with himself. How was it that he, such a clever and cunning man, couldn't conceive of a foolproof way to humiliate both the daughter and her parents without putting himself and his business in harm's way?

Thursday afternoon, with his scheduled appointment with Katya looming, Anton became restless. To calm himself and get clarity of mind, he opened a bottle of his favorite French cognac and had a drink. Unfortunately, no calmness and no clarity came to him. He took the bottle and the glass and moved to the corner of his office where his baby grand piano stood. He had another drink and then started to play.

That was how Katya found him when she arrived: playing a slow, sad melody.

"Hello, Anton Matveevich. I didn't know you could play. It's so beautiful. Where are the other people who are going to be listening to my singing audition?"

"Oh, they'll be here any moment," Anton replied casually. "In the meantime, why don't we start, Katya? What are you going to sing for me?"

Katya named one of the popular modern songs and asked Anton if he could accompany her on the piano.

"I think I can manage that," Anton laughed, but before he started to play, he took several more gulps of his drink.

Katya assumed a pose and began to sing. She sang and danced and stage-acted simultaneously, trying to impress upon Anton that she was a grown-up woman and already an accomplished rock singer. Her body undulated, even if somewhat clumsily, as she did her best to present herself as a provocative woman. It was apparent to Anton, as he was watching the girl's gyrations, that she actually had no idea what she was doing. Katya, as he knew perfectly well, would have been raised on classical music and he suspected she had never had a jazz or hip-hop class in her life.

And yet, Anton was struck by the realization of how similar Katya's voice was to her mother's. Of course she needed to have much more training and learn to control and project her voice, but even so, it was Nina's haunting voice that he was hearing yet again.

In her inept attempts to dance, Katya looked exceptionally erotic without even realizing it. Anton felt himself becoming aroused. He tried to concentrate on the music, but that writhing body and the golden sheet of hair distracted him. He finished his drink and poured himself another.

"Katya," he slurred, "why don't you play to accompany yourself? I think it would be much better."

"Well, OK," the girl replied timidly and they switched places. Katya was glad to sit down. She didn't feel entirely comfortable standing alone before this man; his focused and intense stare was beginning to bother her more and more. It had come to the point where, more than anything, she just wanted to leave this place. She was even sorry that she'd come in the first place but wasn't quite sure how to find an excuse to make her exit.

Katya decided to play one more song and then to leave, unless Anton's other alleged associates made their promised appearance to hear her too. Katya placed her hands on the piano in a practiced manner, thought for a moment, and decided to sing something subdued and safe.

"I'll sing a well-known old folk song," she announced.

"Go right ahead," Anton replied as he continued to nurse his drink. By now he was feeling light-headed and a bit disoriented.

When Katya started to play and sing again, Anton's attention was rekindled. He sat straighter and finished his drink in one gulp. He had heard this song – in the very same voice – on a train years before when he was speeding toward Anatoly's dacha and his unfolding destiny. How happy and carefree he was then! As he was hearing this song for the second time so many years later, he realized that in fact he had lost his destiny. On that prior occasion he had been keeping to the shadows, trying to be unobserved by anybody, and all the while desiring Nina.

And now, Anton perceived that he was hearing the very same voice singing that same song once again. In his mind, quite clouded by the liberal amount of alcohol that he had consumed, Katya and Nina melded into one and the same woman. It was as if Anton was in the presence of his first wife again. At that moment, he was overwhelmed with the surreal belief that Nina was the one and only woman that he had ever truly loved. He felt angry with her and even more so with Anatoly. Sure, Anton and Nina had had a slight disagreement but nothing that they wouldn't have been able to resolve, if only Anatoly hadn't stolen his Nina away from him.

This girl was supposed to be *his* daughter! No! How she could be his daughter if she was actually Nina in the flesh?

She was his wife, he desired her, and he had the right to be with her, right now. Why had she kept him away for so long? Didn't she know how much he needed and wanted her?

Anton impulsively rose and approached Katya, roughly lifted her from the piano bench and kissed her fiercely. Startled and frightened by this unexpected attack, Katya tried to pull herself free and run off, but Anton's strong hands were grasping her tightly and ripping apart the front of her dress at the same time. Katya struggled against Anton's unwanted advance and tried to scream for help, but he stifled her scream with another ardent, deep kiss. He then threw her down on the carpet and fell clumsily on top of her. Anton's passion of the moment was totally beyond control and reason. It was Nina he was now holding so closely and rightfully claiming as his wife. "Nina!" Anton cried out in anguish.

But the more the distraught girl struggled, the more violent Anton became. He couldn't remember afterwards how he had undressed her or himself, but he could remember how Katya had stiffened, stopped struggling and started to sob uncontrollably when he entered her.

When it was over, the hysterical girl quickly gathered her clothing and ran out of the building. Anton stumbled to his feet. The stark realization of what he had done suddenly hit him: he had raped Nina's daughter. *She won't say anything to anybody,* Anton thought, even as the level of panic in his mind was rising. *She'd be too ashamed for herself and for her parents. But what if she did? I'd be arrested. I have to get away from here as soon as possible; I'll have to go to Cyprus. I must get to the airport before Katya can alert anybody.*

Anton's brief moment of lucidity faded and he found that he could no longer think straight. Reflexively, he reached for his bottle. There still was some amber liquid on the bottom. He drank straight from the bottle until he had finished every last drop of cognac.

He took a couple of tentative steps but then collapsed and fell prostrate on the carpet. He needed ten minutes of rest, just to clear his head, he decided. *Just ten minutes.* Anton fell into a deep sleep on the light-colored, luxuriant carpet beside the tell-tale stain from his impulsive actions.

An hour or so later, the police found him half-dressed and still sleeping in the same spot. He was woken up, cuffed and taken to a waiting police vehicle.

It was only after Anton had been booked, while he was being led to a holding cell, that he fully realized the enormity of his predicament. He was permitted to make just one phone call and he used that opportunity to call Marek.

.... and The Punishment

Marek received the unexpected call from the prison as he was reclining in his comfortable armchair and watching some Russian soap-opera on TV. He had enjoyed a pleasant dinner engagement with his personal trainer, after which the young lady had agreed to accompany Marek to his apartment. They had a drink and Marek wanted to proceed to the bedroom, but his lady friend declared that she couldn't miss an important episode of her favorite show. And so, he was sipping slowly on his second drink and waiting in anticipation for the end of the program episode.

Marek had changed visibly since he had met Anton eight years earlier on *The Statendam*. The life of a successful businessman had certainly agreed with him. He had become a vegetarian and a health-nut, and lost a lot of weight. He exercised in the gym four or five times every week, played tennis regularly, and had even learned to play golf.

He enjoyed having his autonomous branch of the agency in Warsaw, but secretly resented his overall dependency on the St. Petersburg headquarters. When Marek was last in Vancouver, he had tried to probe Susan's attachment to Anton. He was harboring the idea of telling Susan about Victoria, winning her trust and convincing Ms. Harper to deal directly with him. In the end, Marek decided against it. The woman was completely smitten with Anton and such a revelation would surely backfire. It would have been silly to bite off the hand that was feeding him.

When Marek fully comprehended the nature of Anton's shocking call, he started to yell on the phone at him. "How could you do this to us? We're ruined, destroyed! None of the clients will stay with us and you can be sure Susan will immediately sever all relationships with the *Pinnacle!*"

Anton screamed back, "Marek, I have no time! Help me. Get me the best lawyer; money's no object. You'll have to tell Peter what happened, but don't let Victoria or Megan find out about my arrest. Don't tell Susan anything either. Just get me that lawyer and get me out of here."

Anton had an interview with his lawyer the following morning. After spending his first night in jail, he felt completely devastated.

The lawyer regarded him with open disdain. Anton wasn't aware that he was already the most infamous man in Russia, and that his picture had been plastered on the front page of the majority of the morning newspapers under large headline banners, including: *Prominent Impresario Rapes Sixteen-year-old Daughter of Nina Kuznetsova*; *Discarded Ex-husband of Nina Kuznetsova Rapes her Teenage Daughter*; and, *Did He Mistake the Daughter for the Mother?*

It was a scandal of major proportions and the newspapers were having a field day with it.

Perhaps, if Katya had made it home and told her story to her uncle, everything would have been quieter. But when a policewoman on patrol observed the sobbing teenage girl in a tattered dress on the street, the officer stopped her patrol car and questioned her. Katya was then taken to the station and subjected to further questioning.

Her uncle was notified and he rushed to the station to pick up his niece. Unfortunately for Anton, a crime reporter happened to be lurking at the station at the same time. He overheard the story and soon realized whose daughter had been the victim of a brutal rape. The reporter immediately sensed that he had stumbled upon the makings of a monumental story. He observed Katya's multiple bruises and was able to take several all-revealing photos.

Katya's uncle arrived at the station and bitterly said, "I want to kill that son of a bitch. He almost destroyed my sister and now look what he's done to my niece!"

The distraught man blurted out the story of Anton's first marriage and the shrewd reporter quickly unearthed quite a few other juicy details that both Anton and Nina had long ago tried to suppress and forget about.

Perhaps if Katya had not had such famous parents, and maybe if Nina had not been so beloved by the entire country, the story would not have been given such a high profile. As it was now, however, everybody had read or heard some version of the story and even Anton's lawyer had formed quite an unfavorable opinion about his client.

Anton, unaware of his sudden infamy, tried to solicit his lawyer's help and sought to explain himself and his actions. "She came of her own volition. I was drunk and I wasn't aware of what I was doing. I thought that it was her mother appearing before me; I used to be married to Nina. I was disoriented and I really thought that it was my wife.

"Get me out of here! Please, I can't stand being here. Whatever the bail is, I'll pay it; just get me out of here. Now!"

The lawyer dispassionately explained to Anton that everything, even the setting of bail, would take time, and indicated that he would attend to it right away. He suggested to Anton that he remain calm, and above all, to avoid getting into any squabbles with other prisoners.

"Anton," he said, "if other prisoners see that you're weak, they'll pounce on you and make your life miserable. Try to be as invisible and unobtrusive as possible."

The lawyer left to initiate the legal process on behalf of his unwelcome client. The trembling Anton was led back to the cell, where five other recently arrested men were waiting for nothing else but to torment him, or so it seemed to the distraught Anton.

Ω

On the same day Victoria received a phone call from a reporter who wanted to know if she had ever met Nina Kuznetsova or her daughter. The reporter started peppering her with questions. What were her plans for the future? Was she planning to apply for a divorce? Did her husband ever demonstrate a violent streak at home?

The bewildered Victoria couldn't understand in the slightest what the reporter was talking about. What would Nina Kuznetsova, a well-known singer and movie star, have to do with her, Victoria?

No sooner had she hung up the phone than it rang again...and again. Frustrated and alarmed, Victoria tried to call to Anton's office, but to no avail.

The phone rang yet again. This time it was her old friend Liza, Peter's stepmother. "Poor Vika," she started, "it's in all the newspapers."

"What's going on, Liza?" Victoria asked, still totally mystified. "I'm receiving all kinds of weird phone calls from reporters but I can't understand what they want!"

Liza related the grim highlights. Victoria was now suddenly frantic and tried to phone Megan but the phone was apparently off the hook. Then she called Marek and fortunately he answered the phone.

"Victoria," he said, "I'm dealing with the situation. Please stay put and look after the children. The papers have blown everything out of proportion. Don't talk to any reporters or to anybody else. I'm arranging bail for Anton and within a day or two he'll be out of jail. Then he'll explain everything to you. Promise to stay put."

Dumbfounded, Victoria promised to stay in Cyprus and wait for Marek's return call. But as soon as she hung up the phone, she decided to act. Her Anton was in trouble. There was no way she was going to sit still in Cyprus and do nothing. She quickly concluded that she must be beside her husband in his time of need. They had had seven years of great marriage; he had always been the most kind, devoted, and loving husband and father. He provided for her and the children and allowed her to live a life of luxury and leisure. Now it was time for Victoria to help her Anton.

Victoria located her mother and informed her that she needed to go to St. Petersburg urgently. She asked her mother to care for the children and not to become engaged in any discussion with any reporters. She explained very little to her mother, because she herself understood very little of the situation. Several hours later Victoria was en route to St. Petersburg.

Ω

At the same time, another anxious woman was flying to St. Petersburg from farther afield to offer a helping hand to her beloved Anton. Susan Harper heard the shocking news from one of the entertainers who had arrived just that day from Russia to join the Holland America Cruise Line. In his hand there was a daily Russian newspaper with prominent front-page coverage.

When Susan understood the gist of the situation, she decided on her own that she would fly to Russia without delay. Several months earlier, purely on a whim, Susan had applied for a Russian visa. Now she was relieved that her papers were in order. She called Marek, informing him of her plans and asked him to meet her at the airport.

During her long flight to St. Petersburg, Susan had a lot of time to think about her complicated relationship with Anton. She had never loved anybody as much as she loved him. Unbeknownst to Anton, ever since she first met him, Susan never even looked at another man. But she was tired of this irregular, long-distance affair. Enough was enough. It was her own fault that she had permitted Anton to live a bachelor's life for so long. Sure, he was lonely and some young floozy took advantage of him and then cried *rape!*

First she had to bail him out. Then she would hire the best lawyer for him and extricate him from this predicament. One way or another, she wouldn't be returning home to Canada without Anton in tow, a resolute Susan decided.

It was late evening when Susan arrived in St. Petersburg. Marek was glad to see her but he was understandably very tense. He felt that the responsibility for the agency, Anton's family, and Anton's own destiny was squarely on his shoulders and he loathed this entire unwanted burden. He still did not feel comfortable in Russia and longed to get back to Warsaw. And now this new development! He realized that he must be very careful with Susan too, making sure that none of Anton's relatives would meet her face-to-face. At least Victoria was far away, or so he thought.

They had dinner together and then Marek drove Susan to her hotel. The next morning Anton was supposed to be freed on bail, and then they would help him sort out all this mess.

Nobody met Victoria because no one knew about her arrival from Cyprus. She took a taxi from the airport to their condo and started to call people. She still couldn't reach Megan or Peter and didn't feel at all disposed towards talking to Anton's parents or his sister. Eventually, Victoria reached Marek and he informed her that Anton would be freed in the morning. Victoria did not reveal to Marek than she was calling from St. Petersburg and he assumed that she was still in Cyprus. He suggested that she should wait for a call from

Anton and then he hung up.

Victoria couldn't fall sleep for a long time. She paced the rooms of the condo and tried to watch the news, but soon turned the television off. She barely slept that night, and early in the morning she packed a fresh outfit for Anton and headed for the municipal jail.

Ω

Anton was having a difficult time adjusting to his temporary quarters. He did not make a good prisoner and he was leery of every shadow. The jests and constant needling of his cellmates terrified him. When somebody shoved him against the bars of the cell, Anton felt like weeping.

Every moment he was hoping that he would be let go; he couldn't fathom why it took such a long time to set bail. When his lawyer informed him that he would have to spend one more night in the jail, Anton fell to pieces. He started to sob and besought his lawyer to arrange moving him to a different, preferably empty cell. He was begging for solitary confinement.

Anton's lawyer was disgusted by his client's display of weakness in the face of adversity but promised to arrange something and hastily left. An hour later, Anton was moved to another cell.

Maybe it was a mistake or maybe it was a deliberate act by the unsympathetic guards (even they were fans of Nina Kuznetsova), because instead of solitary confinement as he had requested, Anton found himself in an even larger cell which was occupied by a number of rough-looking men.

When he sized up his new surroundings, Anton deduced almost immediately that his new cell-mates were quite unlike the recently-arrested, motley crew in the holding cell with whom he had been originally placed. Now he found himself confronted by a group of hardened criminals.

He banged repeatedly on the doors of the cell, desperately seeking to get the attention of the guards. But some authoritative voice from behind a closed door shouted '*Silence*', and so a dejected and disconsolate Anton sat down on the edge of a bench in one corner of the cell.

"And what do we have here? Wow, look at those classy shoes. Can I have them? Hey buddy, let's exchange shoes," one of the prisoners accosted him in a gruff voice, whereupon Anton tried to shrink inconspicuously into his corner seat.

Another of the prisoners exclaimed, "Hey, I know this guy! I saw his face in the paper. He's the creep that raped that young Kuznetsova girl."

The sullen faces staring at Anton now became angry-looking and even more menacing. Anton felt an overwhelming dread and tried to get up and make a move again towards the cell-door. But powerful arms restrained him and pushed him roughly back onto the bench.

"So, you like them young, do you?" Anton heard from a sneering voice. "First you screwed mama, and then her baby, eh? So how would you like to take it, instead of giving it? You want to have fun, do you? We'll give you some fun…lots of fun."

Strong hands pinned down Anton's arms. Somebody was pulling down his pants and he heard a command, "Boys, careful with those shoes. They're mine."

When Anton realized what was about to happen to him he started to struggle desperately, but to no avail. The pain when they took him was excruciating. One after another, to the sound of overwhelming, derisive laughter, the men in the cell tore apart Anton's body and in the process utterly destroyed his mind and soul.

Finally, in a panic like that of an animal being led to

the slaughter, he somehow managed to free his right leg. Without hesitating, he began kicking his one free leg wildly and eventually it connected with some bodily flesh and he heard a scream of pain and then a groan of anguish.

A heavy silence enveloped the cell, and then a gentle voice whispered almost compassionately into Anton's ear, "You shouldn't have done that. It was the wrong man you kicked. It's just too bad for you now, dude... *really* too bad for you."

The last thing Anton felt was the touch of cold, sharp metal on his chest, and then that metal blade was penetrating his skin, his flesh, reaching deeper and deeper inside him, into the very place where his heart was still beating.

Ω

Victoria arrived at the jail before nine o'clock and was asked to wait. She sat down on a hard and uncomfortable bench and anxiously waited for Anton to appear. Every time the door leading to the interior part of the building would open, Victoria's heart skipped a beat in anticipation.

At nine fifteen, the front entrance door opened and Marek strode in with a middle aged, elegant woman at his side. Victoria was very glad to see him and stood up to embrace him but Marek seemed to be both startled and unhappy to see her.

"What are you doing here, Victoria?" he blurted out.

"What do you think I'm doing, Marek? Did you really think I would just sit in Cyprus while Anton was in such a predicament? Be polite and introduce me to your companion," Victoria smiled.

"Yes, of course. Victoria, this is Susan Harper."

"Susan, this is Victoria Zubova," Marek stammered in English, feeling incredibly uncomfortable being caught in the middle between the two women in Anton's life.

"Are you Anton's sister?" Susan inquired with some hesitation.

"No, no! I'm Anton's wife. Anton told me so much about you! You're his most important business associate. He respects and values you so much, Ms. Harper," Victoria replied in fluent English.

"Business associate? He calls me a business associate?" Susan hissed. "Marek, what's going on? Who is this woman?"

"Anton's wife," Marek responded miserably, wishing he was somewhere else.

"When did he get married? Yesterday? Why didn't anybody tell me about this new development?" Susan demanded furiously.

Victoria tried to remain calm and she responded to Susan's barrage of questions with dignity. "This development is not new, Ms. Harper. We've been married for over seven years and we have three children. What I don't understand is why Anton's private life is any concern of yours."

"Is this true, Marek? Has Anton really been married for seven years?" Susan demanded to know.

"Yes, Susan, it's true, but he instructed me in no uncertain terms not to say anything to you about his private life. Susan, please understand. I'm working for Anton. What could I do?"

Susan stared intently at the beautiful younger woman and then said, "Now you listen to me. I'm Anton's lover. We've been together for almost eight years. He's the dearest person to me in the entire world."

"My husband..."

"He told me that he loves me and wants to live with me. He was tired, as much as I was, of our sporadic, long-distance relationship. Just last month in Vancouver, he promised me that before the end of the year everything would change."

"Vancouver," Victoria repeated aloud slowly, trying to comprehend all of the implications in Susan's words. "From Vancouver he flew to Cyprus and spent ten days with me and the kids. It doesn't make any sense, Ms. Harper. Anton loves me and our family very much; he would never do anything like that to hurt me and the children."

Susan chose not to respond and the two women could only continue looking at one another in shock, dismay and confusion.

The hapless Marek, desperately trying to put at least some little distance between himself and the standoff between the distraught women, noticed a young policeman and moved to accost him. "Do you know when Anton Zubov is going to be released? We're waiting for him."

The harried officer looked askance at Marek and replied, "I don't think that the body will be released today; not until after an autopsy has been performed."

There was an audible gasp from Victoria and Susan shouted, "What did he say? What did he say?" Marek turned away from the two women, asked the policeman to escort him to someone in authority, and then disappeared behind the door.

In a hushed voice, Victoria translated the policeman's words from Russian into English for Susan. The two women slumped side-by-side on the bench, without looking at each other and with their hands clasped on their own laps, both hoping desperately that this was some kind of terrible mistake.

Marek followed after the officer and then re-appeared in the waiting area after about ten minutes, his face ashen. "Anton was killed in his cell last night. He was stabbed by some other inmates. The prison authority must conduct a formal investigation, so it may take several days before they release his body. Let's get out of here."

Susan struggled to get up off the bench. Now she really looked old and worn out. Victoria couldn't even bring herself to her feet and Marek had to assist her and then to support her all the way to his car. Susan seated herself in the front passenger seat while Marek helped Victoria settle into the back seat of the car, and then he sped away in the direction of Anton and Victoria's condo apartment.

Marek glanced into the rearview mirror at Victoria, and seeing her pale and dry-eyed, he became extremely concerned. He punched up Peter's cell number, quickly explained the situation and asked Peter to send Megan to her father's apartment. Peter started to protest that Megan needed her own time and space to deal with her grief, but Marek firmly responded, "Peter, trust me. If you don't want the responsibility of raising three small children, you'd better get Megan over there right away."

When the car pulled up near the apartment, Megan was already anxiously waiting. Victoria emerged from the car and the two grieving women embraced and started to wail in anguish together. Then Megan led her stepmother inside. Susan, who had remained seated in the car, hissed, "Marek, get me away from here. Take me to my hotel."

Victoria tried to gather her thoughts but the reality of the situation was eluding her. She struggled to come to grips with everything that had happened in the past two days and everything that she had learned about Anton that she never would have guessed or expected of him. Her husband used to be married to Nina Kuznetsova and had hid that fact from her. He raped Nina's sixteen-year-old daughter. He kept a mistress in Vancouver for the past eight years. He was stabbed to death in prison.

Anton had been killed; Anton was dead. That last fact was the most incomprehensible. Victoria tried to marshal anger towards him for all of his misdeeds, hoping that it would diminish her grief, but she couldn't manage to do that. She loved him with all her heart and somewhere deep in her soul she still hoped that it was all just a nightmare, and at any moment she would wake up from this horrible dream.

Megan made tea for both of them. The hands of the young woman were shaking and her face was covered with streaks of tears. She wanted to be with Peter and to feel the comfort of his hands at that moment, but she was fearful for Victoria's sanity and indeed her life.

Eventually, Victoria said, "Megan, I want to be alone. I'm okay. I will try to sleep."

She kissed Megan, went to her room, shut the door behind her, and sat down on the edge of her bed. She clasped her hands together and slowly started to rock back and forth. Slowly, ever so slowly, Victoria began to comprehend the reality of the tragedy that had befallen her. This was no nightmare – Anton really was dead.

Gradually, resentment towards him began to build inside her. How could he possibly have done this to her and the children? Had he not loved her at all? Was everything he had told her nothing more than a big lie?

That was when he came to her. She felt Anton's presence; she heard his wailing voice, "Oh, Vika, my love, my sweetheart! I love you so much. Don't believe anything that they say about me. Please understand I loved only you. You are the only woman in my life that gave me happiness. Please take care of our babies...I wish I could see them now. Help them remember me. I love them so much! I'm so sorry for everything that happened, darling, so sorry. Please forgive me. You need to be strong, Victoria, our children need you – I need you! I wish I could touch you and comfort you..."

Victoria imagined she could feel the brush of his lips on her cheek. He had lied to her. Even this apparition, this wailing – it was just another lie. She, Victoria, had not been the only woman in his life. How many more had there been? Somehow, the swell of anger that she hadn't felt before now engulfed her from within. She wrapped herself in its cold comfort, and finally she lapsed into a fitful sleep.

The Wake

Marek and Valentina attended to all the necessary logistics in organizing the funeral. Peter spent his time performing damage control, calling all their clients and assuring them that the agencies were alive and well and that it was business as usual. In one sense, Anton's death helped the situation for the agencies in an obtuse way. Now that he knew that there would be no trial, Peter could claim that the media had overreacted and that Anton was a victim of unfavorable circumstances and a media witch-hunt. The media had refocused the captions and the tone of their reporting. Now, their articles where being headlined with such titles as *Crude Justice Prevails*, or, *Crime and Punishment*.

Every reporter in Russia was searching for the Kuznetsovs, hoping for an exclusive interview, but they had disappeared from public view. Nobody knew where Anatoly had taken his family.

So instead, Anton's family was hunted and harassed by the media. Anton's distraught and grieving parents were afraid to leave the confines of their apartment. Valentina, Peter and Megan avoided pesky paparazzi as much as they could, but whenever they were confronted they would briskly say *"no comment"* and walk away.

Throughout this chaotic time, Victoria made only one decision: she called Cyprus, told her mother about Anton's death, and asked her to continue to look after the children. She didn't want them in St. Petersburg. She needed to get some greater clarity around Anton's life and his demise before she would have some idea of what to say to her young family.

The day of the funeral arrived. Victoria, dressed in widow's black, left her apartment and started walking towards a waiting limo.

All that she wanted to do now was to bury her husband in peace. Unfortunately, peace was the one thing that eluded her. A horde of reporters encircled her from all sides as soon as she emerged from her apartment building. Their flash-cameras almost blinded her.

Even at the cemetery, Anton's body was not permitted the dignity of a solemn burial. The reporters photographed a weeping Susan, the frail parents, a trembling Megan, and the beautiful, dry-eyed Victoria with her unfathomable expression which disguised whatever her inner emotions might have been.

Quite a few of the agency clients came to the funeral, although Victoria felt that they had come because they were worried about their contracts and their future, not because they experienced any strong urge to pay their last respects to Anton.

During the ceremony Susan was leaning on Marek who offered her his handkerchief and his shoulder for support. As soon as Anton's coffin had been lowered into the freshly dug grave, Susan and Marek departed from the cemetery.

The wake was held in Victoria's apartment. In the sitting room, Anton's parents and Valentina received condolences from the mourners who attended. Peter returned to the office and was continuing to do damage control.

When the stream of attending mourners eventually departed, Anton's lawyer produced and read the will to the gathered family members. It was very straightforward. Anton had two very large insurance policies. Megan was the beneficiary of one policy; Victoria was the beneficiary of the other. Victoria also inherited the Cyprus house, the St. Petersburg condo, a handsome sum of money, and ownership of the *Stars of Russia Agency*. Megan received ownership of the *Pinnacle Talent Agency*. The school was bequeathed to

Valentina. There were monetary bequests to his parents as well. Neither of Anton's business associates, Susan or Marek, was named in the will.

Victoria, Megan and Valentina were now destined to become wealthy women.

Megan's cell-phone rang. It was her mother, who had just learned about the events in Russia. Carol did her best to be supportive and loving towards her daughter, but her long-held negativity towards Russia in general and Anton in particular only hurt Megan more. Carol insisted that Megan ought to return as soon as possible to Calgary where she had her loving family. Megan listened to her mother's advice, then quietly said, "I'm a married woman, Mom. My husband lives in Russia and so will I." Then she disconnected her phone.

Victoria longed to be left alone. She couldn't face anybody; she was feeling profound shame, anger and grief. The reading of the will upset her even further. She wanted nothing else but to escape from St. Petersburg and to return to Cyprus. She didn't want the responsibility of the agency.

After the obligatory wake and reading of the will, Victoria decided to go for a solitary walk. She hoped that by then all the reporters would be gone. She changed her clothes and now wore her most inconspicuous suit. Passing by the sitting room she curtly announced, "I'm going out." Then she promptly left the apartment. *A good long walk in the crisp air will help*, Victoria hoped.

As she crossed the lobby, Victoria noticed a couple entering the building and so she quickly stepped behind a column to let them pass and remain unnoticed. She didn't want to hear yet another insincere expression of condolence.

Victoria could hear that the couple was arguing. The gentleman wanted to get into the elevator but the woman was trying to restrain him.

Victoria then recognized those two people: they

were members of a group called *The Wandering Stars,* one of Anton's most important clients.

"Larissa, if you don't want to go up, then wait for me in the car," the man was saying.

"I don't think that you should go either, Boris," the woman replied.

"He was my dearest friend for five years in the conservatory. I knew his parents since I was eighteen years old. I owe them this visit. I understand that you didn't like Anton, but he's gone, Larissa. Let's go in together; we'll just stay for five minutes and then we'll leave."

"He doesn't deserve your sympathy, Boris. He wasn't a good man," the woman persisted.

"Larissa, obviously I know that you disliked Anton because of his treatment of Nina and you are right. I have always supported your viewpoint about that. He treated Nina horribly. But he *had* changed; he was trying to be a better man. He cared very much about his wife, Victoria, and their children. And actually, he was a good agent for us too."

"Borya, you... you... you're not simply naïve, you're stupid!" the agitated woman yelled at her husband. "He loved nobody but himself. Do you really think that he cared about his young wife? She was nothing more than a showpiece for him. He took that beautiful, talented creature and planted her in Cyprus! And while she was sitting there as a submissive and obedient wife, he was screwing every young, good-looking female performer who came his way, not to mention that mistress he kept in Vancouver as well."

"Larissa, since when have you started to give credence to such malicious rumors? And why do you think that his wife was talented? Sure, she's beautiful. I saw her pictures in the papers and have to agree - she's gorgeous. But talented is quite another matter."

"She had gone to see Arkady years ago and he was

very impressed with her. He was already looking for a proper placement for her when she went to see Anton, and then your so-called best friend never let her out of his clutches. Maybe that was what the girl wanted: a good marriage and a comfortable, quiet life. But what if Anton had never given her a chance to decide for herself? Maybe he convinced her that she didn't have talent, even though all the while she had been destined to become a great actress?"

"Larissa, this is all utter speculation. I have no idea what Anton's wife originally wanted when she first met him, nor do I care."

"It's hardly speculation that Anton killed Arkady," Larissa retorted gloomily.

"That's enough! I've heard your theories one too many times and I don't buy them. Let's go," Boris said angrily, as he again approached the elevator.

"Okay, but I must tell you one more thing. Hear me out, Boris, and then we will go to see his parents, if you wish.

"Right after the last performance of the tour, Anton and I had a testy conversation backstage."

Boris made an impatient movement to go forward but Larissa stopped him again. "Listen! He spelled out for me the reason why he was after Arkady's agency. He wanted to completely control and to own us - you and me. He told me that for the next four years we belonged to him and that I should take care of my health because every time I opened my mouth to sing, he made money."

Boris looked intently at his wife and solemnly asked, "Did he really say that, Larissa? Anton's dead and buried. Please don't tell fibs or half-truths now."

"I'm not, Borya. As I just told you, he actually said, *"Take care of your health, Larissa, because for the next four years you and your husband belong to me."* I wouldn't make up something like that." Larissa pressed her hand to her brow. She looked worn-out and in a poor state of health.

Boris frowned and shook his head in dismay. He remained standing in the middle of the lobby, reluctant to proceed up to Victoria's apartment and yet not prepared to leave either.

Larissa wasn't done yet. "Boris, he killed Arkady, or at least he was directly responsible for his death, and then he practically stole his agency. Faina called me and was crying about that. He paid her no more than half of what the agency was worth and promised to pay her every month some reasonable percentage of the royalties which the agency receives on each contract, as a lifelong source of income for her.

"But Anton added several critical words to the contract at the last minute: *existing and valid at the time of sale*. Whether she realized it or not, that meant that Faina would only receive a share of the royalties from the existing contracts; royalties from future new contracts and even from future renewals of current contracts would be excluded. So, in two or three years, she won't be receiving any more money, and even now her monthly checks are much less than she had been expecting. What can she possibly do now? She has no way to audit the books of the agency. The sad truth is that Anton duped an unwitting old lady in order to gain his revenge on *The Summit* and on us too.

"I knew that he would never forgive or forget, your Anton. He knew how to hold a grudge and eventually how to gain some kind of ultimate revenge. Don't you see that?"

"We'll go in now," Boris said firmly and he led Larissa to the elevator. "We're going for the sake of Anton's parents, even if not for him."

The couple entered the elevator and Victoria, who had heard the entire animated conversation between Boris and Larissa, continued to linger hidden from view behind the lobby column until their brief visit was over and she saw them leaving the building. Eventually Victoria tried to move but her knees buckled under her. Slowly, after grasping the wall for support, she stumbled toward the elevator and went back up to the apartment.

"Are you back from your walk already, dear?" Anton's mother asked, but Victoria didn't respond. She went directly to her room and shut the door.

Lies, all lies from that spiteful woman, Victoria thought, seeking to convince herself that Larissa was making false and vindictive accusations. But one word that Larissa had spoken remained stuck in Victoria's mind: *planted.* Anton had *planted* her in Cyprus!

Victoria now saw her carefree and luxurious life in Cyprus in a wholly different and more sinister perspective. She reflected on all her childhood dreams and aspirations and wondered now why she had given them up so easily.

Why did I do it? Was the security of a stable salary that Anton offered me years ago worth it in the end? Victoria's mind drifted back to her first meeting with Arkady Levitt. She remembered how she had been intimidated by him, how uncertain she was of his intentions to place her in suitable employment and to help her become an actress. *So, that was it! I was unsure of myself, doubting my own abilities, and Anton took advantage of my immaturity by tapping into that inner fear.*

The nature of Victoria's torment and lingering anger had evolved to the point of total transformation. She wasn't angry with Anton any longer; rather, she was angry only with herself. In the eyes of that Larissa woman and probably in everyone else's eyes, she was just some 'dumb blonde' who was duped by her unfaithful husband. If that was the case, then so be it; she deserved it. But, Victoria resolved, she would change their opinion of her. She must, for her own sake and for the sake of the children.

For the typically good-natured Victoria, anger was an unfamiliar feeling, but now she nursed it. She let it take hold of her. She wanted to use this anger as a powerful force that would provide direction and help her to escape this nightmare and to start a brand new life.

Victoria rose from the bedside chair, walked over to a wall-shelf, and retrieved a CD that Anton had been listening to during his last stay in Cyprus. It was the latest release of *The Wandering Stars* and Anton had boasted that he would make a lot of money from it. Victoria put the CD into the player and settled back in the chair to focus on the sound.

She listened to Larissa's low, haunting voice and wondered how that same voice could have sounded so grating when she overheard Larissa speaking in person, and yet so beautiful when she was singing.

Something in the song on track four touched a nerve, and so Victoria found herself listening to that same song again...and then again. She rose to put the player into repeat mode. and then resumed sitting on her bedroom armchair, totally engrossed in the haunting words of the song and by Larissa's captivating voice.

Somehow, that song gave Victoria a measure of inner peace and even some emerging sense of control over her own destiny. *I won't go back to Cyprus*, she decided. *I will talk to Megan and trade the agencies. I am sure she and Peter would agree. The Stars of Russia is a much more profitable and prestigious agency, but I don't want it. I want to forge some truths out of Anton's lies. Maybe he never meant to help young artists. Maybe that was just one of his lines. It doesn't matter any longer. It's my own intentions and actions that matter now. I'll stay here and help young artists attain their dreams. I will redeem and vindicate the Zubov name and build a true legacy for my family. I'll make this the best agency ever. If Anton could do it, so can I! It's time for people to learn that Victoria Zubova is more than just the widow of the disgraced Anton Zubov.*

From the room on other side of Victoria's bedroom wall, Anton's father held his head in his hands and bitterly complained to his wife, "Why does she keep listening to the same darn song again and again? I can't stand it anymore. That song is going to haunt me forever."

"Please, Matvei, be kind," his wife replied patiently. "Everyone mourns in their own way. The poor girl truly loved our son. It's not easy for her to cope."

"Valentina, do you happen to know the name of that song?" Matvei asked.

Valentina slowly rose from her chair and retrieved another copy of the same CD. She examined the title of track four and in a subdued voice said, *"The Reckoning."*

www.ingramcontent.com/pod-product-compliance
Lightning Source LLC
Chambersburg PA
CBHW060405260626
47160CB00006B/2443